THE OBEAH MAN

THE OBEAH MAN

a novel

Ismith Khan

TSAR

Toronto

Oxford

1995

Thepublishers acknowledge generous assistance
from the Canada Council and the Ontario Arts Council.

First published in 1964 by Hutchinson & Co. (UK).

Cover art by Natasha Ksonzek

Author photograph by Farida Khan

Canadian Cataloguing in Publication Data

Khan, Ismith, 1925-
   The obeah man : a novel

ISBN 0-920661-46-7

I. Title.

PS3561.H35024 1995   813'.54   C95-931676-0

Printed and bound in Canada

TSAR Publications
P. O. Box 6996, Station A
Toronto, Ontario M5W 1X7
Canada

Introduction

The reissue of *The Obeah Man,* Ismith Khan's second novel, some thirty-one years after it was first published, must be a noteworthy and welcome event for all students of West Indian literature, especially for those who were never able to find a copy in book shops or on library shelves. For this reissue makes available what is, to be sure, not the author's most successful novel, but his most ambitious. Therein, incidentally, lies a parallel with the Selvon corpus, in which *An Island Is a World* (1955, 1993), also his second novel, is his most ambitious, though not nearly as successful as *A Brighter Sun* (1952), his first. *The Obeah Man,* in addition, is important because it presents the most effective and satisfying treatment of obeah in West Indian literature. It is, also, along with Selvon's *I Hear Thunder* (1963) and Lovelace's *The Dragon Can't Dance* (1979), among a mere handful of novels that depict stirring images of carnival, that ambiguous cultural extravaganza that defines so much of the Trinidadian sensibility. *The Obeah Man* is important, too, because it opens up for us Khan's widest vision of Trinidadian and West Indian society, an ailing society which must heal itself. Caribbean man, Khan argues, must hone his enormous skills, encourage and develop his prodigious resources in a concerted effort to discover a necessary cure for the chronic, compounded malaise of apathy, overindulgence and aimlessness.

Markedly different from his first novel *The Jumbie Bird* (1961), in which a fierce, intransigent pride in ethnicity is a crucial factor, *The Obeah Man* advocates the need to recognize the truth of the other side of the cultural coin: that there is real strength in and potential for personal, national, and regional growth in mixing the races to such an extent that each individual, like Zampi, becomes 'one of the breeds of the island that has no race, no caste, no colour . . . the end of masses of assimilations and mixtures' (p. 6). This idealism runs counter to the wisdom born of daily living that continually absorbs the lessons of history. Such an advocacy can appeal to perhaps only half of the Trinidad society, for the majority of Indo-Trinidadians, even in 1995, still balk at the idea of miscegenation, though, of course, they welcome a carefully defined creolization, which involves no loss of racial pride or integrity. Unlike *The Jumbie Bird, The Obeah Man*, then, is a comic novel in which the life of Zampi is both heroic and normative, setting a standard of conduct worthy of emulation. At the end of *The Jumbie Bird*, we sense that Jamini is much too young and callow to understand the burdens of adult responsibility in the land his grandfather found so alien; but at the end of *The Obeah Man*, Zampi has conquered negative passions, has won the love of the woman he desires, and seems adequately prepared to minister to the needs of all supplicants who journey up to his humble hut above Blue Basin. *The Obeah Man*, finally, suggests the endless possibilities of a nation and culture in which obeah, the art of curing by natural medicine, is taken seriously to the point where it becomes in a real sense an antidote against carnival.

Ismith Khan's fiction, his three novels, and the collection *A Day In the Country and Other Stories* (1988), establishes the essential isolation of the human condition.[1] It also establishes the necessity of struggling to understand this isolation, for only be struggling does one define and realize self, that basic component of personality in which reside all means of coding and decoding experience. Mere capitulation to the awful isolation is not permitted in this exacting moral world. Kale Khan, in *The Jumbie Bird*, not given to capitulation, is a tragic victim of a consuming isolation, derived in being away from Mother India and from being in an unacceptable Trinidadian experience. His grandson, Jamini, does not feel to the same degree this isolation because the historical process—the passing of generations—endows him with a sense of belonging. Still, he must cope with, what Khan calls, 'outer surfaces' of human relationships which often prove impenetrable. In *The Crucifixion* (1989), the author's most recent novel, Khan once more portrays the individual as essentially isolated from much around him. Like Kale Khan, Manko, the protagonist of *The Crucifixion*, experiences a massive self-deception, that becomes a telling index of his inability to cope with his isolation. His self-styled crucifixion does not carry resonances of sacrifice, only ample evidence of the failure to discover meaning in life's essential loneliness. Both Kale Khan and Manko are finally victims of a closure of vision, an inability to admit and live out the rich possibilities of human experience.

In *The Obeah Man* however, Khan, moving away from autobiography and the Indo-Caribbean experience, creates in Zampi, an obeah man, a hero who conquers isolation not merely through naive philosophy of self control, as Ramchand first argues,[2] but precisely because he comes to recognize, accept and understand the possibilities inherent in all human activity. Khan shows his hero moving from being a creature of negative emotions and narrow vision to becoming a chastened individual who embodies a desired philosophy of wholeness. Zampi's integrative vision is roundly opposed to the blinkered arrogance and the tunnel-visioned monomania of Kale Khan. Ismith Khan clearly affirms the resultant disaster in any attempt to limit or deny the possibility of alternative meaning to any human situation. To reduce the mystery at the heart of life is never to go beyond the 'other surfaces'; to gainsay the wonder of creation is not to grow and absorb the innate richness of meaning and possibility, but to stifle and kill the urge to be creative. Unlike *The Jumbie Bird* and *The Crucifixion,* in which a tragic irony governs the lives of Kale Khan and Manko, respectively, *The Obeah Man* is a heroic work in which the author approves and sanctions Zampi's quest for an integrative vision of human endeavour.

Whereas masking and unmasking—or concealing and revealing—become an implicit theme in *The Jumbie Bird* and *The Crucifixion*, they become perhaps the primary fictional technique in *The Obeah Man.* Set against the temporal backdrop of the two days of carnival and Ash Wednesday, the novel introduces some characters who wear masks and others who do not. In chapter 12, undoubtedly the central symbolic scene in the novel, Zampi unmasks the red dragon's beast. This unmasking is both literal and symbolic, and underscores a unique moment in the unfolding of the novel. There are as well several other instances of unmasking, often more symbolic than literal, and these comprise an integral aspect of Khan's fictional technique. The fictive world of *The Obeah Man* is both epistemological and ontological, establishing knowing and being as heroic modes of human conduct that define self and identity.

Masking necessarily implies unmasking. Accordingly, masquerading at carnival is a time of masking and unmasking. A mask affords the wearer a chance of unmasking inhibitions and whatever else impedes the total enjoyment of the bacchanalian spirit. All human behaviour is in some way about revealing and concealing; masks therefore can be visible or invisible, external or internal. And writing, creative or critical, is an act of masking and unmasking, for words, as far as literate man is concerned, comprise the ultimate mask. The more sophisticated one becomes, the more adept one grows in the use of masks. Both writer and critic, then, are involved in the same business: one masks, the other seeks to unmask.

The Obeah Man opens significantly with Zampi, the obeah man, on a journey of two-fold objective—one, to ascertain the accuracy of rumours about Zolda, the woman he loves; and two, to bring her back to his secluded hut above Blue Basin. The journey is dramatized as a descent into the heart of the city, a struggle there, and a return up the hill to his hut. It is in fact a journey of double return: Zampi returns to the haunts where up to four years ago he continually indulged in hedonistic pleasures; at the end, chastened and wiser, he returns with Zolda away from and far above the wild abandon. I have emphasized doubleness because it seems clear that Khan makes the duality of human experience a central tenet of his fictional world. The opening scene, as so many others in the novel, asserts the need to recognize the essential ambivalence of all we do. Deep in thought as he walks on Frederick Street on carnival Monday morning, Zampi readily confesses to feeling anger and hate towards Zolda, if the rumours are true. This is the beginning of the cumulative unmasking that Zampi experiences during his journey into and away from carnival. Soon his thoughts become entangled with his words, and he is suddenly knocked off his feet, '. . . a sudden jolt sent him sprawling clear off the sidewalk' (p. 1). This jolt, along with many others in the novel, are external equivalents of internal moments of unmasking during the hero's journey of knowing and being.

As Zampi sits up, rubbing his elbow, he notices two figures wearing grotesque masks, and their suits are completely sewn from patches. Such costumes have long been associated with figures of fate, and these two bepatched masqueraders are used with this meaning in this fictional context. The taller masquerader, the tailor's assistant, draws out a tape measure and begins to take the measurements of the accosted clerk on his way to work. The other tailor 'repeated the measurements aloud, pretending to take them down in a notebook held in his empty palm' (p. 1). When the man being measured for the make-believe suit declares that he has no money to pay his way out of his obvious bond, the masqueraders become brutal:

The tall tailor then drove the hard end of the tape measure into his crotch with a loud laugh, and the clerk kicked him in the stomach. The two masqueraders lit out and shoved Zampi off the sidewalk as they raced away, the offended client, who had not yet caught the full spirit of the bacchanal, the savage and profane humour of carnival, in hot pursuit at their heels. (p. 2)

It is not too far-fetched to read this scene as Khan's masked presentation of the relationship between author and critic, in which the author appears to be bested by the hard-hitting, precisely measuring and brutal critic. It is no accident that Khan has an angry Zampi shout at the two masqueraders: 'You playin' mask or you playin' the ass?'(p. 1), which becomes then an early warning to the reader and critic. Here, then, in this initial scene of masks, both Zampi and the reader are jolted into recognizing both the limitations and the possibilities of a particular perception.

Knocked over a second time, Zampi gets up cursing at the gratuitousness of the violence. He is in effect jolted into seeing beyond the mask, something he becomes more adept at as he gathers the wisdom necessary to make him an effective obeah man:

There was something ugly, something cruel, about people at carnival time . . . He wondered if this ugliness was not buried in them all along, and now is showed itself during carnival. Was the city and its people like this four years ago when he left it to become an obeah man? His small thatched hut above the Blue Basin waterfall in Diego Martin was different, people were different—people who occasionally made the climb to the top of the waterfall to get some charm or blessing from him—and now he thought that it was the carnival, that it *did* bring out all the nastiness people had locked up in them all year. 'Is the work of the devil he-self,' he thought as he dusted off his clothes, glancing sideways from time to time to make sure that some masquerader would not surprise him with a nasty trick like they just played on the clerk. (p. 2)

Having confirmed his belief that carnival brings out the worst in men, almost immediately he observes a group of blue devils, stragglers from Jouvert 'ole mas', extorting money from a young girl with threats. Significantly, Zampi is able to confess: 'That have a lesson in it . . . People should be afraid of the devil, they should pay to get out of his clutches' (p. 2). Zampi and the reader are being schooled in the need to understand masks and to see beyond and behind them, and to acknowledge and accept the inherent duplicity of every experience. This doubleness, equivocation and ambivalence form the necessary basis of the worldview which Zampi must attain. The lopsided view of either the ascetic or the hedonist will not suffice, Khan asserts, as he advocates an ideal condition: '. . . a kind of vision which [holds] all things together and [brings] them into a crystal focus that should never be explained or explored . . . (p. 118). Further clarifying his philosophy, he humanizes and personalizes the desired conditions: 'He must know the pleasure in his groin and he must know how to prevent it from swallowing him up' (p. 119).

All of the major characters are, in a sense, unmasked as the novel unfolds. Massahood, an ethnic composite, as Zampi and Zolda are, comes to represent sensual man, living only for what might be called phallic pleasures, for his famous poui stick is but a phallic extension: '. . . all I need is this,' pointing to the stick, 'and this,' grasping a handful of his genitals' (p. 96). Massahood's entire life is spent in accumulating and enjoying visceral and corporeal pleasures. He virtually comes to life when he tastes 'the strange salt blood of his own body in his mouth' (p. 59), after being viciously slapped by his irascible and vindictive grandfather, Santo Pi. Never having enough to eat, Massahood develops a lifelong hunger not merely for food, but for the sating of all his appetites. He is in Khan's moral fable, appetitive man. He nurses a desire of avenging all the humiliation and pain suffered at his grandfather's hand, and when the day comes, he gives the old man a dose of his own medicine, and drives him out of Port of Spain. A victim of a callous and brutal upbringing, Massahood adopts a mask of machismo, taking pleasure at random from anyone who offers.

Encouraged by Zolda, who offers pleasure, but unable to hold himself back when she changes her mind, Massahood wrestles the struggling woman to the floor. The thought that after all she does not want him never crosses his mind, for he sees himself as the desire of all women. During the struggle he is knifed by Hop-and-Drop, the cripple, blinded by jealousy. The fatal confrontation is another symbolic scene in the fictional drama, an occasion for unmasking in a moment of truth. The mask of the easygoing, unruffled macho man is ripped off, laying bare anger, indignation and disgust. He is revealed as a selfish, lonely man, attractive to many, but loved by no one. Khan chooses the most ignominious of deaths for his stick fighter—he is stoned to death, mourned only by Santo Pi. The dwellers on the La Basse, with whom he was so popular all his life, see him finally as merely a coward and bully, who had brutally murdered a defenceless cripple. His life ends as it began, in violence. And when Zampi hurls the magic weapon into one of the smouldering fires on the La Basse, we sense that Massahood has no continued life in the collective memory of the dwellers on the La Basse, now that his greatest admirer, Hop-and-Drop, is dead.

Hop-and-Drop is a more curiously presented character than either Massahood or Zolda. Although he is no match physically for Massahood even when armed with a knife, he is intellectually superior to all the characters, except perhaps to Zampi. He has read widely and accumulated an impressive wealth of knowledge 'from ancient books, old newspapers, magazines some of them centuries old, which he had memorized, quoted, and hoarded in the vast storehouse of that small and tortured being of his' (p. 68). His pleasure is derived from using his knowledge on behalf of others, especially the dwellers on the La Basse, who proclaimed him unofficial mayor of the community. Khan continues his mock-heroic characterization of Hop-and-Drop by describing him as 'an aristocrat' (p. 70), as he forages through cartloads of garbage in the hope of retrieving some special item such as a swollen tin of caviar, which he shares with his fellows. A comic figure, with a suit of castoffs, a blossom or sprig in his buttonhole, he masks a massive resentment, humiliation and pain from nature's violence. His carnival mask of 'a most beautiful face' worn at the back of the head is an obvious symbol of the two-faced nature of the cripple's existence, which, according to Arthur Drayton, in a somewhat confused critique, is meant to symbolize 'the colonial condition.'[3] At times Hop-and-Drop sees his deformity as a mask hiding his specialness, in a manner somewhat reminiscent of Wordsworth in *The Prelude*: 'Indeed the little man had fleeting moments of grandeur, when saw himself a kind of end of all of God's creations, for within this breast were turned to a much higher pitch all of the emotions and feelings of ordinary men' (p. 77). At other times, deformity becomes a mask reflecting a tortured and twisted hatred, which emerges in a heated exchange with the obeah man, who could not cure the cripple's deformity:

What the ass you know? God make cat, and he makes dog and all kind of jackass like you first. And when He see He mistake, then He make *me*. With *all* He feelin's lock up inside of me. I is the last last last . . . the last thing that God make, boy.

He started scraping his tongue against his front death as through he tasted something vile and bitter, then through the wide gap between his stumps of teeth he sent a thin long stream shooting out into spittoon, and as it landed there he looked about with a kind of satisfaction, as if that final action proved beyond a doubt that his statement were so. (p. 123)

The cripple's 'secret,' that defining quality that Khan describes at length (p. 68), is revealed in the violent confrontation in Zolda's hut. Reading, the accumulation of knowledge, and his curious back-to-front carnival mask combine to veil a deeply felt sexual urge, which finally surfaces just before his death. His libido is tantalized by Zolda's frequent invitations to dance with her, and his final frenzied affirmation reveals a feeling never before confessed:

'She didn't want you!' the cripple cried out. 'She don't want you . . . who tell you to force she? She belongs to me . . . to me . . . *me!* The little man jabbed at his chest with the knife which he still held, as he insisted, 'Me me me!' (p. 129)

This sexual urge is itself a mask for a more deeply felt need to belong, to be loved, in compensation for nature's cruelty to him. The final image of the dead cripple reveals the vicious, dehumanized tendencies of a society that perceives life as merely a constant sensual feast:

The cripple lay on the floor with his arms and legs drawn up tightly like an overturned bug that could not right itself. His figure was a strange sight. It looked like a puppet with its head twisted back to front, its arms and legs wrenched out of kilter in the back-to-front carnival costume. (p. 143)

Zolda, one of a large bevy of fictional beauties in West Indian literature, although given a variety of roles in *The Obeah Man,* does not really come alive as do the three other main characters. She is the object of Zampi's journey to Port of Spain; but she is also the object of every man's desire. Even Zampi, who confesses to being in love with her, is completely overwhelmed by desire when she makes her long-awaited entrance on carnival Tuesday. She is part of 'the wildest, dirtiest, and most respected of all sailor bands' (p. 36), when she appears to eagerly awaiting eyes, arms and hearts (p. 37). She seems to embody the spirit of carnival, her boundless energy spent in masquerading, dancing and luring men to dance with her. Neither the cripple, nor Massahood nor Zampi can withstand the devastating allure of this Caribbean Cleopatra of infinite variety: 'And then which man could turn away from this creature whose every movement was calculated to house and harness all the desire a man could possess?' (p. 126). Gifted by nature with surpassing beauty and instinctively taught how to use it in her relations with men, she is for a good deal of the drama the cynosure who, like Massahood, cannot be upstaged. It is no surprise then that jealousy drives all the male characters to be with her, and of course, Massahood and Hop-and-Drop die recognizing each other's brutal jealousy.

Zolda is also given the ability to feel genuine love and to experience the need to change her unfulfilling life. She has her conventional mask as the femme fatale both put on and taken off in the death scene involving the cripple, Massahood and herself. Her toying with their emotions brings them to their death; but in her confession to Zampi we sense her need to move to a new and different experience: 'You tell me long time gone that I encourage him [the cripple], and that I encourage Massahood too, and you was right' (p. 142). Her experience with death is, as one would expect, a soul-making one, and what we are led to believe is her true self, hidden behind socially desirable masks, surfaces. A reflective, sensitive, caring Zolda emerges, and she is able to see behind the mask Zampi wears:

> Meantime, Zolda was looking at Zampi's face. She felt that she could read all the thoughts that sped through his mind. And deep within her she felt a guilt, a feeling of shame, a feeling that insisted in the back of her mind that she was in some way responsible for what had happened, and she was not satisfied to simply say as she had said before that she was this way, or that, that people should learn to take her for what she was; and yet she knew that Zampi was right when he said that it was not her fault . . . Her kind of woman was always to blame, always at fault, and doubly so with the men she did not allow to have their way with her. All the moments of pleasure she knew, all the recklessness that drove her, left her now, and she felt as though she were in an empty house where all manner of debauchery had been acted out, leaving behind only the dirty confetti, the fat limp streamers that she, Zolda, was now left to tidy up, to be haunted by the emptiness, the hollowness, the sight of the two dead men. (p. 143)

This is a moment of unmasking, of transformation, of soul-making, and Zolda is able to move beyond the exhilarating pleasures of her accustomed way of life. This is a moment of discovery for her brought about by her firsthand experience with death, sharing in the blame for two deaths. Only now, having reached her nadir, can she go on. Although we may question the efficacy of Khan's characterization, we cannot slight the sincerity of Zolda's insistent plea to Zampi:

'Carry me far away from here,' she pleaded. I want to see all of the things that you do, hear all of the things that you hear in the bush. I want to see what the nighttime like when it get dark and quiet up in Blue Basin. I want to see if I can't find you again and know you like I used to know you.' (p. 144)

Her final gesture in the hut at the La Basse is a confirmation of her wish to be a woman in love with the obeah man and with all that that entails. The only object she chooses to take with her to Zampi's hut is the red paraffin hurricane lantern, a symbol of the lasting possibilities of their relationship. Her response to the lantern when they had first found and fixed it indicates its symbolic significance not just to her, but to them both: 'She was so happy with it that she had said to Zampi long ago, 'I will only light it when you come to see me' (p. 141).

Although Zolda enjoys a fine moment of recognition and discovery through which she seeks change, only Zampi is allowed to mature and experience change in a way that aesthetically satisfies us. He is Khan's hero, and he embodies what the author considers a desirable combination of qualities. Only Zampi is consciously on a quest for love, and love is at the heart of Khan's fictional world. Zampi is a man of both thought and action, recognizing his aching need for love and doing something about it. He is not always right, and we find him being disabused of many misconceptions and illusions during his journey. His quest for love is approved by his author, and he is successful in winning the woman who embodies the love he desires. His quest is defined as a struggle, during which he must learn to withstand threats to his person and his profession and, and as the artist must learn to do,[4] to accept with as much equanimity he can muster a constant barrage of insults and criticism. He has to learn the value of controlling his negative emotions, through feelings of sympathy for the cripple, pity for Zolda and superiority towards Massahood. In Zampi's instinctive retort to the band of masquerading sailors who fell upon him, pulling at his clothes in an early scene in the novel, we sense something of Khan's technique of characterization:

> 'What you dress up like, man . . . what kind of mask you playing?'
> Zampi felt a mild anger rising in him, but he withheld his temper, and smiled instead. 'I playin' obeah man . . . you know a obeah man not suppose to imitate anything or anybody.' (p. 28)

Zampi's remark masks the fact that he is an obeah man and has been for the last four years. But it also unmasks the truth that at this early stage in his career as obeah man he does not know much about obeah, and therefore, in a real sense, he can be said to be playing obeah man. The novel charts his progress from playing obeah man to becoming one, from knowing to being. Zampi's maturation involves coming to terms with his personal limitations and understanding the limitations of others; but it also involves the recognition that man is a creature of great possibilities. He accepts the need to define limits, but he must be imbued with a sense of personal destiny: '. . . one of the biggest sin in the world is for a man not to know what work make for he' (p. 47). Zampi accepts his role as obeah man, recognizes gradually that he is born to be an obeah man, and seeks to understand as much as he can. When, by his powers he forces the English artist to adjust his closed vision of obeah, and hence, of what is indigenously and essentially West Indian, we grasp Khan's approbation of his hero's mature sense of himself and of his destiny as an obeah man.[5]

Zampi's central task as obeah man is to minister to an ailing society, coming to the aid of the distressed, easing the burdens others experience, and releasing evil spirits that prey upon human potential. Symbolic of his essential role as healer is the climactic scene of the novel, when Zampi, who is able to see behind the mask of the masqueraders and beyond all gathered in the Britannia Bar, unmasks the beast:

> There was something incongruous in the communication between the two, for the monster's eyes in the mask were focused towards the ceiling and yet its movements were directed from eyes low down in its neck. And now the arm was lowering slowly, with the same incongruity, for the beast's mask was ugly, grinning, and vicious, yet inside that front was an exhausted man. His arm descended slowly and Zampi stood in front of him now. His eyes

looking hard into the man's eyes. He placed both hands firmly on the mask and lifted it off gently. And there under the grotesque mask was the man's face, covered with sweat; tears were rolling down the folds of his cheeks, then he started sobbing like a child.

Zampi placed both thumbs against the man's temples and pressed them hard for a few seconds as he spoke some words that were barely audible. Then he said to the dragons, 'Carry him outside where he could catch the breeze and come back to he right senses.'(p. 101-102)

As Jung, Campbell, Frazer, among others, remind us, this is a crucial event in the successful journey of every hero. The monster/beast assumes mythically a wide variety of shapes and forms, but ultimately it is part of the hero's psyche. The conquer the beast does not necessarily mean to annihilate it; rather it suggests the wisdom of accepting its ambivalence, enjoying what challenges it offers, and inevitably transcending it. And to do this, the hero is granted by the gods or fate a magical weapon, whose powers act as an adversary to the beast. Zampi's weapon, unlike Aeneas' golden bough, or Balgobin's cutlass in Selvon's *The Plains of Caroni*, is neither physical nor tangible. Still, Zampi's obeah allows him to combat successfully the mere phallicism of Massahood's life, the conundrum of the tortured cripple's existence, the Circe-like charm of Zolda, and the unbelief of the uninitiated outsider. Put directly, his obeah enables him, when no one else can, to unmask the beast.

This central symbolic scene in *The Obeah Man* is the key to unlocking its fictional world. It provides both the actual reality and the metaphor of unmasking. More particularly, it draws our attention to a specific act and to the symbolic implications of that act. The terms 'beast,' 'monster,' 'savage,' and others with similar connotations recur frequently and significantly. They help us to place the novel's action within a specific context of carnival, not as a celebration of creative energies, but as a ritual demonstration of violence, sensuality and cruelty. The beast is not simply sensuality, nor materialism, nor carnival itself. Rather it is the antagonist of the hero, that which would keep him unfulfilled. Since Zampi's quest is simultaneously for love and wholeness of vision, whatever is divisive or fragmentary is naturally opposed to the integrative property of what Wordsworth terms at the end of *The Prelude,* 'intellectual love.'

Within the context of *The Obeah Man*, the beast comes to signify all that prevents an individual from realizing his potential, from being all that he can be. It is that which prevents him from attaining a balancing vision of life, the 'kind of vision which [holds] all things together and [brings] them into crystal focus.' Having shown proof of his ability to see behind and beyond outward masks, having relieved suffering and discomfort in a supplicant, having unmasked the beast in himself and others, Zampi can leave the low-lying streets of Port of Spain and the wretched landscape of the La Basse, with its sordid garbage heaps and smouldering fires, emblems of the lives of its dwellers, and begin his ascent to his sequestered hut above the Blue Basin, not alone, but with a chastened Zolda. Zampi leaves the endless imitation and masquerading of carnival and moves to a place and life in which there is hardly any need for concealing masks. He is now an obeah man with knowledge and power, living amidst the soothing influences of nature. Aided by love, nature, and obeah, Zampi can remove all other masks and reveal his true self as obeah man, who, during the course of the novel, has presented his credentials, has been severely tested, and has emerged successfully. Having earned it, Zampi can now comfortably and without misgivings wear the mask of the obeah man.

This Introduction is dedicated to my mother

Roydon Salick
University of the West Indies
St. Augustine, Trinidad

NOTES

1. See Lloyd Brown, "The Isolated Self in West Indian Literature," *Caribbean Quarterly* 22 (1977): 54-65, who writes well on this theme of isolation.

2. Kenneth Ramchand, *The West Indian Novel and Its Background* (London: Faber & Faber, 1970), p. 127.

3. Arthur Drayton, "Ismith Khan," in Daryl Cumber Dance, ed., *Fifty Caribbean Writers* (Westport, Conn.: Greenwood Press, 1986), p. 252.

4. Ramchand is the first critic to establish the relationship between Zampi and the artist. See *West Indian Novel*, p. 120.

5. Drayton asserts, reasonably, that "Khan's greatest triumph in this novel is his serious treatment of Obeah." *Fifty Caribbean Writers,* p. 252.

1

HE had to see it with his own eyes before he could believe it. He was tired of rumours, of stories which conflicted and contradicted one another. Each time he heard some new piece of gossip, his mind pursued it to the end of all its possibilities until finally he would ask himself, 'And suppose if what I hear about she is not true?' Then he cursed himself for the hate and anger that rose up in him, and the emotion which he thought was dead in him: jealousy. He was not only thinking now, he was talking out loud to himself, enunciating each word under his breath, 'I have to see with my own two eyes before I could believe.' His thoughts became entangled with his words and he lost sight of the street, the people, and the noise of carnival about him when a sudden jolt sent him sprawling clear off the sidewalk of Frederick Street. He sat up now, rubbing his elbow, and shouted at two masqueraders as they raced away: 'All—you worthless-minded bitches! You playin' mask or you playin' the ass?'

The two figures wore grotesque masks, and their suits were completely made up of patches. They had stopped a clerk, and the tall one, with a great red nose and sad mustachios, drew out a tape measure and ran it from armpit to fingers, arched it around the waist, and began calling out ridiculous measurements. 'Sixty! . . . Forty-three and seventeen-eighths! . . . Two and nine-tenths!'

The little tailor in a pink papiermâché mask, its wide nose twisted, repeated the measurements aloud, pretending to take them down in a notebook held in his empty palm. 'Two and nineteen-tenths!' The small tailor called out as people gathered about laughing at them.

'I say two and *nine*-tenths, man . . . *nine*-tenths!' the master tailor corrected, clapping his assistant on the head to the amusement of a little knot of people who gathered to watch their act.

The man being measured up for the make believe suit was amused at first, but as the crowd gathered he became impatient and wanted to break away from them. 'Sorry, boys . . . I ent have no small change with me this morning,' he said in an attempt to get rid of them.

The tall tailor then drove the hard end of the tape measure into his crotch with a loud laugh, and the clerk kicked him in his stomach. The two masqueraders lit out and shoved Zampi off the sidewalk as they raced away, the offended client, who had not yet caught the full spirit of the bacchanal, the savage and profane humour of carnival, in hot pursuit at their heels.

Zampi got up, cursing. There was something ugly, something cruel, about people at carnival time. He had thought this when he got off the bus at Marine Square. He wondered if this ugliness was not buried in them all along, and now it showed itself during carnival. Was the city and its people like this four years ago when he left it to become an obeah man? His small thatched hut above the Blue Basin waterfall in Diego Martin was different, people were different—people who occasionally made the climb to the top of the waterfall to get some charm or blessing from him—and now he thought that it was the carnival, that it *did* bring out all the nastiness people had locked up in them all year. 'Is the work of the devil he-self,' he thought as he dusted off his clothes, glancing sideways from time to time to make sure that some masquerader would not surprise him with a nasty trick like they just played on the clerk.

A group of blue devils were coming down the street now; there were three of them. One beating a drum, another holding a rope tied to the waist of the third. Their naked bodies were painted blue, and their long tails shook as they rang their lucifer bells, threatening passersby with their tridents. The devils blocked the path of a girl and danced about her, bringing their long tin claws close to her face as they cavorted and minced about, edging up close enough to her to graze her dress with the sweat and the blue that dribbled down their bodies. The girl opened a change purse and handed them a coin, then the beast of the trio made a grotesque grimace and stuck out his tongue at her—it was dyed a deep green.

'That have a lesson in it,' the obeah man thought. People should be afraid of the devil, they should pay to get out of his clutches. How often people had come to him, afraid of the night, afraid of noises and shadows, afraid because they had done wrong to someone. It was he, Zampi, who listened and freed them from their torment, and yet how easy it was for them to be cruel and nasty, all their evil thoughts coming to the surface on these two days of complete abandon. He had only to glance across the street to see this. Two figures were darting in and out of the doorways of Frederick Street, one dressed as a pregnant woman, a huge pillow stuffed in front of her, running away from a man, a pillow stuffed between his thighs. People were worthless-minded in this world. The things they did, the things they said. Why should he believe what anyone told him? He had come down to the city to see for himself and he was glad of it. If what they told him about Zolda was true he would at least have the consolation that he had seen with his own eyes.

The city of Port of Spain was coming to life now. It was just past eight o'clock. Clerks and sales people were on their way to their offices and shops. It would be a good day for carnival. From the distant cross-streets there were sounds of the great bands of steel drums and voices, hundreds of voices singing calypso in chorus, the rhythm of one faster, more sweeping, than the other, the shuffle of one band quicker than another.

And above the great din of music there was laughter, and the loud high-pitched cackle of a woman's voice as she was pinched or fondled. All was laughter today when even the ugly, the shy, the maimed, the too modest, came wriggling, writhing, seeking, looking for that moment of joy, perhaps a lover by evening, hidden behind a penny paper mask.

Zampi stood against a lamppost listening to the sounds of the city. The deep booms of the steel drums carried through the narrow streets, and although he did not see each band, he could hear the heavy beat of the bass drums, a-boom, a-boom, a-boomboom boom. He was idly trying to put together what tune the band was playing when an old woman with a tray full of jetblack blood sausages simmering on a charcoal fire yelled at him.

'You goin' to stand up there whole morning and block people from buying my puddin' and souse? You leanin' up on that post like if you own it,' she said sullenly, then turned her rear to him as she went on fanning the embers of her charcoal fire.

Anger shot through Zampi like a tree pod bursting in the sun. His body shook as the woman turned her back to him. He was ready to curse her, he knew the words. He was surprised at how readily they came to the tip of his tongue, and had she not turned her back to him so suddenly she would have had some choice words from him. Now he forced himself to remain calm. 'But why we black people so? You own the street or what? The white people let you put up in front their store, and now you act like if you own the pavement.'

The woman turned on Zampi, facing him again. She was a quarrel-some vendor who chased away anyone who tried to take her 'spot', and

3

all the other vendors feared her. Even those who bought from her were afraid of her sharp tongue. If they bought three cents' souse, and they felt that it was too little, they didn't dare argue with her, her sour look was enough to drive them off. If only she knew who he was, thought Zampi, as she tried to stare him down in her accustomed way. And then her ugly little eyes drew their loose skin into a tight focus, and a sudden light sparked them wide open.

'I don't want no obeah man shadow to fall 'cross my goods . . . carry your shadow somewhere else before I lose my temper!' she shouted in that high-pitched quarrelsome voice of hers, and she turned to her fire again mumbling to herself: 'Obeah . . . obeah. Huh! I bet he can't even cure a sick goat with a cold.'

The obeah man was not frightened by her sharp tongue, but a small knot of people began to gather as the old woman became more angry and abusive.

'Take care all that obeah you does work don't turn back on you one of these days,' she said. 'You playin' with the devil, you want him to give you powers over other people . . . take care he don't come to call you one of these days.'

The obeah man left and went to stand against another post across the street, where he thought about what the old woman had said. What was obeah? Why could he do the things he did? How could he cast spells on the one hand and on the other exorcize spells cast by other obeah men? Was he playing with the devil? Was his an evil power? The thought had not occurred to him up in the hills; he saw only how obeah worked, he remembered the people who came to him for some little charm or amulet, the reverence in their voices, the humility, and he remembered the time he exorcized the devil from a young girl who had not slept in weeks. Was that the work of evil, of the devil? No, it must be the city, and the people. Why did he have to come? He did not know just when it started, but something began gnawing at him. He had known one woman, he had thought he knew her and all that she was capable of. She had loved him, she had shared his bed, and there was something about that kind of intimacy that makes you know someone and all she is, or ever would be. He could not believe all the tales he had heard about her, and he had come out of the bush to see for himself, he had come to rid himself of blank spots in his mind lately when he could no longer concentrate on what he was doing. He would dive into the cold water of the basin, swim across to the side of the falls, and let a few hundred gallons of cool mountain water pound out the little tightenings of his limbs and bones, then his mind would clear again.

One of the great bands with hundreds of masqueraders was coming down Frederick Street, its savage steel-band rhythm flooding the narrow streets, flowing into the bones of office workers dressed in their quiet business suits. Their faces were chagrined, their bodies longed to surrender to the lewd contortions of the masqueraders. Their instincts and hidden urges were covered up with an air so thin that a moment's rubbing of their bodies in that mass of debauchery would split it wide open.

As the band approached, Zampi felt its savage rhythm steal away his senses, then in a moment he was in possession of himself again. He thought of the last carnival in which he had jumped up; it was four years ago; he remembered how he had led the band up front, writhing his body sensuously when the band passed a few pretty girls. By the end of the day he would have found a girl, any girl, and that last carnival it was Zolda. He shuddered at the thought; he saw all these people as fools, and wondered if that was really he, if he really was like one of the young men writhing and twisting up their bodies in front of the band as it approached him. They were so close now, he could feel the heavy booms of the drums pounding on his chest like physical blows. The masqueraders were wild in their abandon. Here a man had his arms around two women, kissing the one to the left, fondling the breast of the other to his right. Three girls were teasing a boy by dancing about him coaxingly, and then the obeah man saw the steel drummers sweating in the heat of the early morning sun. They alone looked savage, and grim. They alone were not swallowed up by the rhythm of their own music. They mirrored the obeah man's feeling about himself in the city. He knew its very heartbeat, he knew its people, the old vendor who cursed him, the two tailors who ran into him, and he knew the boys and girls and their joy and abandon, because not so long ago he was one of them. Now, in the faces of the drummers, he felt a certain strength, a certain kind of reward in remaining aloof. He had never seen himself before, and now he looked about him as a spectator. When had this happened, and how? Was it because he had turned obeah man? Was it true of all obeah men? He viewed the street and the masqueraders through a special kind of lens, and he held it close like some new and fascinating possession.

As the band drew level at the corner of Frederick Street and Marine Square a woman in a domino mask danced out and grabbed Zampi by the arm. He could almost feel his feet slip into the easy rhythm of the band.

He tried to look beyond the mask to see if he could recognize the woman's features, and for a fleeting moment he thought that it was she, Zolda. With the hundreds of people going past it was unlikely that this would be she, but during that quick moment his heart leapt and pounded. Then when he saw from the woman's shape and undulations that it was not Zolda he gently released her hand from his arm. 'Thank you . . . thank you . . . but . . .' The woman danced away in the tumult and milling of the band.

In a way he was pleased with himself, secretly pleased that a woman should accost him this way on carnival day. He was not really old. It was Zolda who had started him thinking this way and lately he had come to believe it from time to time. She had cautioned him that anyone who lived as he did could never become an obeah man, he would miss too many things. No, he was not old, and he was still handsome in that mysterious sort of way that people in Trinidad spoke about. Mysterious because he was one of the breeds of the island that has no race, no caste, no colour; he was the end of masses of assimilations and mixtures, having the eyes of the East Indian, the build of the Negro, the skin of the Chinese, and some of the colour of all.

The sounds of the brutal music, the shuffle of feet . . . all were dying down slowly, and a strange quiet began falling across the street. Zampi felt alone and empty as the band disappeared; he felt that they had carried away the joy he felt and he saw himself again, standing alone against the lamppost, knowing that he had nothing, no plan in mind. When he was part of the city before he had no such thought, his feet, his thirst, his hunger, all had found places for him to go, things for him to do—and now he was uncertain of the feeling he had of being aloof, it was more one of being cut off from everything.

The day was moving on, the heat mounted, the asphalt of the street softened, and the quickened pace of the music and the masqueraders mounted with it. A masked figure darted out of a band and fondled a woman's breast, a band dressed up as American sailors helped themselves to all the fruit on a vendor's stand, and two red dragon bands clashed at the corner, trying to stomp upon one another's chests with their feet. Their small Lucifer bells, held in the left hand, rang out in unison with their trembling wire tails, their bodies sweated through the bright red skin-fitted costumes. Zampi wove back and forth along Marine Square. He knew that every band would have to pass here at some time, but the chaos and the din became too loud and too strident, his thoughts slipped away from him and he felt tired, and worn. He searched for an empty bench along Marine Square, a narrow strip of green ordinarily, where a tired shopper might rest before going on to catch a bus or a train. But not only were the benches taken, people had brought their own chairs, milk boxes, stools, and ensconced themselves under every patch of shade cast from trees or buildings.

As he moved down Frederick Street he caught a faint aroma of rum. Not rum itself, but the confused aroma of many rums, bitters, limes, disinfectant from the spittoons, and the smell of bodies, large numbers of them, giving off that peculiar odour of living flesh soaked in dark brown rum. The Britannia Bar, why hadn't he thought of it before? He was not the kind of obeah man who gave up smoking and drinking, he felt that was only a sham, that a man could still have his powers as long as he did not fall prey to those things. But this was his reasoning only after he had tried to do without them, and found that he could not. Now he preferred to believe that he had taken away a great deal of the hocus-pocus from obeah.

He pushed through the swinging half-doors of the Britannia Bar, and as the doors swung back and forth they fanned a powerful aroma about him. His body gave a short quiver as it does with the first drink. If he stood there long enough he could be drunkened by the weight of the spirits drifting about the air of the place, he thought, as he wormed his way through the people who stood five and six deep at the bar. Some were dressed in expensive costumes, others in makeshift. If a man was broke at carnival time he had simply to turn an old suit inside out, buy a penny papiermâché mask as ugly as he could find, and he was ready to join the fun.

'Gimme a little nip of fire-water there, boy!' Zampi called out to the bar attender. He looked about the Britannia and was surprised that it had not changed. The same tall water tank stood on the counter with a pipe leading into it. Condensation always ran down the side of the tank, as it did now in small zigzag trickles. The mouth of the tap still had that ring of pale green crust that collected there. The name of the bar was spelled out in many places on a swirling band of ribbon painted on the walls, and on the low ceiling, slightly above the heads of the customers, hung long thin strands of dusty cobwebs which had solidified like stalactites with time, the dampness of many rainy seasons, and the vapours of rum that escaped from the breath and the pores of its habitués.

Zampi felt at ease in the warmth and familiarity of the Britannia as the bar attender placed his order before him: a nip of Black Cat rum in a dark green bottle, a small glass, and water in a pitcher with most of its white enamel flaked away. In front of him hung the same old picture above the cash register. 'I sold for Cash.' 'I sold for Credit.' On one half sat John Bull, fat thighs crossed, glass in the right hand, cigar in the left, beaming before an iron vault from which bills, coins, and $ $ $ $ $ $ floated out. On the other half sat a lean bony man, all jaws and temple-bone, his bony fingers arched up through his sparse hair, his eyes pushing out of their sockets. Behind him stood an open iron vault coughing out torn and tattered bills, papers, notes, IOUs lying on the floor, three plump mice nibbling at them.

The Britannia had not changed, and it gave the obeah man the feeling of ease and composure that he was in search of, but he felt aloof, and outside. He had become an observer, and it was not by choice. He could not slip into the flow of conversation, nor become engaged in those quick friendships over a bottle as he did in the past. He thought of joining a little clique to his left, then another behind him, but he could not think of an appropriate way to begin. And, then, no one had invited him to join them. He had never questioned all the rules and practices that Jimpy, his mentor, had handed down to him, and living alone, as he did above the basin, he never thought that anything had happened to him. Now he wondered, for it was the third time during the day that he felt strange and alone.

It was here in the Britannia that he had first met Jimpy, the old obeah man whose successor he was to become. From the beginning Zampi had been drawn to the quiet old man who drank by himself at the bar. He could never understand why, but he would always go over to the old man and invite him to share a nip, and they had talked easily. Zampi felt as though they had known each other for ever, and that they had known each other intimately. And then one day when the old man said to him, 'Boy, you know who you is?' Zampi swallowed quickly and looked up at him. He was not sure he had heard what Jimpy said. 'You know who you is?' the old man repeated, and Zampi shook his head, more to indicate that he did not understand what the man was saying. 'Well, I go tell you who you is . . . you is the one who have to take my place when I dead an' gone.'

A foolish grin spread across Zampi's face, one that he had put there because he did not have anything to say. But Jimpy did not press him, he simply said that one day Zampi would come to him.

Then some time later Jimpy said to him, 'When the powers call a man it ent have no turning back . . . he bound to go.'

At first Zampi treated the old man as someone in a bar whose whims were humoured, and he decided to avoid him, but each time the two saw each other Zampi was drawn to him, and in time he did not laugh at the old man but he began asking why he was to be the one, and how could the old man know. 'Every time a obeah man die he have to get somebody to take he place, and when the two of them meet one another they know . . . right away!'

'Well, I ent *want* to be no obeah man, and I ent *goin'* to be no obeah man . . . I have plenty other things to do besides—'

Jimpy did not let him finish. He threw his rum down his gullet as though it were a funnel and he turned, saying: 'You have to fight and you have to argue . . . that is the way I was too. It only make me know for sure that I have my eye on the right man.'

And then that day came. Zampi had worked for some people, and as part of the payment they gave him a bunch of those small sweet bananas. It was late in the evening on a Saturday night when the rumshops stayed open until eight o'clock. He went into the Britannia with his bananas, and after he had ordered his rum he tore off one of the bananas and began eating it. As he looked up, there was the old obeah man standing in his usual corner by himself. Zampi only nodded to him.

'It ent good to eat banana and drink rum . . . they don't mix!' the old man said.

Zampi looked at the half of the banana he held in his hand and in defiance he popped it into his mouth. The old man smiled with his eyes alone. Zampi got his rum, rinsed the first shot about in his mouth, and swallowed. He picked up the bunch of bananas to pluck off another one, and a spotted brown scorpion crawled out and placed its venomed tail in his arm.

In three minutes he was stretched out on the floor of the Britannia vomiting green. The old obeah man took out a little draw-string purse he had tucked into his waist and drew out a blue stone which he applied to the wound. Zampi remembered hearing him say, 'Boy, why you don't listen?'

When he saw the obeah man again the old man beckoned to him. Zampi pretended to look over his shoulder. 'Is you I talkin' to, you-self,' Jimpy said to him. 'I have something here for you.' And he offered Zampi a cigarette which he had prepared specially. It was stuffed with a ground-up scorpion's tail, and tasted bitter. After that it was Zampi's sport to let a scorpion crawl across his body in the certainty that the small beast would never plunge its tiny venomed tail into his skin. On the Ash Wednesday after that last carnival Zampi had gone of his own accord to look for the old obeah man, to tell him that he was ready.

'But life is a bitch of a thing, eh!' he said to himself softly as he went over his thoughts. In the midst of the noise and confusion of the Britannia Bar the two swinging half-doors opened slowly, and between them was one of the loveliest masks on the streets that day. The head wearing the mask turned slowly, then suddenly its voice uttered a piercing raspy 'Ahhhhhh.'

Just as was planned, all attention was drawn to the doors, and some-one, recognizing the trick of a cripple who always hung about the bar, called out, 'Hop-and-Drop . . . you old rascal, come and chop a liquor!'

The doors opened, and a little man came in, high on the left foot, low on the right, up on the left foot, down on the right. As the little man went from drinker to drinker he popped up his hands in the air, shouting, 'Ahhhhhh . . . Ahhhhhh . . . Ahhhhhh,' trying to frighten them.

'Hop, you old rascal . . . with a face like yours you don't need no mask,' one of the men called out. Zampi had known the cripple quite some time ago, and he was pleased at finding at least one person that he knew in the Britannia.

'Ahhhhhh . . . Ahhhhhh!' The little man went down and through the crowds playfully frightening the customers at the bar, and when he rasped out 'Ahhhhhh' again his joy and game fell flat, his 'Ahhhhhh' changed to 'Ohhhhhh' . . . is you, Mr. Zampi,' for he had come face to face with the obeah man. The cripple had a way of finding out every-one's affairs and what better place was there than the Britannia? It was he who started the rumour that Zolda was living with another man, someone who knew Zampi, someone who came to him, as a matter of fact, for his witchcraft, his strong obeah.

The cripple took off his mask, showing a face on which were written all of the anxieties that a crippled man knows: ridicule, hunger for love, loneliness, lust for woman, and bitterness—all these things which have their particular ways of lining the face. And since Zampi was driven, on his face too was a particular mark, and the cripple knew how to read these lines as one who knows the secret meanings of lines on the palm of a hand. But beneath all the markings on the cripple's face there was one which spelled great humour and at times it covered up all other lines, for he had learnt that as long as he could make men laugh at him he was safe. The Britannia was a second home to him, and there he was never alone, nor without food or drink.

'What about a little drink?' the obeah man asked. There was a short silence; the cripple was at first surprised, then he accepted with some discomfort.

'So what bring you to town after . . . ?'

'Three years, going on four,' Zampi replied, not saying what had brought him into the city.

But the little man knew, perhaps even better than the obeah man, what had driven him to the city, and the cripple was amused in a strange way. He was wed to humiliation, to ridicule, to keeping his body and soul together by immediately sensing the tempo of a group, the mood of a man as he drank at the Britannia. He knew that Zampi was haunted, driven. Put all this together with the little confidences, gossip, that he gleaned from day to day at the Britannia, the cripple knew that Zampi was in search of a woman he could not hold. He took the bottle by its neck and leaned it backwards, reading off the name on it. 'Hmmmm, Black Cat, eh!'

'Bring another glass over here,' Zampi called, then he poured a little rum in each.

'Water?' he asked the little man, holding the pitcher to the glass. The cripple nodded his head, smiling.

'It have a lot of drinking going on today, and I want to keep it thin.' He sounded pleased with himself as he said this. He was saving himself for better things later on in the day and the thought of this gave him pleasure. There were five or six ground-down stumps of teeth in his mouth that stood like forgotten milestones in the countryside. Today he had them covered over with foil from his cigarette wrapper.

'Why you does do things like that?' Zampi said, pointing to his teeth.

The cripple stiffened. He did not like questions like this. His mouth quivered, then turned down on the left side. He preferred to have people laugh at him for doing these things; asking him why only made him uncomfortable and annoyed.

Four years ago he had climbed the waterfall and gone to see Zampi at Blue Basin. He wanted the obeah man to make him whole. Zampi tried to explain that he did not have the powers to do such a thing, but went on to explain to the little man that he should learn to live with his deformity. The cripple felt that he had gone for help, not for advice, but Zampi was beginning in those days and he did not understand this simple fact. The cripple had resented him since then and he was convinced that the obeah man had no power.

'You know we have all kinds of people coming from all of them far-far places in the world to see this carnival. People coming all the way from America by aeroplane . . . boat . . .'

Zampi nodded. 'But I still don't see why you have to wrap up your teeth with silver paper . . . is better to leave them the way they make, it look better that way.'

The cripple was grinning at Zampi. Not so much at what he said but because he sensed how foolish the obeah man felt after saying that.

'The Yanks don't like to see ugly things . . . you never see in them pictures how American people pretty?'

'Well, yes,' the obeah man said. 'Is true what you say . . . but look at it this way—'

The cripple did not let him finish. 'I does study people, learn what they like and what they don't like, and when the tourists come they always want me to be their guide.'

The foil was slipping loose and the cripple began pressing the pieces around his teeth to secure them. The obeah man looked at him and he felt the same kind of helplessness that he did four years ago when he had to send the little man away, embittered and hurt. He looked out into the street and began stuffing his shirttail into his waist.

'Here,' he said. 'How would you like to finish the bottle?'

The little man waved a Boy Scout salute at him, and when the obeah man left he took up the bottle and waved it in the air.

'Ahhhhhh . . . Ahhhhhh!' he shouted again, pulling his mask over his face. He knew that he had caught the obeah man in a corner and he was delighted to his very bones. He threw up his hands in the air, making wild frenzied gestures, mocking the obeah man's ritual during incantation, then he went off in an eerie, raspy laughter like no one else had.

'Oh Gawd,' he said, laughing as the customers drew around him. 'The blasted world really turn upside down when a big obeah man let a woman make a fool of he.'

2

THERE was no way of telling where the floor of the Britannia ended and where the street began. By evening the white chequerboard tiles of its floor were black from thousands of shuffling feet. The small lamp-bulbs which threw off little pale orange glows seemed paler this evening, the very air tired and filled with a lethargy that the light could not force through. Now that the crowds had thinned out, the proprietor went about throwing handfuls of sawdust where the spittoons had spilled or where the drinkers spat on the floor. Zampi returned to the bar, and although the bands went by less and less often, he rushed to the swinging doors each time he heard the thundering noise of steel drums going past. This time it would be Zolda. He wondered if he might not kill her on sight and the thought horrified him.

He poured a drink of rum in his glass, cupping it tightly, as if he wanted to break it in the palm of his hand. The more he thought about it, the more he realized that if he did see Zolda he did not know what he would do, he did not even know why he felt compelled to come down in search of her. If he was aware of his actions at all his awareness was only that he hated himself for doing things which he did not want to . . . things which robbed him of his self-possession, which would in the end dull his mind and lay his obeah flat. Then he would be the laughing stock of everyone—including Zolda.

Above the swinging half-doors of the Britannia, Zampi could see the sea beyond. The sky had turned from red to purple and in a moment the sun would tumble into the sea, leaving only darkness and a peculiar silence in this section of the city. Across the street was the huge old railroad station, on the other corner an old fort, dating from the time of the Spaniards, lined with old cannons, flanked by great iron cannonballs mounted in pyramids. To the right another ancient edifice, the Customs House with its little fountain in the middle, and at the end of Frederick Street the tall lighthouse. At the water's edge were great mountains of lumber that smelled of pine and forests, a strong and pungent aroma of wood thinned and fanned by the smell of the sea. This particular combination of odours and buildings gave to the dock area its unique feeling of business. But when night fell, and the sounds of the busy people once more moved out, all the ghosts of the past came to haunt the waterfront. The docks and wharves of the island belonged to another world that built them and ran away when it gave freedom to its slaves and learnt how to produce sugar in its own climates. The clock had stopped in the Caribbean, only the flotsam remained.

Zampi put his change in his pocket and walked out. The silence along the dark streets was a depressing one, broken only now and again by great rats as they scurried for the nearest manhole. It was not the silence of wind in the trees and the voices of bullfrogs and bats with which he lived, and as he went on to Marine Square in search of his bus he looked forward to his hut in the bush with longing.

At the far end of Marine Square stood the two tall structures of the wireless station reaching far up into the sky, a million voices of all the world coming to this lost island to jam into the wires. Perhaps on some rare occasion, and then only for a second or two, one of the voices flooding the wires would be the voice of this island . . . Trinidad.

'But life is a bitch of a thing . . . one *bitch* of a thing,' Zampi murmured as he approached the tall weblike structures piercing into the black night, hearing now one vast sound made throughout the city by all those voices, feet, drums, throats, and wild bodies that had taken their frenzy indoors after dark, soaking their wild bodies in dark brown rum all night only to return to the streets the following morning at the break of dawn.

'Well, tomorrow is another day,' Zampi said to himself, as he spotted the Diego Martin bus off the wireless station. 'Tomorrow we will see what we will see . . . tomorrow.'

'Tomorrow what, pardner?' The bus driver startled Zampi.

'Nothing—just talking to myself, man.'

The bus driver was a little shrivelled-up old man dressed in a khaki uniform with brass buttons down the front. His coat was open, showing a dirty brown merino. He sat on the foot board of his bus, smoking, the bus empty. Ordinarily he cursed and swore at people when the bus and the city were crowded. His was a deep-seated hate for all humanity . . . but now that there was no one about, now that humanity had gone off and left him all alone with his bus, he welcomed the sight of Zampi, he yearned for company, for conversation.

'Man, where you goin' at this hour?' he questioned Zampi in his usual sullen way. And Zampi answered him in the same cutting manner.

'The bus say Diego Martin . . . where else you think I goin'?' He knew that he had an advantage over the driver. He was accustomed to silence for days on end. Sometimes weeks went by without speaking to anyone and he sensed the hunger in the driver's mood, the same hunger that drove him in the early days of his seclusion.

The little wizened driver, dried out from the hate that consumed him, remained firmly seated on the running board at the entrance of his bus. He would let Zampi wait. He smoked his cigarette with gestures of deliberate leisure, taking long-drawn-out puffs, letting them out idly, his eyes relaxed, staring out into the darkness of the evening. When his cigarette burnt down to his fingers he pinched its very edges between thumb and forefinger as if informing Zampi that his wait was good for another five minutes. He looked Zampi straight in the eye with this last gesture, then screwed up his leathery face as he drew out the last puffs from his cigarette.

'People making bacchanal all over town . . . who want to go to the *bush?*' he said, as if talking to the air, then he rubbed out his cigarette.

If no one came to ride the bus he would not have to make the run, he could go to one of the many rumshops of the city and curse at people as they danced and sang in their drunken stupor, dressed up in foolish costumes that sagged after the day's toll.

Zampi remained silent. He did not want to get this give-and-take of conversation going. Lately he had found himself slipping into this very kind of talk, and after a few times back and forth he was soon immersed in it, finally losing his patience, then his temper; but the evening was still and he felt that he could almost hear the voices from all those other worlds humming through the wires overhead, and he barely heard the driver say: 'You want to stand up here whole night? . . . Nobody else ain't comin' to ride this bus.'

Zampi got into the bus, and as if taking out his anger on the machine, the driver jerked it forward, mumbling curses under his voice, then the bus settled down to a regular speed along Wrightson Road after he had changed gears with angry jerks.

'Bad things does happen on the Diego Martin road at night. Nobody else want to take this shift . . . is only me . . . is only me who ain't 'fraid of all kind of things.'

Zampi let him ramble on, occasionally stealing a glance through the rear-view mirror whose line of vision he had fallen into as the bus leapt from its standstill.

'You never hear 'bout the obeah man who livin' top of the Blue Basin waterfall?' This time he caught Zampi's eyes as he looked in the mirror.

'No,' said Zampi simply.

'I hear he does turn people into dog and cat . . . make them run out in the road from the bush and get kill by motorcar.'

Zampi flushed. He could not help letting out a little titter. He wondered about the things he could do with his powers. The bus was running past the length of the Mucuraop Cemetery now; its high white wall rose up and down with the level of the bus window as the driver speeded up when they got to the beginning of the cemetery. To the left was the sea, black, the sky was moonless. There were a few stars in the heavens.

'The man who had this shift before me give it up after that night . . . you must be hear 'bout it if you livin' in Diego Martin long time.'

'Yes,' Zampi said. That was enough for the driver to launch into his story.

'Bullin . . . Bullin was he name . . . you see, I still remember he name.'

Zampi, still silent, was watching out at the stars in the sky; one of them seemed bigger than the others. Although he was on the bus, he was already thinking of his return to the city the following morning, his search through the streets for Zolda, and as he thought of her again he wondered if he could not cast some evil spell on her, make her come down with a fever or something, anything to spite her.

'Used to like woman . . . all kinds of woman, 'specially fat woman.'

'What? . . . What you say?' Zampi inquired.

'Bullin . . . Bullin . . . this Bullin I tellin' you 'bout. I tried tell him, "Boy, is woman you like, is woman who go *do* for you" . . . but he have hard ears . . . he ain't listen to me. He park the white people bus on the side of the road and he in some orange grove lovin' up with one of those Diego Martin girls.'

Looking back in the mirror, the driver could see that Zampi was not listening, his eyes were turned up to the stars. In his complete familiarity with every turn of the route he let the bus run close to the edge of the narrow road. The front wheel pounded into a hole and he swerved the bus back onto the road, pressing a fiendish little grin between his lips. Zampi looked up startled, to find the driver staring straight ahead with the indifference he had spread across his face as he smoked by the wireless station.

'You mean to say you never hear 'bout Bullin, man? Is right up here at the end of the line dat it happen. He park the bus waitin' till twelve to make the midnight run when this pretty woman come out from the footpath leadin' up to the waterfall. He say he thought he hear something funny when they walk into the bush and when he went to take she clothes off he bawl out like some old cattle. The woman had one human leg and one horse leg . . . She was a La Diablesse. He get in this same bus and for two weeks he had the ague . . . couldn't even tell people what happen. Ha . . .' The driver laughed sardonically. 'I like to see some woman try to make a fool out of me like that. Horse foot or cow foot, I would'er give she something . . . anyway.'

The bus wormed through the corkscrew roads of Diego Martin. There was the death sound of nocturnal insects as they struck and splashed against its windshield. In the distance were more fireflies, mosquitoes, and gnats, caught in the fascination of light as they rushed to their death along the beams. Hunched like the backs of great animals were grey galvanized roofs of drying sheds used for cocoa and tonca bean. The powerful aromatic odours from the sheds wove about in the night air, and suddenly a pair of eyes like burning emeralds shot out onto the road. As if paralysed for a second, they shone back at the oncoming headlights, and then, with the same swiftness, shot off into the bushes. A little way beyond, the brown eyes of a manicou pierced the blackness as the bus approached. It too disappeared. The night was filled with eyes. The countryside was awake, giving birth each second. A billion new cells were moving, straining to be born. Zampi wished the driver would stop talking. His mind was plagued with so many thoughts. Now he wondered if life was born faster than the whip stroke of death. Now he could hear the old woman's voice at Marine Square, 'You playin' with the devil . . . you callin' on his name . . . take care he come to call you one day!' His mind seemed as alive as the night, the thoughts as confused and as swift as the urge to live and the fascination with death about the land.

Now a voice, his own voice, began whispering in his ear as he thought of Zolda with contempt. 'Work a obeah on she, make she sick, make she come down with a fever or something. She is a blasted whore . . . you could do it, you have the power.'

Was it really the devil's voice? What did the old woman at Marine Square mean, where did he get his powers, were they evil, was he working with the devil?

He tried to shut out the voice, but it only came back more persistent, more urgent, as the bus swung onto open country, now running along a narrow road with swampland on either side, marshes filled with watercress and the smell of half-sea, halfmountain air, an odour of confused life that dwelt in the marshes, life that did not belong to the sea two miles away, nor the dry land that rose gently to the hills of Blue Basin.

The driver shifted gear to speed up the last rises in the land so that he could spin along the road at the end of which was a huge silk-cotton tree, 'the devil tree' as it was called, because it was the abode of all evil spirits. Zampi noted this sudden speed of the bus as the little wizened driver perched on his seat strung tightly like a snake sensing danger.

Overhead the stars burned on, and one of those sudden angers rushed through Zampi. He began speaking his thoughts out loud. 'The bitch . . . the li'l bitch . . . I go *do* for she.'

No sooner had his anger burst out of him than the great star in the heavens unhinged itself and came pelting with a piercing, searing, tearing of cloth, exploding in the silk-cotton tree which burst into a great whirling ball of flames lighting up the countryside as small burnt cinders of the silk-cotton balls went shooting off like fireworks. Zampi felt his heart struck by something hard, and for moments its beating stopped. He plunged his hand into his bosom and began gasping for air as the driver sped on insanely to the end of the road which was not far ahead. The bus skidded as it hit the loose gravel of the U-turn, and he then put it into reverse to get back on to the road. At that moment Zampi, his hand clutching his breast, rushed to the door and jumped out. The bus raced away, swaying crazily from left to right along the narrow road until it disappeared in the black night.

Zampi, all the energies drawn out of him in what seemed like seconds, reached out for the bushes and shrubs along the stony footpath that led to his lean-to above the waterfall. He fell to the floor and began retching. 'Oh God . . . Oh-God-oh-God-oye . . . What happen to me?'

Minutes, hours, how much time had gone past he could not tell. Slowly his senses began returning to him. At first, sounds. He could hear the dull heavy croaks of bullfrogs, then the steady gushing sound of the waterfall. He opened his eyes and glanced about. The great star was still in the sky shining through the lattice work of the large wide leaves of a banana tree outside the hut.

3

HE awoke with a sense of strangeness, surprised to find himself lying on the damp earth, and wondered at first if he had not fallen from his bed. He looked towards his vine-strung cot which was too far away, and then, as if trying to piece a dream together, he remembered slowly, recalling the blaze of the silk-cotton tree, the sensation of that hot bolt of fire that stopped his heartbeat and throttled his breath for what seemed like an endless night. The blaze of the silk-cotton tree, the wisps of burning cotton balls in the night, came back to him vividly, and now he was afraid. Afraid of something vague and intangible, something dark as the night with fists of fire that could reach out and drag him into the un-known inferno from whence it came. What was it? The island was a burial ground after many, many battles . . . bones bleached chalk-white in the tropic dust grew out of the earth after a heavy rain. Zampi did not fear the dead whose ashwhite bones were plentiful as stone. The Caribs, the Arawaks, the Spaniards, the British. An ancient history had walked this land. A cold sweat broke through the skin of his back, his chest, and his forehead.

'My obeah turn against me or what . . . soon as I did think of doing something bad to Zolda it look as if . . .'

The thought was not clear in his mind and, looking about him at the stillness of the earth in the morning, smelling the pungent aromas of dew, just beginning to escape from the dampened earth as the sun rose higher, he felt lonely in the bush, as if saddened by some massive beauty that he could not possess.

The morning sun wove through the thick growth of trees in long hazy shafts that fell on the clearing in the bush that was his abode, and in the centre of the clearing Zampi fanned a small fire over which he boiled water for coffee. His eyes flared wide as he stared into the fire. The smoke rose straight up in a thin blue wisp that mushroomed high up above the trees. At the back of him stood his lean-to, a small thatch-roofed hut with a front section open to the sun and rain. There was one door in the middle over which an old burlap sack hung to keep out the wind and the night draughts when the rainy season came. He was content here once, he recalled, looking about him. It seemed like only yesterday, although more than four years had gone past, since he came to see Jimpy, the old obeah man whose place he had taken.

'So you make up your mind, after all,' Jimpy had said to him. It was the Ash Wednesday after carnival, and after the fete and bacchanal, after the wallowing in rum, sin, and women, Zampi was seized by a mood. He felt that all about him was flat and colourless; even the thought of the body of the woman he loved left him cold.

'If you make up your mind . . . you make up your mind! It ain't have no turning back for people like we,' Jimpy reminded him.

There were times when he felt that he was a part of all the great Saman trees, part of the fragile magic that made the flower of the Poui . . . the sounds of the rushing water of Blue Basin and the sounds of the earth giving birth at night. All these were one with him. And then there were moments when a jealousy stole across his soul. A jealousy of all the world's beauty, the everlastingness of its life in which he was plunged for a short moment. Suddenly he would become filled with a strange rage. He did not think of love at these moments, he reached into the darkest corners of his brain and tried to tell Zolda how he felt. But she had simply said that she loved him more for this very reason. Did he feel differently because he was a man?

A woman in love is in love twenty-four hours a day each day of the week each week of the year. No dark of night, no fall of rain nor thunder-clap, injects the evanescence of the universe into her brain. He remembered only the firm grip of Jimpy's bony fingers upon his arm that day at the Britannia Bar as he said, 'Is you who have to take my place when I dead an' gone, otherwise . . .'

'Yes,' Zampi had said that Ash Wednesday when he went to Blue Basin to commit himself, and Jimpy taught him all the things he could. He showed him all the little nooks and crannies where he could hunt for lizards' eggs. He passed on to him ancient and worn sheets of parchment with strange writings in blood, he showed him how to grind old bones to powder between stones; always reminding him: 'When I dead an' gone you go have plenty things to figure out for yourself. That is the real test of a obeah man, but I know you have it in you, you have the mark on your face. When a obeah man time come he know it . . . and when he see the man who have to take he place the two of them know one another, right away!' Zampi could not deny that the old man held a hypnotic fascination for him from the start.

And then Jimpy, as if without warning, had stretched out and died above the Blue Basin waterfall one morning, leaving Zampi quite alone.

'Must be 'bout seven o'clock,' he said to himself as he heard footsteps coming up the path.

'Zampi. . . Zampi-O,' a voice called. In the stillness that followed there was the sound of a powerful person moving up along the path which was difficult and stony. By now Zampi could tell what kind of person was coming by the sound of the footsteps.

'It must be Massahood,' he reflected. He had promised the burly stickfighter to place a charm on his stick for this Carnival Tuesday.

With a leap and a bound, the stick man jumped into the clearing like a deer, startling Zampi as he landed on his feet in front of him. He had a kind of energy that Zampi envied, the very manner in which he dressed himself suggested something of a wild animal. His blue ducks, faded to the pale blue of the water in the basin below, were drawn tight across his thighs, his buttocks fitted in them so closely that the trousers looked as though they might stand up by themselves when removed. He was small at the waist, but his torso widened showing massive shoulders through a sleeveless vest that someone must have discarded on the city dump where Massahood made his home. His great arms were wet and shining from the hike up to Zampi's hut. These two could have been brothers, both built as powerfully . . . from the waist upwards. Their chocolate brown faces bore the same question mark of lost races and cultures. But in their eyes they were different men, and if it is true that men are responsible for their faces then these differences were written on each. Where Zampi's eyes seemed mysterious and a little tortured, Massahood's were keen, quick, the kind of eyes that could act swiftly without stopping to think. Again, their faces smiled differently: Zampi smiled inwardly, as if to himself, but Massahood smiled for all the world, and where Zampi was slow to find this kind of expression, Massahood's face was formed by a constant readiness to find laughter and amusement with all of life. Had he not a few years ago, when struck down by a more skilful stick man, burst forth in riotous laughter . . . a small stream of blood running down his forehead?

'You had your coffee yet?' Zampi asked as he watched him sprawled out beside the small fire, taking deep breaths, his chest expanding, his nostrils dilating. A small vein stood high on his forehead, running from his hairline and disappearing above his eyes.

'Yes,' said the stick man, but he would join Zampi in a cup, and they drank together.

The obeah man could tell that he was anxious to get his stick blessed and head out for the grand bacchanal of rum, savage steel drums, and the smell of female flesh worked into its frenzy and sweat. For reasons of his own, Zampi too was anxious to set out. He disappeared into his hut and brought out some black dried-up toadstools, three tiny yellow lizard's eggs and a bottle with water scraped from his body after a swim in the basin when the moon was full. Amid some eerie chanting and muttering he ground up the fungi, working them up into a paste with the contents of the small pale yellow eggs which he broke open, removing their sticky contents as some rare and elegant liqueur of which every drop should be saved; adding from time to time drops of water from the bottle.

Massahood looked on with an awe that resembled fright as the obeah man touched the paste to either end of the stick, holding it up to the sun now, pointing it to the earth, muttering, chanting. Finally he kissed the yard-long copper-wound stick and placed it between Massahood and the fire, into which he threw a pinch of something that looked like salt.

'Don't touch it yet, let the obeah settle for a while,' he warned as he went to a small ravine behind the hut to wash his face and hands.

'If you fight clean you bound to win! Remember that! Don't have nothing to do with woman till the sun go to sleep, otherwise you get your head bust open.'

It gave Zampi a small satisfaction to place this restriction on Massahood. The cripple had rumoured that Massahood was frequently over at Zolda's shanty on the La Basse, as the city dump was called. Zampi was not unaware of the hungry eyes that all but devoured his woman when she danced the Limbo, her great breasts rolling loose under a horizontal bar which was made lower and lower, the dancer trying to writhe under without touching it.

Massahood, still squatting before the small fire, stared at his stick in wonderment. Whether he always came out of the carnival season un-scathed because he was a good stick man, or whether it was due to Zampi's strong magic, he was never sure. He came to the obeah man as an added precaution, just in case there should really be something to it . . . he would have preferred to have Zampi along with him on his escapades, as they did long ago.

22

Zampi in his own way knew this, yet he could refuse no one who came to him for help. And although he did not resent the stick man, there was an indefinable emotion aroused in him by the stick man's popularity, his cocky sureness of himself with the stick, and the near idol worship for him by all.

'Pick up the stick . . . Pick up the stick and let we go to town, man.'

With that they were off to the city, Zampi hardly able to withhold the anxiety and turmoil that stretched his mind to breaking. As they arrived at the gravel path where the bus made a U-turn, he became anxious. What if the driver were the little man from last night? He walked behind Massahood. No, it wasn't the little man from last night. He felt greatly relieved as they entered the bus, and as they moved through the country-side he was filled with great apprehensions about the silk-cotton tree. All of Diego Martin would be asking what happened to the tree, who was so worthless as to burn it down . . . and then the scamp of a driver would tell what had happened.

The bus swung onto the straight road, and there . . . there was the great tree . . . standing erect and intact, its small balls of cotton sailing through the mild zephyrs of the morning. Zampi let out a sudden gasp of surprise. Was he dreaming?

'Wha' happen . . . wha' happen, man?' Massahood demanded, looking out to the countryside racing past and seeing no one.

'Nothing, man . . . nothing,' Zampi said gruffly now that the bus had left the great devil tree in the distance.

'The bitch gone an' dead without a word of warning . . . without a *single* word 'bout this. Now what. . . ?' Zampi wondered where he could turn for some explanation, some answer. Obeah men hated one another. They hid little secrets from one another. They constantly tried to outdo one another, to steal clients away from one another. They would only laugh and jeer at Zampi if they knew of his shortcomings. They might even spread rumours that would make people berate him as a quack and a charlatan. If only he could bury himself in his practice he would be all the obeah man that Jimpy swore he had in him. Yet . . . here he was, on his way to the city again, in search of a woman whose image haunted his nights. He felt irritable this morning. His body ached from having slept on the cold earth. Sitting next to him, Massahood was running his fingers longingly along the stick. His eyes betrayed an intense anticipation that irked Zampi. 'Soon as we get to town he goin' 'bout he business,' Zampi thought. The day ahead of him seemed colourless in comparison.

23

'The bitch goin' to get he head bust open one day . . . then we go see who is more man,' Zampi fretted to himself as Massahood shifted from left to right, foraging in his pockets. The stick man took out a package of Anchor cigarettes and elbowed Zampi, offering them. Zampi faced him sternly and Massahood let his eyes drop to the cigarettes in his hand and Zampi took one. As the stick man lit it for him he felt ashamed for all the little irritations he felt.

Massahood smoked greedily, he drew the smoke into his lungs, making a loud hissing sound as the air entered his mouth and flooded his tautened lungs. The hunger of all of his senses was the same, not an avaricious one, but one which savoured all things with a magnificent gusto and relish. He was looking out to the docks now as the bus rolled on its tin frame, banging and clanking as it jogged along.

'But look how this place change, eh!' he said out loud, as if talking to the air. When he and Zampi were boys and ran away from school they came to swim here. A few fishermen with knee-high rolled-up trousers used to tie up their boats here, taking out many strange-looking creatures of the sea. There was a fish market, half on land, half jutting out on to the sea, and the boys swam around the stilts below. They would buy a three-cent length of marlin and two blue steel fish hooks and let the lines dangle from their big toes.

' 'Member that time when we get black oil all over we skin?' Massahood asked.

Zampi laughed as he used to laugh in the old days. 'You know, I never know up to today where you get the pitch oil we used to rub off that black oil.'

His smile tapered off as he looked to the sea. How the docks had changed. It was filled in now, lined by large warehouses and cranes that made an ugly sound. There were piers now, with great ships standing alongside, and the sky was blackened by soot and fumes from the cranes and the ships at anchor. All along Wrightson Road there now stood a tall lattice-work wire fence topped off with vicious-looking barbed wire, and only those who had official business and a pass could enter the area. The bus drew closer to Marine Square now; that combination of tar and salt-sea air became richer as they sped along. A market vendor in the bus with a round basket of chickens, tied six together by the feet, sat dozing two seats ahead of them. One of the chickens wet the floor, and a rooster tied in the same batch, as if intoxicated by this, tried to mount the bird. But tied together as tightly as they were, it fell back flat into the basket.

Zampi shifted his weight in his seat.

Ahead, at the foot of Wrightson Road, a great band of costumed masqueraders depicting Samson and Delilah moved slowly to the beat of steel drums. The band was a good hundred strong, with members of court, slaves, kings, queens, all decked out in rich brocades and wild colours. They jumped in the air to the music as the bus squeezed through the thick crowd. They began beating out the rhythm against the noisy tin body of the bus, and now that the bus was in the middle of the band Zampi could hear the words of the calypso, 'Iron something bust up my something . . . Oh, Man-Man-Ti-Re.'

Massahood was half hanging out of the bus drinking brown rum from a bottle of Vat 19 one of the masqueraders handed him. His swallow of the rum hardly completed, he shouted above the din: 'Play mask! . . . Play mask!' pounding out the rhythm with his stick on the floor of the bus.

Someone in the band shouted out, 'Give the Hood a drink,' and Massahood shoved the bottle in the air, showing that he had one, then put it to his mouth again and drank. His face lit up as he caught the savage ecstasy of the crowd. The driver was a man with a great belly. He threw his arms wide apart, his stomach touching the steering wheel, and it moved from left to right as he writhed in his seat.

'Oh, Iron something bust up me nothing, Oh, Man-Man-Ti-Re,' he bellowed in chorus over the din of steel drums, the bus wedged in the very core of the drummers now. Not far away was the bus stop at Marine Square. They could have been there now were it not for the band, and as the tail end of hangers-on who followed the masqueraders shuffled on to the still audible music, the sound of the driver pressing on the starter of the stalled bus could be heard making a slow and grinding sound.

Massahood jumped up from his seat. 'Let me go and see if I can't lend a hand, man,' he said as he tried to go past Zampi.

The obeah man looked at him sternly out of the corner of his eye, not moving to let him by. 'Boy, why you don't keep your backside quiet? You is stick man? . . . You is sweet man to all them woman? . . . Now you is best mechanic? What happen to you at all? You know 'bout everything? It look as if you have a spring inside of you. You can't keep your tail quiet for one minute? From the time you come up by me you prancing around. Let the man fix the bus . . .'

With a loud explosion the bus started up and the driver wheeled it round under the shade of a large spreading Saman tree at the kerb of

Marine Square, and Massahood, completely silenced by the obeah man, said simply, 'We go pick up later,' as they got out of the bus.

Zampi watched him walking up along Marine Square twirling his stick between his fingers. As the stick reached the little finger it stopped, then started counter-clockwise, the shiny copper wire wound around it glinting in the blatant sunlight.

4

TIME lingers everlastingly in the tropics.

The new-born day barely blows its birth water from its nostrils when the great amber ball of the sun lashes the pale pink-tongued hibiscus to a shrivelled purple blue with its whipstrokes.

At nine o'clock young buds hide in the shade of stronger leaves and a man wandering the world all alone feels old, as his marrows run to hide in the columns of his bones.

For the sun, as if taking oath, promises more and more punishment.

At ten o'clock the small urchin devils. They alone, so far, begin their dance along the sizzling galvanized rooftops. The air above the tramcar line has caught the jig, and now the asphalt road begins to soften to the hoof marks of a donkey cart.

Oh, but there's rum to belt and blister the tongue, and ice water in small flaked-up enamel pitchers at the Britannia.

But the sun is master of all the streets and alleyways . . . all the backyards, still and empty . . . all the lampposts standing still . . . all the burrowing beetles . . . the mighty Saman tree with its bats hung upside down.

All still as sleep.

All but the hunted bodies of men, hungering for a whole year, hungering for the ecstatic frenzy of carnival, hungering for tumult that will tease and tickle their throats until it screams for rum.

Dark brown rum . . . and breasts, dark and amber brown . . . like sea foam in the cupping hand. And thighs with smouldering fires in their clefts.

Then the fire in the thigh bone will be soothed and put to sleep for another year.

All these things, then, drove the obeah man, yet he was unaware of them, for all his restlessness told him that one thing and one thing only would quiet the discordance that rang out from his eye sockets to his ankle bone . . . find Zolda. What things had she done with other men? Had she known another man? All these would wait. As he walked up through Marine Square, a narrow park that stretched parallel to the docks from one end of Port of Spain to the other, he reminded himself to avoid all entanglements with people, that he should try to shut out the very sounds of voices, the din of savage steel-drum rhythms, so that he would not be swept up as he was yesterday and carried along until he lost his senses to them.

On either side of Marine Square small bands were going past. The music and the shuffle were still slow. As the day moved on, the bands grew as they collected their members throughout the city. A small group of masqueraders dressed up as American sailors were coming up along the park. They had small handwoven baskets filled with fruit, long red noses with spectacles as masks on their faces, and printed on their jumpers the name of their ship, *USS Bad Behavior.* The small group of sailors, about six or seven of them, were chasing a girl, pulling at her hair, her blouse, and one of them kissed her on her neck. She ran, screamed, swore, but all with that tingle of a giggle of enjoyment. She finally broke away, and now they passed a green bottle of Black Cat rum around, wiping their mouths on the back of their wrists, tottering back and forth, grunting 'Ahhh . . . Ahhh . . . Ahhh' as drunken American sailors on leave are supposed to sound. As they spied Zampi, obviously not in the spirit of carnival—no costume, and facing the day with that look of doom—they fell upon him, pulling at his clothes.

'What you dress up like, man . . . what kind of mask you playing?'

Zampi felt a mild anger rising in him, but he withheld his temper, and smiled instead. 'I playin' obeah man . . . you know a obeah man not suppose to imitate anything or anybody.'

The sailors laughed heartily at this, tottering back and forth as though drunken with rum as well as laughter. They offered him a drink of their Black Cat, which he accepted with the same composure, and then they were on their way. Zampi was pleased with the manner in which he handled them, it was so much like his old self.

Ten o'clock was striking at the Trinity Church in the distance, so it was a little after when he pushed open the swinging half-doors of the Britannia which was not far off. The bar attender nodded on seeing him and, knowing his likes and tastes, brought him a nip of Vat 19, a small enamel pitcher of ice water, and a slice of lemon on a tray. The bar, although not jammed, was filled with people. A loud murmur rose as if out of nowhere when he entered the place, and now it divided into individual little groups of drinkers scattered about the Britannia.

Standing with a small knot of people across from him was the cripple, who turned his gaze in another direction to avoid Zampi. The little hunchback whose right leg was shorter than his left had a small four-legged stool strapped about his right foot. His clothes were on back to front and on the back of his head he wore a mask of the most beautiful face. He was always in the company of women, who bought him drinks, and in the small knot of drinkers a woman was the only one talking and joking with him. No one else seemed to care whether he was part of their company or not. She filled the little man's glass from time to time, dividing her attention with a noisy man to her right. And when no one was looking the cripple helped himself to a small shot, laughing at all the jokes in the group, smoking and puffing his cigar butts (he collected cigar butts only) as though equally a friend of everyone about him. He reached out his hand for the bottle of rum, and the man caught him this time and slapped his loose hand. The cripple pulled his hand up into his sleeve as he did to amuse people, but the man was not amused and the cripple smiled with a foolish grin on his face.

'Why you have to go and do that?' Zampi asked, coming over to them.

'The little short-cut bitch thiefin' and thiefin' my rum. You see when I hit him 'cross he fingers, but you ent see how he squeezing my bottle dry?'

'You ent have no right to hit him,' Zampi said. 'He smaller than you, and besides—'

'He smaller than me! But the li'l break-back bitch could put 'way ten times the amount of rum I could hold. He is a blasted sponge. You know why he back make with that swellup part?'

Zampi felt ashamed for the cripple. In the old days he would start fighting, now he tried to remain cool and indifferent. He was a mere sounding board through which the lives of other people moved back and forth.

'Is a sponge he have there . . . a sponge that could suck up all the rum in town,' the angry voice shouted.

The cripple looked straight ahead, twirling his empty glass between his hands.

'Broko!' the man shouted.

The cripple was standing an arm's length away, but the word seemed to jolt him like a small slap, and he winced with his eyes alone. He still looked ahead with unconcern, feeling all the pangs that only a cripple knows when some new and ugly name has been coined for him . . . these names were like slow-healing ulcers that festered. They were like his very deformities, he would have to carry them with him through his life. When, where did they start calling him Hop-and-Drop? He could not remember; a great surge of fear, of confusion, fell over him each time a new name was coined and thrown into his face as if for measure. 'Broko! . . . Broko! You li'l bitch! Let we see what you have there,' the man said, reaching out for the hump on the little cripple's back.

Zampi stretched out an arm and collared him. His other hand gripped the man's arm before he could touch the cripple.

'Take your hand a-*way*,' Zampi warned, jerking the man's hand down. 'And take care something bad ain't happen to that hand of yours.'

The man drew back sullenly, his body arched forward, his head jutting forward, his mouth pouted. One of his companions whispered in his ear, reminding him of a character called Hands-up who hung about the Britannia Bar. It was rumoured that he had lifted his hand to strike his own mother and an obeah man from Tunapuna had placed a hex on him. His arm remained frozen in that uplifted position.

'Take care, he bust a bad obeah in your tail, boy! Don't argue with him.'

'Let me go . . . let me loose, man.' The man tore himself free of his friends who held him back.

'You think I 'fraid? . . . You think I 'fraid you just because you is obeah man? Hai-aye-ai,' he said sarcastically.

Zampi was surprised at this. He never thought of himself as one who should be feared. Respected, yes. But feared because he might work an evil spell?

'Is your woman who offer him a drink . . . ask she,' he said, about to turn away.

As if suddenly drunken now, the man's eyes became stupidly wild and filled with an intense hatred, his tongue heavy. 'Is my woman you worried 'bout. What about yours? You can't even hold she. This same little break-back *bitch*—' He reached out suddenly and clouted the cripple across his mouth. There was a loud crack and the cripple fell along the yellow brass rail, his mouth dribbling red.

The two half-doors of the Britannia flung open, and before anyone turned to see who was entering they heard a loud flat crack that landed across the buttocks of the man who had knocked the cripple down. He writhed and coiled like a snake, uttering a low moan as he twisted down to the floor.

Massahood stood with his stick poised above his head. He placed his foot on the man's jaw, pinning him to the floor with it.

'Oh *God* . . . Oh-God-oh-God-oye,' the cripple screamed. 'My pardner come . . . at last my pardner come.' The little man scrambled the loose limbs of his body like a puppet whose strings had been given a sudden jerk.

'Is only the *Hood* who is my friend . . . nobody else,' the cripple railed in his raspy voice.

Zampi drew back a little. He knew that he should not have interfered, that life takes care of itself one way or another. One did what one could in the world, and to do that best one had to avoid all other involvements. Now that the stick man had arrived the cripple turned all attention to him.

'He would of get kill if I . . .' thought Zampi.

'Where he hit you?' asked Massahood. 'Where? Show me. Show me where.'

'Is here . . . is right here . . . look, look at my mouth.' The cripple turned his bleeding lip inside out. The skin inside his mouth was an inky blue-black. His few teeth stood like crooked headstones in an abandoned cemetery.

'Hit him,' Massahood commanded. 'Hit him just the same way he hit you.' No sooner said than done. The cripple fell on the man as Massahood held his head pinned to the white chequerboard floor and began raining blows on his mouth. With the first cuffs, the skin under the man's eyebrow burst open and the heavy veins on his temple pulsed and throbbed as if pushing his blood out in spurts and starts.

'Let him get up, man . . . that is enough,' Zampi pleaded with Massahood, and the cripple, hearing this, started gouging at the bleeding wound, now trying to gouge out the man's eye with his gnarled fingers.

'That 'nuff,' laughed Massahood. 'That 'nuff now,' he growled as he removed a bottle which he had tilted to his mouth.

But the cripple had gripped into the man like a louse embedded into the pores of the skin. Massahood threw down his stick and bottle, grabbed the cripple's coat at the scruff of the collar, and lifted him off. 'That 'nuff, man . . . 'nuff!'

And now the cripple began kicking at the man's genitals, wringing out of that collapsed and beaten body those slow and final movements that only intense pain could draw from it. Soundlessly the man, only now

31

receiving the body's message in his brain, drew up his two quivering legs into his stomach, as if to protect his parts from the blows that had already reached their mark. The cripple's face was wet. His great bloodshot eyes were covered with sweat as Massahood held him up by the scruff of his coat almost bodily, his loose little arms and legs dangling out of his clothes, like a puppet held up by its strings.

'You is a worthless li'l bitch,' Massahood chided, admonishing him for his behaviour. 'Why you ent stop when I tell you to stop . . . eh?' the stick man grinned.

And the cripple smiled with a wild joy on his face as the stick man lowered him to his feet.

'Give the Hood a drink on me,' he called in his raspy voice, still panting from exhaustion. 'My *onliest, onliest* pardner in the *whole, whole* world,' he sang out.

Zampi and one or two of the small knot of masqueraders who clung about felt suddenly turned away by the cripple. Yet he and Massahood enjoyed the centre of attention. The stick man gave the cripple his stick to hold. It was about as tall as the little man, and he ran his black overgrown thumbnail along the copper wire. It gave him an ecstatic joy as it vibrated into his thumb and up along his arm, and each time a band went past outside he kept the rhythm, now with the little stool strapped to his foot, now with the copper-wound stick, thumping upon the floor of the Britannia.

Zampi had forgotten what brought him to the city in the wild moments that went past before. He looked out over the swinging half-doors at the bands, hoping that he might see Zolda, hoping that of all the streets, rumshops and dancehalls, she might pass by here now.

'Everybody should be friends . . . today is carnival,' exclaimed Massahood with his lordly air. 'Fix up some firewater for we, man,' he ordered. The bar attender had slight misgivings about these orders for rum, but the chaos of the fight was just dying down, and then, whenever Massahood was about, the drinks were always paid for; somehow, no one stinted as long as they could be in such company. For the rest of the year, perhaps the rest of their years, they would be telling of how they were drinking with the 'Worse-worse stick man' and how he said such and so.

Similarly, great quantities of food greeted the stick man. Someone had gone outside to the kerb of the Britannia where there was always stationed a vendor with a large pan of frying black blood sausages over a charcoal brazier. The aroma of the blood sausages, and that of many rums and the old wooden casks that stored them, worked back and forth upon one another, confusing the senses. Was it another drink? Yes, then was it another inch of black pudding? And so, on and on, it was the measure of time at the Britannia.

The oyster vendor, as permanent a fixture as the spittoons and the brass rail at the Britannia, opened the delicate shells with quick sharp flicks of his knife, laying plateful after plateful along the counter. The cripple poured a pungent mixture of vinegar, crushed tomatoes, and bright yellow peppers over them, and in the same motion that he threw his head back to down his shots of rum, so he threw the small oysters down his gullet, wincing a little from the burning of the fire in the peppers. He would then stick out his long purple tongue and scrape it along his front teeth as he drew it back in, then make a loud smacking noise as his tongue slapped the roof of his mouth with great relish.

'Zampi!' Massahood called, his mouth stuffed with bread and black pudding. 'Zampi-O,' he called the obeah man again when he had made a hard swallow. He pushed his index finger up into his jaw teeth, took out some food that had lodged there, then licked it. 'Today is not a day for a man to drink all alone by he-self . . . Come and fire a liquid with we.'

The cripple's fast swallows, now of rum, now an oyster, halted abruptly and his deep-set eyes flashed to Zampi. The two men looked at each other for a second, then the cripple let his eyes fall back to his plate of oysters. And, breaking off a small piece of bread, he sopped it onto the rich juices of the oysters in the plate, rubbing it in slow circles, then popped it into the purple void of his mouth.

In that moment Zampi's mind imagined the most fantastic and far-reaching of all things. What did the man they had beaten unconscious say? (Someone had dragged him out into the canal outside of the bar.) He thought he saw something in the little man's eye that made the impossible seem true. He joined the crowd around Massahood, feeling curiously drawn to the cripple, who ignored him and addressed himself, as before, to Massahood only.

'Oh Gawd,' the cripple said, 'but look at how they did want to come and kill the old Hop-and-Drop today. *Nobody!* . . . and *nobody* to pick up for me.'

Massahood placed his hand on the cripple's head affectionately.

'Nobody touch you so long as I name *Massahood . . . nobody!*'

Zampi was annoyed now. Why . . . why was he lying? Would the old scar never heal? Were the wounds in the heart of a twisted man harder to

33

heal? He couldn't make the cripple whole. Was that why he bore this malice still?

The cripple whispered something to Massahood. The stick man smiled. 'You telling me that for donkey years now . . . what it is you have to give me?' Massahood asked the little man.

'He have a thousand dollars tie up in the hump back . . . that is what he going to give you, Hood,' one of the drunken masqueraders jeered.

The stick man flashed such a cutting glance at him that no one in the crowd dared to roar in chorus as was intended.

'I have to give it to you . . . to you only, Hood. One day . . . you go see.' The cripple spoke insistently, drunkenly, in that voice of urgency that confession takes when it becomes soaked in rum.

'Well, tell me . . . tell me, man, what it is you have for me,' Massahood begged teasingly.

The cripple pulled him lower and whispered in his ear again, and this time the stick man's eyes, as if registering the rise and fall of the cripple's voice in his ear, burst forth with his bellowing laughter until he began coughing and choking. He slapped the little man fondly on the head.

'Hoppy,' he said, 'one of we more drunk than the other . . . but the thing is, I can't tell who more drunk than who . . . ha ha ha ha ha ha,' he laughed, thrusting his hands into the cripple's breast and tickling him like a small child. He lifted the little man and seated him on the counter and, looking straight into his eyes, said to him:

'But all joking aside, man . . . you must never talk like that . . . never. Your life is your own, it belong to you only, and you can't give to anybody.'

5

THE human body is savage . . . it is saint. It cries out for vast varieties of
sensations . . . It weeps at sunrise on beholding a crystal dewdrop
balancing in the hammock of a spider's web, then plunges limb and bone
into a savage pounding of feet to drums and music, writhing, sweating in
an ecstasy that is at once a punishment. The ball of the sun has burnt
away the senses and burst forth in the bowels of men, and all sensations
centre there.

Only the sea beyond the half-doors of the Britannia seemed cool and
silent, as if its silence would indeed outlast all these cries and shouts and
milling men dressed up in the omniscient characters of their dreams for
which they had stinted and starved all year. A red dragon band going past
outside caught Zampi's attention. He could not understand why men
wanted to play the part of the Devil, dressed up in red skin-fitted suits,
ugly horned masks, armed with pitchforks, bells, and trembling tails.
They leapt and bounded, trying to stomp upon one another's chests. He
shook his head, his attention returning to the bar again. He was not really
with the group of people about him. Earlier on his head had spun a little
and he tapered off the size of his shots. How much easier it would have
been to slip into the bacchanalian mood of the Britannia and allow
himself to be carried along on the back of the wild spirit that had been let
loose in the city!

The Britannia was full now. No one could stand a few feet away, aim,
and arch their spit into the brass spittoons. There was only a great noise
that rose and thundered from time to time as a band went past. A few
masked faces would pop up over the swinging doors, see the crowds
inside, then race back to join the band they left. The old cash register
pinged, its long jaw jutted out, its little rusted plates, 12 cents, 60 cents,
popped up and down. The owner of the bar was shouting: '*Ice!* Get more
ice, somebody,' and then someone stood on the counter trying to lower a
twenty-five-pound block into the huge cauldron that stood kitty corner of

the counter. Zampi, as if closing out all the excitement about him, became rapt in these little activities that went on. Beneath the spigots of great wooden casks of rum stood small catch pitchers. He could not remember ever having seen them full, but today more than twice he had seen them emptied out, so brisk was the flow of rum!

Those who saw the tight crowd at the Britannia but came and squeezed in just the same were habitués. The place had a particular kind of darkness, an odour of a special combination of old rums, bitters, and walls that became a part of all these which drew them here. About ten sailors were coming in now, pushing through the packed crowd. They called out to comrades in the bar. A stranger would be lost and lonely here, but for those who knew a familiar face the crowd loosened up and made room, as they did for the sailors whose suits were black from rolling in the charcoal bins throughout the city. The letters on their jumpers were barely legible, *USS Bad Behavior.* One of them had a purplish cocoa-pod which he placed between his legs as he waddled about the floor flailing his arms in the air. The cripple went over and touched it and the sailor wriggled. The 'Bad Behaviors' always won the prize for the most authentic depiction of some group. They were the wildest, dirtiest, and most respected of all sailor bands. As they came in they spoke in short, gruff, drunken grunts, as American sailors do.

'Say . . . say . . . how about a rum . . . I mean ah rum . . . AH . . . Ah . . . Ahhhhhh . . . Ahhhhhh.' Their long red-nosed masks hanging off to one side, they entered the bar one by one. There was a great uproar as the two last sailors entered piggyback, the one on top brandishing the Stars and Stripes, and as the doors flapped back and forth, fanning the blatant sunlight until they stopped, it was now possible to see that the sailor on top was a woman dressed in tight bell-bottoms, her taut flesh splayed out as it pressed over the man's shoulders, and instead of the regular jumper she wore a midriff type that knotted below the great fullness of her breasts.

'Miss Zolda . . . Oh-God-oh-God-oye!' the cripple shouted, scrambling his bag of loose limbs together.

The sailor who held her on his shoulders put his arms around her thighs and pressed them close together so that they held his face tightly in a kind of embrace.

The bar attender looked up at this woman towering above the other heads and faces with that strange look of a man who has run a place like the Britannia and knows when he smells trouble.

36

Zampi felt a shiver steal across his heart. His hands were cold and his stomach rose and fell. He felt as though he had overeaten. He tipped two shots down, one after the other, rinsed out his mouth with ice water, then let it fall into the spittoon at his feet. Massahood threw his arms wide apart in front of the sailors as if waiting to catch Zolda as she lifted the wine-coloured domino she wore on her forehead.

'She too blasted good-lookin',' thought Zampi, looking at her face which had often set his mind to wondering from what lost race she had been called forth. Her father was a puny little Indian from the sugarcane plantations. Zampi had never known her mother, who was the product of an English overseer's drunken night with an Indian peasant woman. There were rumours that Zolda was not herself sure who her real father was, and whenever Zampi looked at her face he felt that he was looking at one of the sculptured mermaid faces of water fountains in the parks of the city. And looking at her waist now, the way the eyelets and the laces of her sailor suit drew in her flesh tightly, giving a voluptuous form to her hips, Zampi felt that kind of anger a man has when he meets a woman he has had at such a distance in a crowded place that his only wish is to have her there, as if to insist that the past was real. And as he thought this his body tautened from his eye sockets to his ankle bone. 'Oh woman, woman,' he sighed under his breath, 'if you only know what I would do with you body.'

Her lips were full and symmetrically formed, the skin lineless and smooth. They were strange lips, painted an orange red that livened the kind of bronze the sun drenched her face with, and on her large eyes, up to her eyebrows, she wore a turquoise tint like some of the tourists wore nowadays.

She was patting the small beads of sweat off her forehead with a handkerchief that she had wedged tightly in her waist and now her eyes met Zampi's. The smile and carefree pleasure in her face vanished instantly, her expression telling that in some way she would find some means to irk him, to taunt him.

'Put me down,' she said softly to the sailor. And as soon as she was standing on the floor—tall, her bosom firm, her smile calculated, as if she were the only person sober in the midst of the drunkards at the Britannia—the cripple danced out to her, his one foot stomping, the other clacking. He circled around and around her, his head thrown back, a bottle of Black Cat rum in his hand, which he offered each time he danced in to her, then out again.

She flung out her arms and, leaning as far back as she could, joined in the dance of the cripple while the masqueraders sang out, 'Iron something bust up my nothing . . . Oh-Man-Man-Ti-Re.'

Her breasts rolled slowly with the movements of her hands as she arched her body farther and farther backwards, her legs wide apart, bending from her waist. The crowd let up a roar as the end of her pigtail touched the floor of the Britannia. And now, as she arched still farther back, the sailor pants drawn like the skin of a drum over her thighs, her breasts slipped backwards so that now the pale light brown of her skin where the sun had not reached and played could be seen, and as if sensing that eyes were on some part of her body that should be chaste and covered, she flung herself forward, throwing her arms about the little man with a shrill laughter of such happiness in her voice that it made Zampi feel wretched, alone, and as if saddened by the thought that there were certain things in life he would not be able to do ever again. He knew that he would not be able to laugh as she did just then and he wished that he were as drunk as everyone in the Britannia. His thoughts raced so swiftly that in the next moment he wondered if he would ever be able to house in his body the joy of all these people about him. It was a feeling of instant desperation. He felt rushed . . . overwhelmed by a million things that he should do before it became too late.

He had had his first glimpse of this desperation a few months after he took over Jimpy's hut in Diego Martin. A beautiful American woman, her shoes hung around her neck, wide skirt, a peeling nose that wrinkled when she laughed, had made her way up to the top of the waterfall and playfully asked him to give her a charm which would enable her to find love. Zampi went through his ritual and gave her a small amulet to wear. He was conscious of her eyes devouring him, his body, his muscles working snakelike beneath his skin as he moved back and forth in the naked sun. As she made her way down the path with her guide, the obeah man stole glimpses of her from between the large wide leaves behind his hut. 'What a perfect waste of a beautiful specimen,' she had said. It had sounded foolish to him then. He had smiled foolishly all to himself in the bush. He never thought that the same foolish feeling he had that day would return, and now it had, with a keener edge, a sharper intensity.

The crowd meantime clapped, rapped spoons on bottles, banged on the counter to the tune of 'Iron something bust up my nothing' while Zolda and the cripple danced back and forth. Each time the dancers approached each other there were shouts of 'Hop . . . take care you hurt yourself, boy . . . that woman too much for you!'

Zolda only smiled, as if with a vengeance. 'When you get tired let me take over, boy . . . I love that body too bad-bad-bad,' they jibed, but the cripple, as if defying all, danced with all the energy his little body could provoke. Sweat ran down the folds of his face, caught in the stubble of unshaven beard in the crevices of his face, then rolled down the little veins of his neck that stood out like knotted bits of cord. Zolda, sweating on her forehead and cheeks, seemed only more vexing as her face became filled with the rich blood in her body, reminding the obeah man of mornings when she lay curled up on her side, the great ball of her hips curved so gently, making him feel that he could overpower her body in that lax state. He remembered her too with her legs stretched and tautened as he lay inside of her. He would seize her thighs then, pressing his fingernails into them, but beneath the thin skin of her body stretched ironlike bundles of muscle that finally left him powerless to do her that love hurt, to work a kind of passion and havoc on her body until finally desire seemed small.

Massahood pounded on the floor with his stick. His eyes were wild and insane with a joy that few men in the Britannia knew, for no other man in the Britannia was robust enough, bold enough, to house the madness of his joy. As Zolda catwalked backwards in her dance, her back came close to him. The stick man wove both hands up and down, simulating the shape of her body, then, as she danced away, he threw his arms out, his stick in one, a bottle in the other, and with his head turned to one side, his eyes pressed tightly, his face contorted as if in great pain, he shook the muscles of his breast alone, shivering as if he had caught the ague.

'Oh God, man . . . Aye aye aye!' he screamed as he tossed his head from left to right. He then glanced at Zampi as if to measure the extent to which he could go without angering him. But the obeah man was without reaction; he only smiled with a kind of resignation as he wondered whose woman she was. Was she the cripple's? The remark of the drunken man they had beaten up came back to him and he tried to recall the exact words, but they would not come in the din of the strange display between these three. For whose benefit was this dance? Zampi wondered.

'Boy . . . ha!' he said to himself as he downed a fast rum.

'You begin to think and think and after a while anything begin to sound true.'

39

Zolda danced back towards Massahood this time, and the stick man handed his stick and bottle to someone, and he waited, rubbing his palms together. His nostrils dilated as he took deep breaths, and when she was closest to him he threw his arms around her waist. Zolda tried to shake him loose, but the stick man had plunged his hands into the tight waist of her bell bottoms. One hand slipped in and she bit hard into it. Massahood pulled his hand out, rolling with his bawdy laughter.

'You is a ugly bitch . . . You make from stone or what?' she said sullenly, adjusting the waistband of her trousers. But her words fell weakly.

The stick man tensed the muscles of his breasts and quivered them in reply. His body seemed to be indeed carved from stone—amber brown. He knew the delight it had given women to stare at him, to touch him. 'That is the way woman like me, and that is the way God make me. Is only you who 'fraid me, but one day you go come beggin' with your tongue hanging down.' He grabbed his bottle from the man who held it and swallowed. 'And I going to make you beg and beg . . . I going to make you crawl on your hands and knees and beg me . . . wait, wait and see.'

There was loud cackling from the voices of women in the Britannia, and the stick man felt strengthened by this.

'You think is man I want?' Zolda said to him. 'You think is man I hard up for?'

The stick man leaned forward, almost breathing in her face; he could smell her breath. 'Doo Doo,' he said. 'I know you ain't had a man for a long, long time . . . I could smell it in your mouth when you get so vex-up and heated.'

She thrust the palm of her hand into his face and pushed him away as hard as she could. The stick man reeled a step backward, but that was all. He bellowed with laughter, knowing that he had really struck hard. What could she say? That she had had dozens and dozens of men? It simply was not true, and what if she had said so? The women in the Britannia were not the kind who liked other women, especially if they were as tempting as Zolda. They were at once on the side of the stick man, and he knew it.

'Darlin', drink up your rum and take your time . . . You could wait, and I could wait *longer*. Is only God in heaven who will know why he put two people like we in the world . . . like if we make from the same mould. You know how it does take fire to fight fire . . . you kind of fire and my kind of fire? What do you say we make a blaze?' He ran his fingers teasingly across her cheek, and she pushed his hand away again.

'Your mouth stink of rum.'

But nothing she could say would affect Massahood. As unsure of Zampi's obeah as he was, he knew that if he could once have the obeah man's woman he would no longer have to go to him. If the stick man's lust was bold it was not his fault. His body and his bones were made for love, women smelt it from his nostrils, tasted it from his mouth, and knew it in that amorphous way that animals in heat single out each other. He had loved with hate, anger, revenge . . . he had loved with a bitter taste in his mouth. He had had women plead with him to tie their hands and feet and love them brutally, obscenely . . . What did he care if she said he was made of stone? If anyone spoke of tenderness to him he would laugh quietly all to himself. He knew the very fibres of a woman's nerve centre, he knew that it could not distinguish between pain and pleasure . . . all was one . . . all was love. Love was a sharp thorn gnawing in his thigh bone. Woman was the only thing that could loosen the tightness in his loins. With his bottle in one hand, his stick in the other, he threw one arm about her again.

Zampi stepped up and took hold of his arm in which he held the stick.

'Let go of she,' he said. 'She don't want you, you can't see that?'

As Zampi touched his arm, it rose instinctively over his shoulder, poised, and the stick man's eyes were upon him.

'What you goin' to do . . . kill me? Go ahead,' Zampi said. And then a strange thing happened. The stick man let out a howl like a wounded hog.

'Oh Gawad!! . . . Oh Gawd . . . my hand freeze . . . it cold, cold, cold like ice!' he said, his stick held in midair.

The cripple who stood off to the side popped his eyes open wide. There was some low whispering in the Britannia. The obeah man had frozen Massahood's arm. In a flash the cripple thought of 'Hands-up,' he thought that Massahood would get a nickname like that; his mind bolted and he was not sure if he was glad of this or not.

Zampi pulled the stick man's arm down, saying, 'Put that stick down and don't make a jackass of yourself.'

'My hand dead . . . Oh Gawd!' Massahood screamed. A sudden fear filled his voice as he cried out, and the cripple cowered in a corner as if there was something going on which he did not understand, something that frightened him.

'Is only your own stupid mind that workin' on you, you fool,' the obeah man said as he turned to Zolda. 'Come on, out of here.'

She shrugged sullenly, sipping from the cripple's glass. Zampi put his hand on her arm and spoke more forcefully this time.

'Come on out of here, I tell you!' He reached for her, and as she tried to pull away, his hand caught in the midriff she wore, tearing it. Her great breasts spilled out, and, wild with panic, she clasped her breasts, trying to cover them with her palms as Zampi pulled her out of the Britannia into the street.

6

THE pool of Blue Basin is a low bowl hammered out deep into the ground by its pounding waters. Its blue water rarely sees the daylight. In the afternoon the basin grumbles in near darkness, the earth around it cool and damp, and a fine spray of the hammering waters scrubs the thick wide leaves a glistening green, covering them until the tiny droplets, hugging one another, caressing one another, rush finally to become one. They stand still for a moment in this ecstasy, roll into the fork of the leaf, then into the earth where they are absorbed thus locked together for ever. By evening, at the first dewfall, the ground is pungent with an aroma of the great, wide, waxy leaves that hide the face of the earth from the thirsty mouth of the sun. It is a strange odour that rises from the basin . . . one that is so close to life, yet not living. When the obeah man first came here he had thought, as children do, that this odour was 'life', that all the shades of meaning of the word 'life' were contained in this smell of the basin, and in such moments he was happy, pleased with all the world about him, for the earth in this spot seemed as if awaiting a single breath into its nostrils for life to begin in all its shapes and forms in an otherwise uninhabited planet . . . or so he often felt as he sat on a large stone above the basin in the evenings.

As he and Zolda walked up to his hut this evening this familiar odour of the basin enveloped him, and he thought that if the choice were his he would not blow life into it.

'You comin' or you ain't comin'?' he turned and asked her gruffly.

She hung back a few paces behind him, slashing at the bushes along the path with a switch she had picked up below. She stopped abruptly, her hand on her hip. 'Is so a man does get quarrelsome after living in the bush?'

Zampi walked down to her. He wondered if something had not indeed happened to him since he came here, and to hear someone else remark upon it troubled him even more.

'Yes! Is so a man does get quarrelsome . . . You want to go back? Go! Next bus leaving in a hour.' He turned and began walking up the hill again.

'I didn't ask to come here, you know. You drag me . . .' She was talking in that childish way she had which made Zampi smile. Most people thought that she was filled with fire and a wild rage. No one would think that she could sound helpless.

'If I had any sense in my head I would never . . .' she mumbled, following him up to the hut.

Zampi teased her about all the little things that frightened her. 'Take care a big snake ain't crawl out of the bush and give you a good bite,' he called out as he reached the top.

Her sullen whines halted and she scampered up the hill to the clearing where Zampi stood laughing at her. When she saw him laughing she started cuffing him, but this only made the obeah man laugh more heartily. He held her hands, then threw his arms around her, but she still wriggled with enough strength to break loose. Zampi then lifted her off her feet and now her legs worked on, loosely flailing at the air as she grunted out at him. She bit into his arm and he had to let her go.

'It have plenty snake hidin' in the bush, you know.'

She sat down heavily on a large stone beside the fireplace in the clearing while Zampi went into the hut.

'I don't know why you didn't leave me to mind my own business. I ain't like you, you know. I was having a good time at the Britannia with my friends till you come and spoil everything.'

Zampi came out with some food in his arms. He stood still for a moment and looked at her. The teasing of a moment ago had fled somewhere.

'That is what you call having a good time? A man have to shove he hand inside your crotch and a dozen others watch and laugh. You can't have a good time here . . . No, you have to have people to see you and you see them. The bush too dark for you . . . who you would have to show off to here?'

'And what business it is of yours? You must be think you own me?' she asked, turning her head away, throwing her nose up in the air.

It came to Zampi that he had no business questioning her actions. He knew that she would only remind him that it was he who had left her without a word.

'The only thing you know what to feel with is your body. Now shut up your mouth and help me light the fire.'

She got up from the stone where she sat and dusted off her bell-bottoms, slapping at her thighs. Zampi stood in the doorway watching her. He had a great desire to touch her body, slap her thighs, as she was doing just then. A moment ago it would have been all right, but now that moment was past. She walked sullenly to the edge of the clearing to pick up some dried twigs for the fire, and as she walked away she swayed her hips, Zampi thought deliberately, and each time she bent down, the flesh of her body taut against her tight pants outlining the shape of her thighs, Zampi shuddered a little as if slapped by a cold breath of air.

In a few moments she had a lively fire going, and she sat, elbows on her knees, chin in her palms, watching the small twigs fall and crumble. The smell of burning twigs was enough to make her hungry. Zampi hammered out an old five-gallon can into a sheet. He scrubbed off the rust with a corn husk and some sand, then placed it above the three rocks where a nice fire glowed. He rolled on four inch-thick black sausages. They sizzled and emitted thin wisps of smoke that smelled of chives and thyme at first, then there was a maddening odour of the black pudding itself, the thyme and the chives of a moment before mildly blended together with the blood and breadcrumbs of which the sausage was made.

'You hungry?' he asked.

Her eyes were fixed on the tin sheet, the fire, the sausages. She didn't hear him for a moment. She looked up suddenly, swallowed, then said: 'Who, me? Is not the first time I see food, you know.'

The obeah man laid on two crispy loaves of hops bread, and when they were warm he broke them open with his hands and slapped some dark yellow butter in each. He closed the loaves and let them steam for a while, as if he had all the patience in the world.

The food still lay untouched with a small smouldering fire below the sheet. It was dark enough now, and the fire gave off a pleasant glow, lighting their faces a pale orange as they sat, as if each were waiting on the other to break the silence, until Zolda finally said: 'So this is the way you does live? You could do everything for yourself—cook wash . . . you really don't need nobody.'

At first Zampi was annoyed at her, that she should begin to chatter. There had been a quiet beauty about before she opened her mouth; now it was broken. It was the kind of statement that people make when they have nothing to say, and Zampi was aware, all over again, of a vast amount of what he called 'slackness' about this woman.

'And what about you? Perhaps you would like to tell me what and what you do with yourself for the past two years . . . and don't tell me that you was a saint.'

She threw a cutting glance at him, then looked away. She was still for a few seconds, and he knew that she was boiling, that she had not cast the glance as her reply. She turned and faced him again.

'You think that a woman is like a bitch in heat . . . that as soon as a man leave her she have to go out and get another man to comfort she. You think that is the way I did want you? You make me shame . . . shame for you. If that is the kind of picture you have in your mind 'bout me I don't want to see you so long as I live. You don't understand woman, you ain't even begin to know what does go on inside of she . . . Zampi, you don't understand people. I don't think you even know what make them laugh and cry. I learn something today. Something I did never know. I uses to think that you had so much feelin's, but I don't think you know the first thing about people. What a mistake I did make in you. I think that the feelin's that you have is for yourself.'

Everything a man did was done in the name of ambition, she thought. A woman stood in his way always, and she was swept aside. It was her fault that Zampi was whittling away his life on the La Basse. She stood in the way. When he decided to become an obeah man he simply said so and left one day and she was expected to understand. Now that he had come into the city and dragged her here she should be ready to do his bidding, and what was that? Did she understand what compelled him now? Could she ask? But she loved him and that was why everything worked in one direction only. She wished that she did not need this man who could make her do anything without being able to expect some return of affection from him. Was this what was called love? Or was that something that only people in faraway places, like they show in the films, knew? In these islands people lived with one another so that they would have someone close by to strike or curse each day when the sun was too hot or the rainy season too long . . . Who knew love?

Far removed as the obeah man was from people and their ways, he was not unaware of her feelings. What she said about him seemed to have more and more truth to it, and he wondered if he truly understood people. He could only fall back on the few people whom he had helped with advice and medicine, and, even so, that seemed to be a small proportion of what he thought he could do as an obeah man.

'Well,' he said, after a long reflective silence, 'my life is nothing. I just here for other people. To come in the way of all kind of people and all kind of things. I is like a sounding board . . . like a conch shell that people could put they ears to to find out what thing they have to do. All of the foolishness I do, all of the nonsense I talk, I do them because I think they right and good. Whoever laugh at me, or whoever believe in me, who get hurt and kill because of me . . . I is only here to make they life complete. You ask me what is my reward . . . what uses I have? That is the onliest use I have . . . like a sieve that the whole world pass through and leave nothing behind . . . is not a bad thing. Is only one in a million who born to do something. The rest of we born only to cross they path for a second . . . that is we life . . . four, five seconds when we path cross with somebody who have a big work to do.'

Without realizing it, the two of them had started eating the food. They talked on as if unaware of each other's presence, as if there was a strangeness in the woods at Blue Basin that took hold in a peculiar way. The obeah man had held many a conversation with himself, laughing now, muttering now, talking back to himself. Perhaps Jimpy, its previous tenant, had left some spell on the place; perhaps this was why he chose it. Anger came easily here, and so did tenderness.

After Zampi spoke she felt sorry for what she had said to him. She did not think that she could penetrate the cold shroud of aloofness that took hold of him. Now she had, and she was sorry. She said gently to him: 'You have a big work to do, Zampi. I meet somebody only the other day down by John-John who say that you is the best obeah man in the island, that when nobody else could rid him of he headache he come to you, and now he is a new man.'

Zampi laughed to himself. 'So, I have a big work to do,' he repeated. 'I *used* to think so. Now I see for myself what I is, and I glad, glad too bad! Is good for a man to know he limits. He mustn't aim too far. That is the biggest thing wrong with people, they don't know how far they could reach. I hear people say that this is a sin, that is a sin. Well, one of the biggest sin in the world is for a man not to know what work make for he. A man who waste he life always chasing behind something that ain't make for he, something that too big for he, always feeling he-self, believing, feeling like if it close by. One more day, one more day, and is so he spend he life, never reaching that thing. We like to say, "But look how five years done gone past in my life and I ain't do nothing with it!" That ain't the way life does waste away . . . It does waste away day by day, day by day. I see it and I know it.'

Zolda listened quietly to his rambling. At first she was kind; the thoughts he expressed moved her with the kind of tenderness a woman has when a man talks this way. When she first met Zampi it was just this kind of melancholy brooding that touched her. As he was about in the middle of his talk, gesturing now with one hand, now with the other, she felt that there was something weak, something evil, about the way he allowed himself to slip into this kind of mood, and as he spoke on her temper grew and grew so that by the end she almost wanted to scream, to shake him by the shoulders.

'The trouble with you is that you can't be happy, you don't know how to enjoy yourself any more, and when you see other people having a good time you sour up your face. Nothing ent wrong with people, boy— is you! It have everything here that you could ask for. You know better than me how much people does come here from all them far far part of the world to see this island. I hear some say that they would like to spend the rest of they days here. What wrong? What wrong with Trinidad?'

The obeah man stopped chewing. He spat out his mouthful of food into the small fire. He was ready to tell her. The words were on the tip of his tongue. 'What the hell you go say if I tell you that the island dead!' he lashed out at her.

There was only silence.

'Eh . . . answer me that!'

Silence.

'You dead and I dead,' he said. 'The people who put up all them buildings, them big big churches with clock to tell time by . . . they dead and gone. They did plan to stay and they build them things to last for ever, but Trinidad blight. Oh, yes, it nice for white people who have money to come here and spend a few days and laugh and enjoy they-self . . . When I was a boy . . . run 'way from school and go down to the jetty, I used to say, "One day, one day I go study a big work." Well, I get a job in a doctor office cleaning it up for him. The man say he go teach me how to be a doctor. Where the hell I know you have to go 'way to learn doctor work? I sweep, I clean, I scrub. "Good man . . . good man," he keep telling me. "A fine doctor one day . . . You're going to be a fine doctor one day, lad."

'A fine doctor, my ass!

'Then you . . . you come wiggin' your tail under my nose. I say to myself, "It look like if the only thing left for we here behind God back is more rum and more woman," and then . . . it look as if that have a end to it, too.

'Down by the wharf, where the big ships does come in, I was talkin' to a tourist one day. The man is a big professor or something, up in England or America. He say: "Man! you fellers don't know how lucky you are. All you have to do is put your hand outside your window, pick your banana and grapefruit off a tree, have breakfast, and go on back to sleep." He say, "Man, you are the mixtures of all the peoples of the world . . ."

'I wish I could see the old son of a bitch now. He really full up my head with a lot of nonsense. It ain't have no place for we. The islands drowning and we going down with them—down, down, down. One day the clocks in the big church and them go stop and nobody here to fix them or wind them up. Time stop then . . . time stop . . . and we just waiting for that day. I only want to say one thing. We is nobody, and we ain't have nowhere to go. Everything leave me with a cold, cold feeling in my insides and I ain't have no uses for you or nobody nor nothing— nothing . . .' He stopped briefly to look at her, as if all that he had said was general, now it was his turn to speak to her personally.

'. . . and who the hell you think you is to come here and tell me who I is and what I have to do? I done give you everything I have inside me till I ain't have no feelings in my insides . . . and that over, too . . . it dry up like a blasted calabash shell that have only seeds rattling round inside.'

Zampi felt his throat go dry. He pulled the cork off a bottle and wet his throat with some rum. He gargled it about his mouth, then spat it out into the fire. The embers blazed up purple and blue, making a faint noise, then died down. He placed the bottle to his mouth now and had a good swallow. Although he did not look at her, he knew that her eyes followed his every action. He turned his face away from her, lit a cigarette, and puffed leisurely.

'You know what I think, Zampi?' He looked at her disdainfully, his eyebrows, his nostrils wide, the smoke of his last puff curling slowly out. 'I think you frighten. I think you 'fraid something. Like if you have something lock up inside you that does come out in the night and make monkey-face at you in your sleep.'

The obeah man laughed at her scornfully. 'Huh . . .' he said. 'So is frighten you think I frighten, eh?' He looked away from her. 'A woman is a hell of a thing,' he mumbled to himself, adding: 'I frighten, all right. Frighten like hell. I 'fraid to dead. I 'fraid to come into the world and go out of it like Hop-and-Drop and Massahood and you. The only thing that count for me was the first time a woman come here with a sick child . . . roasting with fever. She say somebody put a bad spirit on the child, and I make that child get well, well, well. It ain't have no feeling in the world like that for me. All I want is more and more of that feeling. It have a taste like a good rum in my mouth and I want to get drunk with it day after day . . . nothing more.'

She screwed up her mouth at him as if she was envious of something. She had told him that he would crave for her . . . for her body. She had told him that, knowing him the way she did that he would spend sleepless nights wondering if she hadn't someone else to warm her bed. All of these warnings had fallen flat with his last remark. She had the feeling that she could not touch him now. 'What about me?' her heart kept saying.

'I think you 'fraid; I think you is coward!' she screamed.

'Think what the damn' hell you want to think,' he said coolly. 'Is only your body that talkin' now. So long as it can't have what it want it have to find fault with everything. Yes, Zolda, I 'fraid. I 'fraid people like you. You livin' from day to day like if you goin' to dead tomorrow. You want to squeeze everything out of every minute of the day. I ain't forget the way you used to like to drink . . . the way you used to like to love. You goin' to kill yourself one day, and I don't want to help you do it. You say it look as if I have a spirit inside of me. Tell me what kind of spirit you have lock up in you? You 'fraid to sleep, you 'fraid to be by yourself, you . . .'

She wouldn't listen to him any more. If there was one thing she feared, or respected, about Zampi it was that he knew her. She wore a face for all the world, but this one man knew her, and the truth he made her face was unbearable.

'*I* should come and sit up here in the bush like . . . dat it?' Zampi didn't answer, he only looked at her. 'My body young and strong and I don't want to wait till I get old, old, old and dry up. Nobody want to watch you when your flesh hanging from your bones like wet clothes on a clothes line. If you ask me, it look as if you ain't a man no more . . . that is the whole thing that wrong with you.'

The obeah man stood up now, he jumped up from the stone he sat on.

'You think I is not a man . . . that what you think?' He threw one arm round her bosom, gripping her breast with a kind of savage love. With the other hand he ripped the front flap of her trousers and the four buttons

50

that held it snapped and rolled away in the grass. She hammered upon his shoulders with slow, deliberate blows. With each blow of her clenched fist Zampi felt his arms weaken, but he held on to her breast so firmly he could feel the hard meshwork of muscle fibre between his fingers. He knew that he would have to throw her on the ground before her deadening blows could numb his arm.

'I hate you . . . I hate you so bad!' she screamed at him, her legs firm on the ground, digging into the earth as she fought.

In a flash Zampi's hand had shot into the flap of her trousers. He felt her knees buckle suddenly as her defences shifted from one part of her body to another. He pushed with all his weight against her and they were both on the ground. Their thighs locked in love beside the fire on the cool earth that was beginning to dampen with the heavy fall of dew. He felt his face wet against the side of hers, he felt her fire die, he heard her say, 'Love me, Zampi . . . love me . . . just make love to me.' And as his body worked, he felt the rhythm of hers growing closer to the phase of his movements, and then he heard her say: 'Bite me, Zampi . . . bite my breasts. I want to remember this love tomorrow.'

7

TIME too will run out in the end and all the worlds go to their cold and quiet sleep. The human body tuned to the ping-pong pan, the base booms of the steel drums that run through the streets like a maddened beast, its tempo mounting in unending rhythms . . . on Tuesday night at twelve o'clock shrill whistles of the constables echo through the streets; there is a tap-tap-tapping of their night sticks on the front doors of the city and a quiet fills the night.

But sanity does not return with the blowing of a whistle. The stretched nerve coils back slowly to its size. The bodies of men, still tuned to the pitch of bacchanal, hunger on. And in the quiet that falls a distant scream will fill the night as someone lying drunk in the gutters hears the great sound of a steel band coming down the street and staggers up to plunge into its massive noise only to find that the sound is in his ear, the rhythm buried in his bone begging to break loose. The drug has been snatched from the fevered nerve and leaves it weeping in the empty streets of Port of Spain with only the low grumbling of the mule carts clearing away the scattered confetti, broken rum bottles, and coloured streamers of the past hours.

Throughout the city, as the end of carnival burns itself out on Tuesday night, there is only a vast noise echoing through the night. It floats up through the valley of Diego Martin, and at Blue Basin there are two great sounds: the waterfall, and the din of the drums and ping-pong pans. Both are equal at this point. You could tune your ear to either one and tune out the other. If you were close to the hut, or seated on its step as Zampi was, you heard the waterfall, the small noises of frogs, and the humming of the sand flies. If you stood at the edges of the clearing as Zolda did, looking down to the dark city, you could hear its shrill cry as it drenched its appetite with rum, trying to squeeze out the last dregs of a frenzy already spent. Another hour or two more and the bacchanal would have to leave the streets. But for those whose bodies hated the abruptness of

52

this end there were clubs like the Scorpion Tail or the Manicou around Charlotte Street and George Street where night joined day around the Eastern Market, the one slipping into the other so smoothly that no one could tell the difference.

'You think that just because you done gone and make love to me you could keep me tied down here. People does wait a whole year for this fete and you have to come and spoil it,' Zolda said to the obeah man.

He looked at her crossly without saying anything. There was something that triggered off in her. She seemed possessed by a strange spirit when she spoke up this way; her face, her eyebrows, her lips, her mouth, all acted independently of her—what she would say at moments like this came from another tongue, Zampi thought. He wondered if she knew how other people saw her. He wondered if she had any kind of picture of herself at all.

'You is a funny kind of woman,' he said to her. 'It have some kind of women that men like and it have some kind of women that women like. I don't think that either men or women like you . . . What kind of woman you is at all?'

'Don't worry 'bout me, boy. Man like me, all right. Woman—who the hell care if they don't like me?'

The last bus would leave from the foot of the hill at twelve o'clock, she thought, wondering what time it was, what she would do if she left now. The lively smoky air of the clubs was in her nostrils. 'The least you could do is go back with me . . . It done gone and get so late already,' she complained.

Zampi could feel the haunting silence of the streets that carnival left behind, that peculiar silence in a place where great activity had taken place . . . a broken mask, a stray sash from some colourful costume, trampled by hundreds of feet in the dark, confetti mixed with dust.

'What business I have in Port of Spain?' he asked.

She sat down heavily on the grass, breaking a piece of twig into tiny pieces, and when it was all broken she began breaking the pieces into still smaller pieces.

'You have all your spirits that you does call up from Blue Basin to come and talk with you. I ain't have nothing here, you know.'

Zampi was always amused by what other people thought obeah was, for deep within himself he did not know. With time he had learnt many things with what Jimpy had taught him, yet he knew that a day would come when some special problem, some special issue, would fall before his very eyes like the small bones he threw out on the ground to get his cue for the cure of some ailment. There were times when he wished he knew everything about obeah, yet there were times when he was afraid that its meaning would be too sudden, too staggering, too unusual for him to shift his ways and thoughts to encompass it. 'What the hell left for a man if he wake up one day and find out that he workin' for the devil?' he questioned himself. But since there was so much to learn, so much that worked for him from day to day, each day improving his knowledge of herbs, chants, places where he could find the little tools of his calling, he moved about with a kind of conviction that in the end all would be well. Spirits he did not—could not—call up from the basin. Perhaps they dwelt there. He often had the feeling as he ministered to some client of his that there were eyes watching him he did not know. And then there was the shooting star that night when he came close to working a bad obeah on Zolda out of spite. Looking at her now, he saw where debauchery, love, sex, rum, all acted on her like a catalyst. But for what? Her eyes were alive and filled with a new sparkle, her body seemed to crave only more and more vexation, cruelty too, all of which only left Zampi feeling alone and anxious to set himself to things which would yield some kind of statement for him.

'If you have to go, why you don't go 'bout your business and leave me alone? . . . You can't see that I don't want to go anywhere with you?'

If she could only get him away from here, she thought. If only he would come with her to the city, go to the places that they used to frequent, have him see all the walls and doorways, the colour of the morning light after a long night at the Scorpion Tail, have him know again the sound of the tramcar bells as it rattled along the early streets, the taste of green coconut water. If she could only do this she was sure that she could find him again.

'Tomorrow everybody that we uses to know down by the La Basse going to be feting . . . why you don't come? You think that you better than everybody else down there?'

Zampi recalled how it was after carnival, how everyone on the dump went from one shanty to another trying to keep the mood of bacchanal from dying out, hanging on to its tail, feeding it like a dying fire whose vital centre had burnt out leaving only pale and warm grey cinders at its edges.

'They didn't get their bellyful yet . . . two days ain't enough to kill them!' he said.

'Zampi . . . Zampi, you used to do all of them things yourself. What happen to you at all? Nobody would believe how you change. Your face even beginning to change. You look like a different person. When you meet me the first time it was at one of those same fetes down on the La Basse after carnival. It was your bottle I did drink from. It was for you that I did dance whole night. You don't remember?'

She spoke on quietly, her hands still now, her eyes fixed at a point in midair, focused on nothing. 'It look as if you come to hate me for all the things you liked me for in the beginning. You like the way I dance, the way I sing, the way my voice sound when I laugh, you like the way my body move, and now . . .'

Zampi pushed the cinders of the dying fire with a twig as he listened to her.

'. . . And then, after you have me, after you know that I belong to you, you begin to wonder all kinds of things; who who I do this for; who who I do that with. The same thing that you love me for, soon as I give it to you it look as if it turn you sour. The same foolishness that I used to listen, make you laugh, make you happy, and then later on you say that I foolish, and slack. What a woman have to do to please a man in this world at all?'

What she said had some truth, Zampi reflected as he stared into the fire, puzzled. After she was his he did not care ever to do that kind of frantic dance with her, nor did he want her to dance that way with anyone else. Had he let her down, had he disappointed her?

'All right . . . all right,' he said. 'Tomorrow night I going to come down there.'

She looked up, surprised, at him. 'You will come, you really mean it?'

'Yes,' he said, 'I really mean it.'

Down along the valley of Diego Martin there was only black night. The small houses, the thatched-roofed huts of estate workers had gone to sleep buried in the ground in the midst of thick black shapes of trees that hid them from view. Beyond, heaped together like a mass of small shoe boxes, was Port of Spain, its streets lined by straight rows of dim lights, with an occasional tiny eye of light burning in a house here or there where someone had taken the fete indoors. The voluminous sound of the city was almost gone now. It took only the smallest whisper of a mosquito sawing the air to drown out the sound that came up along the valley. From this Zolda could tell the time, that it was getting close to midnight, that the last bus had no more than part of an hour before it would leave the foot of Blue Basin.

'But you won't come in town with me tonight!'

'No,' he said. 'I see 'nuff people make a fool of they-self for one day.'

'Well, go to hell, then!' she shouted at him. She drew a string of vine tightly about her waist to hold up the flap of her trousers.

Zampi watched her lips working like her fingers as she tied two knots in the vine. 'What you going to tell people when they ask you how your pants fall down?'

She stopped tying the string for a second and gave him a cutting glance, then returned to fixing her clothes again.

'You ain't have no uses for me. That is all what you bring me here for, to laugh at me. Is only that that you did want from me, nothing more, now I could go.'

She was pouting her lips the way she always did when Zampi teased her.

'If you stick out your mouth that way somebody go plant a kiss on them for you,' he said.

'Why you don't leave me alone and mind your own business? All of you men is the same way. A woman can't do nothing, she can't walk down the street with the body that God give she before all of you start picturing all kinds of things. What wrong with me lips? That is all you could see when you look at them and after you plant that in the back of your mind you make up all kind of things that I does do. *Man!*' Throwing her eyes to the heavens, '*God ?*' She looked at Zampi again. 'You don't know how I hate you . . . I hate you too bad!' she said, and started walking down the path.

As she turned her back and started walking away, the obeah man felt suddenly alone, sitting on the steps of his hut. He felt that carnival and the mounting passions in her had not reached their climax. He felt that somewhere down in the dark city there was someone whom she might find, someone who would know instinctively that her whole being yearned for pleasure, for love that had only started and would have to run its wild course. He knew that he would be plagued by all the visions his mind could conjure up in that lonely place. If he did let her go this night something might happen, something like love, something that would change Zolda for ever in his eyes, and although he would not do all that she wished, although he would not leave Blue Basin and go back to live the life they led on the La Basse, he could not bear the thought that she might sleep with someone else this night. He ran to the path and listened.

He could still hear her footsteps on the loose gravel.

'Zolda . . . Zolda, wait for me!' he shouted, putting his hands to his mouth like a funnel so that his voice would carry, and when he heard his own voice in the quiet of the woods he felt it was someone else's. His body was seized with a wild excitement as he listened.

He heard her footsteps stop and he heard her say, 'You coming down in town with me?'

'Yes,' he answered, his heart throbbing. 'I don't want no other man to finish off what I start,' he said to himself. All the dormant hungers of her body that had been awakened plagued him, all the pleasures they could yield were his, his, and though he did not want to go into the city with her, he felt compelled. He rushed into the hut and took down a small silver box with a string attached to it and tied it securely around his arm, then rolled down his sleeve to cover it. 'This going to protect me from all kind of bad bad things,' he said as he buttoned his sleeve. He darted out of the hut with an agility and abandon such as his heart and his body had not known for a great while. When he reached her he threw his arms about her, pressing her body close to his, slipping his thigh between hers as they embraced.

'Come on and hurry up, man, before the bus go 'way without we,' she said.

Zampi placed his arm round her, his thumb slipped into the tight waist of her trousers. He stood a little above her. He could see her face in the pale moonlight looking up into his, and as they walked, the light, breaking through the trees above, caught her pearl-white teeth, giving them a quick lustre. His hand cupped her breast and she pressed closer to him.

'You happy?' he asked.

'Yes, too bad,' she said. 'And you?'

Zampi felt for the charm on his arm. Yes, it was there.

'Yes,' he said, 'me too.'

'Look,' she said, running away from him, 'the bus! Come on quick before it leave.'

And Zampi started running after her to a small circle in the grass at the foot of the rise to Blue Basin which the buses had cut out as they came to the end of the line and turned round to face Port of Spain.

8

NOW if the human body were to be exposed to all the noises of bacchanal . . . all the small notes and the large notes of the steel drum . . . the bamboos . . . all the smells of bodies sweating in the sun . . . if the hungry thoughts of one mind in the crowd broke loose and lashed themselves to all the objects of its lust, it would explode like a calabash in the sun. In this seething chaos there is order, thin and hidden from the eye. Each man narrows down the wide and open field, his focus falls upon a single flask of rum, a pair of breasts, a pelvis that arcs and circles wide. The rest of the world does not exist save as background for most men. But not so for Massahood . . . where most men set the limits of their lust, the stick man's knew no bounds. Every woman was a potential lover, and given the right moment he knew that their bodies could hunger like any other. The Britannia was his home. It was where he was weaned from thick heavy condensed milk to Black Cat rum.

As a boy he had grown up with his grandfather who worked as a night watchman for the Trinidad Electricity Board and the first sounds the boy uttered were 'T-E-B.' When his mother disappeared and went to Venezuela, Santo Pi, the child's grandfather, was glad to have someone to shout at, someone to run his errands, someone to rub his bony back when it ached with the dampness of the rainy season. Massahood would never forget the first day of his life, the first time that his senses awakened to consciousness. He was rubbing his grandfather's back. The old man's joints ached more from rum than rain. The boy was looking out of the tiny window, absentmindedly watching the thin, long threads of grey.

'Gramps, is who does make the rain up dey?' he asked.

The old man was lolling half asleep from the delicious massage of tiny hands along his loose shanks. He woke up suddenly when the sweet sensation stopped. He saw the foolish look in the boy's eyes looking out into the rain and he slapped him across his mouth so hard that Massahood went spinning like a small rag doll across the tiny little shack which the TEB provided for the watchman and the boy as their home.

'You li'l bitch! You does ask too much question. Keep your blasted mouth shut and you go learn more that way!'

Massahood was only five years old then. He cowered in the midst of dozens of hurricane lanterns which they kept in the hut, tasting the strange salt blood of his own body in his mouth. It seemed that he discovered himself that day. He heard his own voice, a part of him; something which was only a series of noises before, was now he . . . Massahood.

The blow had choked off the boy's breath somehow. He could still feel the bones of the old man's knuckles raw against his tiny adam's apple, and as the old man looked down at him in rage, the boy, stricken with terror as he was, tried to let pass a small column of air through his throat so that he could hear his voice again. It came out as a faint whistle as the air painfully went past his throat, the sound that was he, Massahood.

He heard for the first time that day, too. He heard the cascading clatter of all those hurricane lanterns with red glass chimneys as they rattled for an endless moment when his little body was hurled into the heap of them.

That night, as Massahood lay sprawled out on the floor at the old man's feet, he saw with his eyes for the first time, too. He saw the cold grey colour of the watchman's hut. He had never seen a single colour before in his life. His whole body ached, for it had jammed against all the sharp angles of the scattered lanterns. His arms were bruised. He was bruised along his spine, his head had hit the floor, and then his face, his throat, and the little reddened teeth of his mouth. He lay as if paralysed for seconds as all these sensations stormed through his little body. Santo Pi grasped him by the arm, dragging him up with a sharp tug.

'Come here, you li'l bitch! You playin' dead. . . eh!' The boy was speechless, his head hung lifeless off to one side. Santo Pi gripped him by the ear and held him up that way.

'Tell me,' the old man shouted close to the boy's ear, 'is dead you playin' dead? I ain't want you to dead now, you know . . . you should'er dead long time . . . long, long time ago. You have to live now . . . is live I want you to live. You have to pay me back for all of my troubles, you hear!'

The little boy seemed suddenly to have a strange kind of sense. He saw the rain, he saw the dim grey light of the watchman's hut, he tasted the salt of his blood, and he tasted the salt water the old man was forcing down his throat, which pained with each swallow. He felt the pains of his

59

body and he felt the damp wind coming in from outside drying up the blue-black bruises on his shins. He smelt the old man's breath, sour, black tobacco, and rotten rum. He smelt the wet grass growing in the slippery red earth that came creeping through the crevices of the floor. His body had crushed a few blades of the grass in the hut as he tumbled and fell.

All these sensations joined together, and the boy felt in a way such as he had never felt before, a feeling of sadness . . . and loneliness that in its peculiar way resembled the rain.

The old man was shaking him by the ear again. 'You want more cut-ass? Tell me! Is that what you want? Eh! Answer me, you little vagabond.'

Finally the boy forced out an answer only to release the old man's tugging of his ear.

'No, Gramps . . . Oh-God-oh-God-oye . . . I beg you, Gramps . . . I beg you!'

'All right, then . . . hush up before people hear you. Hush up before I give you some more licks!' And with that the old man shoved him by his little chest on to the bed. 'Don't ask too much question in this world and you go learn plenty! You hearin' me? If you keep your blasted mouth shut you ain't go hear all kind of nonsense talk from people who like to talk talk talk. Let other jackass an' them talk and ask question 'pon question, you stop easy and listen.' Santo Pi tugged at his ear. 'You hearin' me good?'

'Yes, Gramps . . . yes,' the little boy said, and then the old man sent him out into the rain to buy a nip of Black Cat rum.

'And come back quick-sharp befo' I give you another cut-ass, you hear?' Santo Pi hollered as the little figure ran slipping and sliding along the path of bright red mud that the thin long threads of ragged rain melted into a soft red slime.

Is there any meaning to all the pale pink-tongued hibiscus shrivelled purple in the sun? . . .

If there is any direction in the struggle of the great black ants that wrestle by the hour in the damp darkness dismantling one another's triple spheres of life with their tiny claws . . . If the hibiscus petals, the great black ants, and the sound of rain do not scratch upon the senses of small boys with their puzzling, haunting, questioning, saddening ways . . . then the whole wide world is a bowl of dust that settles with the rain.

Not set in course, but a whirling mass that lost its way. The only voice in all its darkness is surprise. Surprise that seed will root . . . that seed of man will yearn for cell wall, bury there, and grow full blown.

Surprise that a small and fragile child with arms so thin, and rag-doll legs, fed on the refuse of the garbage pails, refuse used to fill in the land of the city dump, will burst forth into a man whose body has six feet of power and muscle by the yard.

When Massahood was sixteen years old he was a surprise to Santo Pi, to himself. The boy's body grew long and bony first. He slept curled up in a ball, cowering in his dreams from the old man's curses. The old man had a stick which he kept at his bedside. In the middle of the night he would poke the boy in his belly and send him off on some errand.

'Aye . . . aye,' Santo Pi would call, nudging the boy. 'Wake up . . . wake up, you li'l bitch. You like to sleep too much. You eatin' my food and livin' off me and I can't get you to do a thing for me.' Massahood would still be rubbing the sleep out of his eyes, vaguely hearing the mean old man's instructions. 'Now run and bring me some hot hot coffee from the Chinee shop . . . and come back quick-sharp 'fore I give you a good cut-ass!' Santo Pi would say, jabbing the boy with his walking stick until he was running in the night, still half asleep.

But now the boy's body widened and filled. He ate voraciously. He went through the city dump picking up swollen cans of foods, spoilt fruit, and stale loaves of hops bread. He caught great blue crabs with a long wooden pole at the edges of the dump where the mangrove met the sea. With his powerful arms he would block the crab's escape by plunging his long staff deep into the ground, cutting off further burrowing, then prise up the earth, and snatch up the crab by its back, its wild claws clenching vainly at the air. He broke off great clusters of oysters from the mossy rocks and the mangrove roots and ate them with hot peppers and lemon juice. And yet when he ate with Santo Pi he was still hungry. The old man ate little sometimes, and he looked upon the boy's hunger with disgust.

'You does eat too blasted much . . . where you puttin' all that food?' he would ask as the boy ate boiled breadfruit, green plantains, and dried codfish in the evenings.

'Take care your belly bust, you hear? You like to stuff-up too much.'

The boy's chewing would stop momentarily, then he would go on eating, no longer with relish, but with a flavour of sawdust in his mouth.

61

And the only time Santo Pi offered him anything was when he had finished eating. He would then say to Massahood: 'Come, come and eat . . . you is a li'l dust-bin. Come and show me how you could finish up what I leave on my plate.'

And Massahood would eat the leftovers while the old man watched him, counting each chew and swallow, each bite and taste, with a kind of sour disgust written all over his face. The boy felt like an ugly sore on the old man's body that he hated to look at in these moments. But he was hungry, and he ate. His body cried out for food, and he ate.

'Now go on . . . get out from my sight and wash up the pot and them before I bust a lash in your tail,' Santo Pi would say, lifting up his walking stick threateningly.

Massahood, still chewing the last mouthful of food, would scramble out of the hut hurriedly to wash up the enamel plates and cups at the public standpipe some distance away.

Often Santo Pi was drunk and his appetite weak. On such evenings, if the boy cooked a good hearty meal of crab callaloo and pounded plantains, the old man's anger would rise to a wicked venom when he knew that he would not be able to feast on those orange-red crabs sticking out of the pale green callaloo sauce.

'You playin' like if you cookin' for me, but all the time you know damn' well that is for yourself you cookin'-up all this nice nice food!' Santo Pi would say, screwing up his face, his ugly little eyes bloodshot and drawn.

Massahood ventured to offer, as meekly as he could, 'But, Gramps . . . is for you I does cook . . . is for you to eat and—'

'Oh-ho . . . so you answering me back now, eh!' Crack! 'Take that.' Crack! 'And that,' Santo Pi said, as he whacked the boy on his arms, his legs. 'So you learnin' to talk back now, you damn' little worthless rascal . . . Well, take some mo'.' Crack! Crack! Crack!

Massahood, still squatting on the floor, tried at first to break the blows from landing on his face, his head, where Santo Pi aimed. Now he tried to catch the old man's stick with his hands each time it came down on him. The boy's body, so young, so full with all the secrets of life, annoyed the old man. The blows of his stick could not burst open the youth and vigour of the boy's body, and it left the old man still more angry. He took the plate of crab callaloo which his weak appetite could not find delight in. He rolled his spit slowly into a great ball, then hacked it out into the plate. He pushed the plate under the boy's face, standing over him with his stick poised in the air.

'Eat, you worthless little bitch . . . come and let me see you eat up now. That is all you know how to do, *eat, eat, eat.*'

The boy's neck began to ache with a tightening kind of feeling, as though a tourniquet was being twisted about it. And now the old man dipped his gnarled fingers into the thick green callaloo sauce and forced it into his mouth. Massahood clenched his teeth and kept his mouth closed tightly.

'You belly well full-up today . . . Your little woman feedin' you good these days. You think I ain't know what going on behind my back.'

Massahood looked up surprised. He wondered how Santo Pi knew about the little woman he spent his time with. But Santo Pi, as if aggravated by all the pleasures the boy's young body could house, made wretched by all the pleasures which had soured for him, became more and more angry. He rubbed the callaloo against the boy's face, inserting his index finger between his lips to open his mouth forcefully.

Massahood sprang to his feet and snatched up the rod he used to go crabbing with, and now he began to parry the old man's blows. While on the La Basse, he used to play a joking kind of stick fight with boys his age. His body and his limbs were suddenly in danger of being hurt, a sharp thrill searched through his spine as he held the staff; he felt a weird comfort, defence. It was as though he knew deep down inside of him that as long as he could hold and feel this stick nothing could hurt him or pain him. Even if a blow did land on him he knew that he would not feel it the way he did when he crouched in the corners of the hut so many times from the old man's blows. The strange excitement spread through his veins, his thighs, and the points of his breasts. He felt a kind of pleasure in the danger as he dodged the blows. Each time he parried well, his body vibrated down the column of his backbone, and now his whole body yearned to land one good blow.

'O-ho . . . so you is a stick man, eh! Why you didn't tell me?' Santo Pi grinned. Then suddenly from his cunning laughter, Crack! he landed a blow on Massahood's arm. 'You is best stick man, but I is *better* stick man! . . . Come on! Come on, let we see!' The old man laughed as he moved back and forth, cavorting, circling like the stick men do when in battle. Massahood was still rubbing his arm. He still held his stick, watching the movements of his grandfather. The boy's eyes shifted for a moment to look at the welt the blow on his arm had made; he could feel the thin strip of his flesh throbbing in unison with his heart. And in that split second Santo Pi landed another blow, on his legs this time. He felt the stick lash with a burning blow.

'Take that, you li'l bitch,' Santo Pi said. The boy coiled up like a snake winding down to the floor. As he looked up, he saw the old man steadying himself on his feet, making ready to come crashing down on his head. Massahood lurched at him as swiftly as a mongoose, and the old man fell.

'Get up, you old bitch . . . get up and fight now . . . That is what you beggin' for? That is what you go get.'

But Santo Pi only crawled cunningly into the corner. Massahood threw a blow at him, only testing his reactions, and Santo Pi raised his stick in the air, holding it with both hands above his head. So simple it was, the old man thought. This nice parry strengthened him. He rose to his feet. But no sooner had he done so than Massahood slashed at his feet. Santo Pi shrieked like a small pig in the slaughterhouse. Massahood then began cuffing him and kicking him until he was sure that all the cunning was out of him. The boy then rolled his spit into a large ball and let it fly straight into the old man's face.

'See how it feel now, you nasty old bitch!' Massahood said to him, turning away from him. But as soon as the boy turned his back, Santo Pi began shouting.

'Murdah . . . murdah . . . Oh-God-oh-God-oye!'

Massahood turned on him again, but the old man made for the door and landed outside without touching the steps. He kept bawling: 'Murdah . . . murdah . . . Come and see, everybody . . . Come and see how I is a sick sick old man and I gettin' beat by my own grandchile.'

Massahood stood at the door, his stick in his hand. 'I don't want to see you face so long as I live. I warnin' you. *Leave* Port of Spain or else any time I see you in the road I beat you like a old snake.'

Santo Pi was all eyes, ears, his whole being waited to run, to scream, to anticipate anything that would come his way. The boy was surprised by the old man's agility as he stood breathing hard, enough steps away from the hut so that he could make a run for it if Massahood attacked, but since the boy just stood there in the doorway Santo Pi started railing again.

'Come and see, everybody . . . come and see with you own own two eye. I bring up this chile in the world today and he chasin' me from my own door. That is the thanks . . . Oh Lawdee-Lawd. Look how children worthless minded in the world today. I put clothes on he back. I feed he and take care of he when he own moomah ain't care for he and this is what I gettin'. Come and hear my troubles, everybody . . . come and hear!'

Three or four people who lived nearby heard the commotion and came to see what was going on. Ordinarily they would have said, 'Is the old watchman giving he grandson a cut-ass.' Then they would turn over and go back to sleep, but this time they heard the old man's voice, and they came to see and to see only. No one said a word. They listened as though they knew that the day would come, they had awaited it, and now that it had come they stood dumbly satisfied that their predictions had come true. It remained only for the boy to come running out at Santo Pi now and it would be all over.

Massahood jumped down the two steps on to the ground and smacked the earth hard with his stick. Santo Pi jumped back a few steps, almost falling into the arms of the onlookers. A man pushed him forward so that he was now almost within striking distance of Massahood's stick. The boy laughed at the frightened little man, laughter like he used to laugh in the middle of the night after dreaming that Santo Pi was chasing him all through the dump with his stick and waking up to find that it was only a dream.

And with a wicked laughter in his voice, a man's voice now, he shouted: '*Go* . . . I say *go* . . . I say *one, two, three, four, go!*'

There was a short silence, the onlookers giggled, and Massahood began.

'One . . . two . . .' and he started moving towards Santo Pi. The old man looked left and right and burst into a sudden bolt such as Massahood never dreamed his wretched old body could summon up.

9

THE streets of Port of Spain are filled with faces, the benches in Woodford Square at evening taking on their familiar look . . . a huddled figure waiting for darkness to fall before he makes the bench his bed. To this city have come all the lost and lonely faces from all corners of the world. Lost like the sugar that they came to harvest, lonely like the tracts of idle earth their generation has forgotten how to plant. The park benches seem empty when the rainy season comes and pelts its pitchforks with their ringing tines into the earth. The park-dwellers disappear into the crevices of the city, leaving behind only a vast silence filled with many questions. Who are they? Who bore them? From which distant corner of the earth did they come, what fickle fortune did they come to seek, marooned, cast away, waiting out their time?

Some men's faces lend themselves to story easily. It is not difficult to find a place for faces that people the streets, to construct their lives, filling in each detail of time and place until they are known and silently fade into the dark landscape of the mind.

And then . . . there are faces like the cripple's. An ageless face of stone! As restless as the dead spirits that haunt the island, wandering past its streams and waterfalls, bleating at midnight in the massive silk-cotton trees as if waiting for their day of judgement to come, whispering in the night air of the haunted countryside, just faint enough for a late passerby to hear them say, 'Eternity is a long, long time . . . eternity is a long, long time, and we have to wait that long.' And like these voices hushed below the level of a whisper, these timeless ageless voices, so was the cripple's face. It did not have time stamped upon it.

Someone would say: 'Who you talkin' 'bout? Hop-and-Drop? Man, I don't know . . . He uses to be here in the Britannia since I come in first, one long long time ago . . . I hear he say one time, "God ain't make me, you know . . . is me who make God." The bitch must be old old old for so!'

Or someone else would say: 'Who he? Man, he was the first man who put up a shanty on the La Basse, and when some stupid health inspector come and bust a case in he ass and carry he up befo' the magistrate the case get dismiss. Since that time other people gone to live there and make a whole town out of the place . . . and like if he is the mayor of that town.'

And then some newcomer to the Britannia, trying to worm his way into its tight little clique, would add: 'Yes, man . . . yes, man, is true . . . I hear 'bout the case. The old Hop-and-Drop argue like a lawyer from London town befo' the magistrate. He quote so much law that the white man head begin to spin like a tennis ball and he had was to bawl: "Oh, God . . . case dismiss! Case dismiss!" '

And when the clique at the Britannia looked silently sceptical and scornful at the newcomer he would jostle his position quickly, adding, 'Man, you could go down to the *Guardian* newspaper and read 'bout it if you think is make up that I makin' up this story.' And then, sensing that he had shaken off their disbelief, knowing that he was now on the edges, almost the centre, the very heart and nucleus of this group, that any moment now he would be one of them, he pushed on his advantage, saying: 'Yes, man . . . yes . . . I hear 'bout the old Hop-and-Drop long, long time gone. I hear he uses to have a work sweeping up the Empire Theatre till they give 'em the sack when the manager catch 'em playin' with he-self whilst watching one of them technicolor pictures that had Marilyn Monroe in it.'

And then there was a great guffaw. One of the Britannia boys kept slapping the back of his neck to hammer out the fits of laughter that seized him, and then the laughter died slowly, and they became sullen and angry now at this outsider, who stood with his eyes down on his glass, turning it slowly, lifting it off the dark mahogany counter, dropping it down again, trying to place one ring of the wet glass close to the first, until one of the boys spoke up and said, 'Yuh lie . . . you lie no ass!'

And then another said, 'Why you don't haul your ass from here and drink you blasted rum in a corner where you can't disturb decent people.'

And the newcomer would take the nip of Black Cat he had bought and steal away as quietly as he could to a dark corner of the Britannia where the sunlight never played, knowing that he had at least made an entry, no matter how small, into the closed clique of the Britannia . . . he knew Hop-and-Drop.

And yet no one really knew where the cripple came from. Turning time back and back there would have to be a moment when he was, when some lust or love had sucked him from the unknown, yet, looking at his face, there was only a feeling of void, of no point in time where he had his beginnings. No one knew his past or present, no one knew the architecture of his soul; yet, if it is true that all of a man's actions, thoughts, and deeds will exhibit themselves in some way, in some small movement of the lip or tongue, the cripple had given his secret away. For each man has one secret. Like the skin he covers himself with, he shares it with no one. It is like the skin he wears because it is exposed for all eyes to see, heart to love, lust to desire, mouth to spit upon. A man buries his secret deep within his wishbone until the day he dies . . . or so he thinks. In all things he does, in all his words, actions, passions, sweat, he is spelling out his secret. Too much rum and he feels it inching out of him, burning in the coils of his brain to break loose, to say to all the world, 'This is what I am.'

Some men know their secret, some hide their secret well, others spit it out. But the little man's secret spelled itself out for all to see. It stood in the open sun beside the bilgy water of the sea. It was rewritten like a carbon copy. The architecture of his soul was one with the architecture of his shanty. Built from hundreds of odds and ends. The best of hard woods and nails. The finest of broken glass and china. He laboured, working all the discarded ends of other people's lives, their refuse on the La Basse, into some delightful pattern which he used to adorn his home. He made a lovely little mosaic path of seashells and china which some little vagabonds destroyed one day. He did not remain angry long; he was glad in a way: it gave him a chance to work on some different pattern.

'A man must always have something to keep he mind off things with . . . he must never live with one thing too long, otherwise it make he bones turn cold cold cold like ice.' Whether he fitted in these thoughts as a result of each incident, or whether he really believed them, was hard to tell, for they always had that ring of appropriateness that was difficult to dispute. In a word, all of life either seemed to happen or was put together, as one great plan which the little man understood as he drew upon all the sources of remote ideas that he had accumulated from ancient books, old newspapers, magazines, some of them centuries old, which he memorized, quoted, and hoarded in the vast storehouse of that small and tortured being of his.

On the walls of his shanty was repeated the same pattern of bits and pieces from which he packed together his life. Pinned, glued, or hanging from corners of the walls were fragments of pictures which he had cut out from magazines and books. Here a segment of a woman's buttocks, a picture of a pair of crossed thighs, a pair of eyes only, a hand from the wrist down, a pair of lips.

There was no complete representation of any human form among the cut-out stickers that adorned his walls. But this is not to say that they were not without beauty, for had not the little man said to himself: 'But life is one hell of a thing . . . it ugly no-ass. Who like a ugly thing . . . who? I don't care what they say 'bout liking people because they pretty inside, I like something pretty that I could feel and touch . . . and see with my own two eyes. The world have 'nuff ugly thing in it and a man have to surround heself with pretty pretty things.'

There was nothing exaggerated or perverted in the picture of pinkish ivory breasts that dominated the largest wall of the shanty. They were not like the Amazonian or bovine calendar pictures in the barber shops of Port of Spain. They were breasts which beggared the cupping of the hand, that invited the sensation of a lightness of touch, their size small, as of some virgin girl, lacking the rude, suggestive tilt of the nipples. They stood in a quiet manner of dignity and beauty; the beholder would take delight in them for themselves without having his attention wrenched by the perversions of size, the exaggeration of colour, or the wicked lines of some hack artist's brush. Yet it was a picture of breasts alone from which the rest of that no doubt beautiful form had been snipped away.

The cripple's appearance was striking, not because of his size or deformity but for other reasons. He was always neat in spite of the old cast-offs he wore. There was always tucked into the band of his old felt hat some sprig of fern or rosemary bush which he plucked from the wayside, the hat blocked and tilted at a rakish angle. In his buttonhole he would wear a blossom of purplish blue bougainvillaea. The coats he chose from the lot of cast-offs were deliberately too large for his shoulders; the same was true of the shoes he wore, and his trousers were bunched up by a wide leather belt with a great, gleaming brass buckle. His appearance, then, was of being a man of great proportions, and the limp of his leg caused him to throw his body in a kind of swagger as he lumbered along, not lugubriously, but as one who indeed owned the world and understood the hearts of all men. Thus he would move along in the late morning to the Britannia, laughing at the sunlight, twirling his great bunch of keys around his index finger, the very soul of contentment.

The little man was an aristocrat. The taste he showed in his dress, the jauntiness of his walk, the small pains he took to pin some little sprig of fern or flower to his person, all spoke up as evidence of this fact. In his foraging at the La Basse he was particular in the types of garbage he picked through. Years of living off the refuse of other people's lives gave him an extra sense of discrimination so that his instincts led him immediately to the refuse of the rich. He could quickly size up a load of rubbish which the collection carts of Port of Spain dumped out on to the La Basse and tell instantly whether it had come from a section of the city that was wealthy.

One evening he had brought a small tin of blue-black caviar to Zolda's shack as his donation to the party. He had found it months ago, along with several swollen cans of food, and locked it up in one of his many footlockers for some special occasion. Zolda had danced with him, an event which he prized above all things. There was nothing he would not do for her.

He held forth expertly on the delicacy of caviar. Aristocracy, being an all-pervading quality of character, extended to the cripple's taste in food as well. His shanty was better stocked than any other on the La Basse, and, in short, he was a grand gourmand.

'What is this black poison you bring here to kill we with?' one of the guests at the party jibed.

The little man put him in his place, for at Zolda's he enjoyed a breath of power over the others, which they knew. And when someone tasted it and asked: 'It spoil, or what? . . . It taste rotten, man,' the little man put him down.

'These are the eggs of a rare specimen of fish that do not haunt Caribbean waters,' he exclaimed.

There was a short round of applause, and the little man was himself again, the guest with carte blanche. The man took up the small tin and examined it, saying: 'Let me smell it, man, let me smell it to see if it still good . . . I never hear fish does lay egg.'

The cripple snatched it away from him, saying, 'Take out you big nose from my caviar . . . you hear!'

And with a foolish grin on his face, the man could only explain to the others present: 'Man, I never did know that fish does lay egg . . . that is all. I never hear that fish does lay egg.'

The little man was more literate than his fellows. He read newspapers and books no matter how ancient they were, whenever he found them on the La Basse. He saw himself as a great wedge which could crack open the British Empire, and lately, with all the odds and ends of information he gleaned, he became an expert on independence for the island.

'Hop, why you don't haul your ass with all this talk? . . . You think independence go put rice in we mouth?' his fellows would counter. But the little man dismissed them as fools, and barren of the broad vision he had of what lay in store for the islands.

'When we begin to *talk*,' he would say, '*boy!* White man go *trimble*. White man up in England go TRIMBLE. They go hold they head and *bawl!*'

A voice popped up and said, 'Hop, you mean *tremble*, man, *tremble*.'

There was a small titter, and when it died down he said, 'When I say TRIMBLE I mean TRIMBLE . . . you are a bombastic ass!'

And with this silencing remark he went on: 'Wait and see. We days comin' and even if I dead an' gone when we put a black man in Parliament . . . ANTS GO BRING THE NEWS TO ME IN MY GRAVE.' The last sentence he would pronounce with such theatrics and gesture that it would bring a little twinge in the hearts of the Britannia Brigade.

For the most part, however, the La Basse dwellers, the Britannia Brigade, only laughed heartily at the cripple's philosophizing, or sometimes they goaded him on to stronger and stronger elocution. The little man had a way of drawing all his strong veins into a fit of grotesque laughter that would then lead all to believe that he was only joking. And then, when he had their attention again, he would say: 'You know what politics mean? . . . That is the thing that puttin' food in your guts and rum in your throat . . . all yuh fool don't even know which way the wind does blow.'

'What you mean we don't know what puttin' food in we mouth? . . . Is the mule cart that does come to the La Basse every mornin' that feed we.'

'All right, all right,' the little man would say, ending his lecture. 'Don't listen to me . . .'

And then, 'Hop, you old bitch, you reap more livin' off the La Basse than anybody, and still you tryin' to give we all this talk,' they would answer, for they all knew that the cripple's shanty was well stocked, well made, and his footlockers filled and closed, with padlocks on them, for which he carried a small jingling bunch of keys which he twirled about his index finger as he made his way through the dark and quiet streets of Port of Spain, as if in deep meditation.

71

Why did men think that they could find an instinctive kinship with him? he wondered. Why was he forced into being confidant and sounding board for the misguided, the lovesick, the lonely, the anguished? He became vexed when people pounded upon his ear with their petty problems.

He would be standing at the dark mahogany counter of the Britannia having a quiet one, all by his lonesome, watching the square of last light falling upon the counter, the dark rich wood almost translucent as the warm sunlight dried out its moisture of many, many rums. The aroma coiling up to his nostrils sent him who knows where? To his childhood? To some night of glory? To some vision on a street? Who understands the human heart? And then he would be startled out of his reverie by some warm and friendly sounding voice: 'Ah-ah, man . . . you standing up by the counter with a look on you face like if you moomah dead . . . How about firin' one with me?'

And before the little man could answer, the voice had slapped its arm round his shoulder and ordered something good . . . no green bottle through which you could not see the colour of its contents, but a small white nip with a warm translucent draught that looked like fresh honey. And then to add to the luxury there would be a soda water for three cents instead of 'pipe-water' for the mix.

Then no sooner would the first one be down when this voice, like all the other voices, would launch out upon its escapades, its lust, its hidden desires. And after the first nip was gone they would begin mutilating themselves, saying what asses they were, what fools they were making of themselves, what ugly beasts they were. The simplest, plainest soul who sold stamps in the Government Treasury all day—dressed in his white shirt and necktie . . . a man of respect and high rank in the island— would begin elaborating, fabricating all his fancies, stuffing them down into the little man's craw like the worthless chicken vendors in the Eastern Market who forced 'corn coo-coo' into the guts of birds to add to their weight. And the little man would only wince and grind his teeth together as the voices rolled on and on like the surf at Ballandra Bay.

'Man, I is not the kind of fella you see standin' up here at all . . . I different different. Everybody in my office respect me, they think that I is a quiet fella . . . but Gawd, the things I does think sometimes . . . the things that does go round and round in my head is only me and almighty God who know . . . Sometimes I myself does have to tremble in my shoes . . .'

And the cripple's mind would wander. He could smell the sea breeze now; the land breeze had shifted and as the sea air came up along the jetty and mixed with the aroma of the boards and counters of the Britannia, he wished that he could be left alone, but as the voices went on and on he would only nod. When he felt that he should be more affirmative he would say, 'Um-hmm-um-hmm,' until finally he would have to ask, 'What kind of things does go on in your mind?'

He knew the stories from beginning to end, yet he would have to go through them over and over again; and when they started the cripple's mind would wander a bit, his taste buds uppermost in his mind . . . 'But is a nice brown colour that this rum have today, man . . . I wonder if these bitches in the Britannia ain't colour it with raw leather or something? . . . I wonder if it really colour-up so from standing in the vats? . . .'

Two worlds as distant as the constellations of the heavens struck into orbit for a fleeting second with a nip of Brown Skin Girl.

'Hai-I-aye, boy . . . if you only know how woman is . . . if you only know, padnar . . .'

The voice at the Britannia waiting for his commuting train would exclaim, shaking his head with wonder.

'Man . . . this is one of them reel nips . . . a reel reel nip what ripen by itself in them dark wood puncheons.'

The cripple speculated, hearing the voice only thinly, dimly. 'Now the second nip comin' now the temperature go start droppin',' he thought. And as surely as he thought this, so swiftly, so accurately, it came.

'It have a young girl in the office that I livin' with, ha ha ha . . . You see, I is not the kind of fella you think I is at all at all, ha ha ha ha ha. Man, sometimes I want to say haul ass to the old people who I have to carry my salary to and bust loose and go 'way to Venezuela with this chicken . . . I goin' to do it one day, you know . . . I goin' to do it, wait.'

So here it was, the second nip, and then: 'Man, you know what I talkin' 'bout . . . you understand what what I mean . . . I mean, er, you understand the position. I is not one to turn my back on my people when they done work so hard and send me to college with white people, and things like that . . . I mean I would like to take care of them till they days done and over, but you see the position . . . Tell me, man, what the hell you would do if you was to be in my place.' The man would again clap his hand around the cripple's shoulder, slapping only the great amounts of padding of his oversized jacket.

But the cripple was not one to drink a man's rum and egg him on and

sweet-talk him and agree with him simply to keep the liquor flowing. He
had his scruples. Each time someone came up to him this way he re-
pressed all his disappointment of the past, and that tiny mite of hope
would set itself aglow. He yearned for some kind of true comradeship,
some equality with other men. It broke something fragile deep inside of
him when this moment came, and then he would speak up.

'Now, listen,' he would say. 'People like to get they ass in all kind of
hot water. They like to mix up with a little little thing like a piece of
backside and tail. They think that they carryin' the world on they shoulders and the load too heavy . . . then they want to unload it on somebody
else shoulder. When it too late to do anything they want advice.' The
little man would then push the half-finished drink over to the voice that
bought it, in a kind of return gesture, as if to imply that since he was not
going to be able to pay the price of the drink in sound advice and
confidences, he would no longer drink. He would go on to add: 'In my
long, long years I find out that people don't want advice. All they want
is "old talk" and "old talk", and "old talk". They mind make up from
long time before and what they goin' to do is what they goin' to do and
is regardless . . .'

And then suddenly, as suddenly as the temper of the breeze of the land
changes to the breeze of the sea, so too the temper turned at the Britannia,
and the man who had been all gentleness and confidences before began
shouting: 'But look at this bitch . . . look at this short-cut bitch nuh . . .
He drink up my rum and now he ready to 'buse me. But look at my blue
crosses today! I buy 'em a rum and he ready to 'buse me upside down
. . . What it is at all . . . tell me . . . what it is at all at all?'

Where the little man was ready to forget the whole incident, to forget
the deep hurt, the snatched hope for some kind of real friendship, he was
angry now. 'Who the hell ask to hear you troubles, eh? Who? You invite
a poor cripple like me to drink, and that is the way you want me to pay
for it. You have to twist up my ears with your troubles. You want *me* to
tell you what to do. What the hell you think I is . . . you must be think
that I is God, or something. You can't see I have troubles of my own?'
At this point he lifted up his shorter foot, all twisted and bent, and jerked
up his trouser leg, driving his point home like sharp nails into tough
wood.

'You want to hang on to me till I fall down to the ground. If you like
backside so much and you want to go kissin' it up and smellin' from
pillar to post, why you ain't go ahead . . . go . . . go Venezuela. What you

see in me that make you think that I could give you the correct correct answer?'

And the man, sobering up now, seeing that all eyes were upon him, knowing that his intimate confidences would be blurted out in the raw, that they would be judged by the crowd, not with the soft and mellow romance with which it was told, began to calm and quiet the cripple, saying as he put his arm round him: 'Man, you is my friend, man . . . is who else but a friend a man does have to go to when he have troubles? You is my friend.' As he said these words, his eyes stole furtively from the swinging doors, to the crowd whose attention was slowly returning to their own drinking and conversation, waiting for that moment of calm which was breaking his nerves with waiting, then he would slip out of the Britannia as gently as the land breeze had slipped out to sea.

And now night had come and crept into the corners of the Britannia to nestle there with the pitch-pine sawdust of the floor. The small yellow bulbs were on, their cords thick and heavy with the droppings of millions of flies that had rested there in the past, and those who were nestled now for the night. A feeling of tiredness, of the burnt-out edges of the day, was floating in beneath the swinging half-doors. An oily moisture from the sea seeped into the rusty hinges of the half-doors and they swung back and forth smoothly, they lost that song and squeak, that little melody they sang out when the sun was still high, and the little man shook his body in the oversize cocoon of his clothes, up on the left foot, down on the right, up on the left foot, down on the right, slowly making his way to the WC.

He absentmindedly walked up to the trough. It had always been too high for him to reach. He remembered once how he had come in by mistake and two drunken American sailors offered to buy him a nip if he could arch the stream of his urine with enough pressure so that it would land inside the trough. He had won the nip that day, and he was tempted to try it now; instead, he walked out of the WC and went round the back where he always went, and in the mild darkness he tried to make out the pattern his urine made as it splashed on the dry dusty earth, seizing the loose dust into perfect balls which rolled away like a shower and sunburst, then settled and flatted as the dry earth sucked up the moisture of his entrails. He then waved his shorter leg three times over the sunburst splash and spat on the spot. It was an old habit left over from his boyhood which stemmed from a rumour that if one did this over the urine of some careless person one would get their strength. As a boy he had never failed to wave his leg over the urine marks of other boys, hoping and praying that they had forgotten, and over his own he always performed this ritual. But as time passes all of life becomes illusion and the little man was left with the hollow shell of ritual only, which, although it did not strengthen him as was believed, protected him in some strange way as if compensating for the vague nostalgia of parting with part of his very being . . . something that had been housed in the poor-house of his body, traced through the innermost intimacies of his limp flesh, hugging the cells of his body that contained his life's breath, then became expelled and lost in the foolish earth that did not care a hoot.

The feeling of agelessness and timelessness was not in the cripple's cold stone face alone. It was woven into the fabric of his bones as well. His meticulousness with his body and his being suggested a man who was waiting. Waiting for some great event. Waiting for his great day. Meantime he was saving, collecting, storing, sorting, and, above all, constantly polishing up himself for that moment when all his learning and living, his strange kind of loving, would all come together and spell out the great destiny and climax that all the loose threads of his life would draw into some focal point like the random zig-zag spider web that had its centre despite the myriad meanderings of its fragile fibre.

He loved the morning sunlight best of all lights, for he had read somewhere that the afternoon and evening sun in its tropic power could burst open the pigment of his skin, leaving it a mottled dark purple against its black cocoa-brown. He had also read somewhere that the salt water of the sea contained great quantities of nutrients if allowed to dry on the body and soak deep into its marrows. So of a sunny morning then, like the lazy blue crabs that woke drowsily and went down to dip their feet in the sea as an instinctive reminder that they belonged completely to neither world, the little man would seat himself on the steps of his shanty, his trousers rolled up above his short little twisted legs, sunning himself.

'Ah Ah . . . but yuh sunning yourself early, man! It look as if yuh does get up with the chicken and them,' some passerby on his way to his day's pickings on the La Basse would hail out as he went past. And the cripple in his secretive way would only nod and smile, thinking that he had one up on the foolish fellow who did not know of the richness of his actions. It pleased him to feel that he was strengthening his body for the great day. He would not share his knowledge that the sea could put power in his bones. Life was, to him, a mild form of handicap race in which he was at a disadvantage. Any small advantage which he could glean from his tattered books was simply the natural due which a superior kind of animal had over the others, so that it could thrive and prosper among them. Indeed, the little man had fleeting moments of grandeur when he saw himself a kind of end to all of God's creations, for within this breast were tuned to a much higher pitch all of the emotions and feelings of ordinary men.

As the morning wore on, he would go into the shanty, and from one of the many padlocked footlockers he would take out a phial of coconut oil in which many herbs were soaking. He would hold up the little phial to the sunlight, shake it vigorously, look at it in the sunlight again, then smile all to himself, humming a little tune just above a whisper. He would then go back out to the steps, wiggle his buttocks until he felt comfortable, and then begin to massage his little legs, running his thumbs firmly, lovingly, along the knobby little muscles until they shone mirror-bright. As he massaged his body this way his lower jaw moved from left to right, much like a cow's movement when it is chewing its cud, and deep down in the echo chambers of his soul his heart was singing an old, old rhythm the Negro slaves sang out before they ransacked their white masters' houses and set fire to the sugarcane fields. His jaws minced out and his heart sang out:

> One-day-One-day . . . Congo-Té!
> One-day-One-day . . . Congo-Té!
> Ah say One-day-One-day . . . ?

He would then stop his chanting and wait a moment, leaving the half-formed rhythm floating in midair as if waiting for it to resound against the walls in the deep chasms of his soul, and when he heard the echo of the rhythm's full cycle returning to his ear he would sing out loud:

> *Congo-Té!*
> *Congo-Té!*
> Ah say One-day-One-day? . . . *Congo-Té!*

He would then leer all to himself, absentmindedly slapping the stopper on the phial as he surveyed the eternal smoky hazy expanse of the La Basse, take a few deep breaths of its odours of eternal burning garbage mixed with the sea, and a quiet ecstasy would steal across his very soul.

10

THERE is a desperate bid for life in the tropics. The hues of flowers are more violent. Overnight, razor grass roots and soaks the vitality out of the tilled soil. The long-tongued lashes of the sea lap up on the edges of the earth as if waiting a chance to swallow the island—the sun rushes into men's bones, igniting them like fireworks, rushing on their slow flicker into a quick burst of flame, hurrying them on to their cinder bed as if all of life wishes to rush headlong to its end.

The outsider sees and feels only the deep sleep of the tropics where waves play and time lingers long. The pale pink-tongued hibiscus blows for ever for their eyes—they do not see the numbers of their dead beneath the bush. The quiet of the streets is not a restful slumber, it is the toll time takes in its frenzied rush—the tiring of hurried flesh that runs too fast, it is the compulsion of time—it is tropic sleep.

You have told yourself that you would gather your life together, wind it tightly with a strong green jungle vine like a cord of bright red mangrove wood—but the sun comes up too soon, the tomorrows of your life are always upon you—you are never ready—you have not sorted out your thoughts into neat tight bundles, and deep within you you know that you will not be ready—not ready for rum, nor rain, nor tomorrow nor decision.

But decisions will be forced, tomorrows will not tangle, tumble, twist their course. Tomorrow will come—rum will flow.

Only the bones know the irony of your being; the gap in your soul yawns like new music hungering for a scale; new mathematics hungering for a different yardstick. You see the patterns of its melodies, feel its strange new shapes. With enough time a symphony, perhaps, an order that will make the melody stand still long enough so that you can look it face to face before it slips like sand between your fingers.

The obeah man felt the swift motion of the earth about him as he and Zolda raced on to the Diego Martin bus. He wondered if a man might not

78

spend his life out without ever finding that task, that one niche. He was not ready to go into the city with Zolda, and at the last moment when he saw the bus driver, the same little wizened man as before, he almost turned back and ran to his hut.

'A man should never get a woman start up unless he could carry through to the end,' he thought. Then he thought not about himself and his desires, but of Zolda, in whose body he had aroused some dormant thing which should not be left to go searching through the streets this night.

'Come on, man, the bus go leave without we!' she cried, tugging at his arm as she raced ahead. Zampi knew that the driver had seen them and that the bus would wait. He could see the driver dressed in his old khaki tunic, its brass buttons buttoned up to his neck to keep out the cool air and the thick dew that washed the deep green leaves in the valley. As they approached, the driver pinched off the pale red head of his cigarette and tucked the zoot behind his ear for a later smoke. He stared at them with his sullen readiness to abuse. And then suddenly, as his scowling little eyes recognized Zampi, he beamed, his mouth tilted up in one corner; the other side of his face through years of scowling was straight, ready to fling scorn in an instant's notice.

'Chief—is you?' he queried Zampi. The obeah man knew that he had put two and two together and reasoned that he, Zampi, was the lone dweller above the Blue Basin waterfall. What would anyone else be doing here at this hour, especially on Carnival Tuesday night?

'Yes, is me,' Zampi answered. He wondered what he would say if the driver asked him what happened when the star shot out at the bus. He wasn't sure himself.

The driver sat on the running board, his eyes about the level of Zolda's loins, and Zampi watched his tiny manicou eyes run from her firm legs and thighs slowly up to the indentation of her belly, then move down to her feet staring at the deep incisions the leather laces of her sandals cut around her ankles and calves, then his eyes moved up to her breasts, her face, and when his eyes met hers his whole face changed. The scowling corner of his mouth touched into a smile and he got up, motioning them into the bus. He appraised Zampi with a kind of envy. 'He must be a real powerful obeah man to catch the pretty pretty ones like that,' he reasoned. With his own eyes he had witnessed what power the obeah man had over the heavens. The very stars did his bidding!

'Boy,' he mused, 'it have obeah man and it have obeah man. This man is Obeah *poopah* he-self.'

With a sweeping gesture of his cap and a low bow he ushered them into his bus.

The brief acquaintance he had with Zampi gave the little man not only a sense of importance but one of invincibility in all things. He was certain that this obeah man could endow his presence with such irresistible charms, fill his bowels with aphrodisiacs of power that would render him a Don Juan on the Diego Martin road, such as in the many lurid tales he heard from the other drivers like Bullin. He had never had any luck so far; yet the valley held him to it with a strange hypnotic spell, with a lust in his veins that he knew must be sated here. At last he had found the key, the secret of the night, in this obeah man.

Zampi entered first and headed for the seat at the rear of the bus when the driver called out: 'Why you don't come and sit up here so I could have somebody to chat with, man? It does get so quiet on the Diego Martin road at this hour . . . A man does be glad to have nice nice people like you to keep a li'l company with.'

Before Zampi could reach down the aisle of the bus Zolda took his hand and pulled him towards the seat directly behind the driver. The obeah man said nothing. How obliging she became after she had been loved, he thought. There was indeed a vivaciousness, a wild kind of beauty, which he remembered after they had loved. All her world was in order, nothing could check the contentment of her soul.

The bus rolled along the highway, its lights picked out some stone, some shape of the turn, then pelted them back into the black night, which ran like something gigantic behind the bus, for ever reaching out to catch it in its jaws and swallow it, digest it . . . The images caught in the headlights came and went so fast, the obeah man felt that he did not have enough time to examine them, to let them play upon his senses.

A kind of tiredness seized Zampi now. He felt as though he had been working physically. It was not unusual for him to feel this way after he had ministered to some sick person. An obeah man's body took on all the ills that he purged someone of, then came the second and more difficult leg of his task: to cleanse himself of these ills, these aches and pains of humanity which he absorbed like long dry roots of Blue Basin that carved through stone and rock in search of water.

'You must be brave to drive this big bus by yourself all up through Diego Martin Valley,' Zolda said.

The obeah man reflected how pleasant it was to encourage little fears of the darkness; he would have enjoyed teasing her about it at one time, now it seemed stupid for a woman of her age. And now he looked at the bus driver; he could hear the bravado waiting to burst forth from him. Had he not been in the bus that night, what a story the little man might tell.

'The things that I see happen on the road at night . . . hai . . .' the driver replied, slapping the gear-shift in fond confidence.

It was enough to impress Zolda that he was no coward. At the same time he did not go into details. Zampi laughed as he recalled that picture of the bus swerving crazily as it pelted off into the night, its little red taillight swaying from left to right along the road as the driver sped away in fear.

'I wonder why he ain't talk 'bout that night,' Zampi wondered. 'He must be understand better than me what take place—why he so full of sweet talk all of a sudden?' What understanding, what interpretation, the bus driver made up for himself about the shooting star was beyond Zampi—but what absorbed him was the faith the little man had in him. His power was boundless and there was nothing he could not do. The manner in which he addressed Zolda, his appraisal of her, was one which said that he too, this puny little stunted wizened butt-end of a man, had a new vigour and new belief in himself.

Should he encourage this little man into believing that all he needed was a good obeah man—that all the girls of Diego Martin would be his? He had thought vaguely that he might even hear Jimpy's voice coming from the depths of the Basin calling out: 'Zampi—Zampi-O—that is a good thing you do! Oh, Zampi—Zampi-O—why you do that? Do this— is a bad bad thing you gone and do.'

The feeling of a terrible sense of responsibility enveloped him and he suddenly understood what Jimpy meant. So the day had indeed come when he truly understood what his task was like, what lay ahead of him. Now he was afraid that in not knowing the best choice he would fail miserably as an obeah man.

'A man have to be really something to understand and pick out the good from the bad in other people life. More and more people coming to believe in me. Gawd, I wonder if my shoulder strong enough?' he wondered, as the bus sped along.

As his mind raced on this way, he overheard only snatches of the conversation between the bus driver and Zolda.

'I know the road with my eye shut!' the driver said. 'It ain't yesterday that I driving this route. Time was when the Diego Martin road used to be only a small dirt track.' He swung back to Zolda and smiled, adding, 'I is not a young man, you know.' And just as he expected, so quickly Zolda disagreed with him.

'What you mean, you is not a young man? I bet you have plenty more years in you than you think.'

The conversation went back and forth this way.

Zampi felt as though he could foretell each banter as they talked on and on, with a friendliness between them which grew and grew; they sounded like old friends. And now the obeah man heard the driver ask Zolda, 'You think he would do it for me?'

'Do what?' Zampi asked.

Zolda leaned over to Zampi and whispered in his ear what the driver wanted. She had a way of letting her breast work close into his side. She looked up at him with a wicked little smile which he did not return, then she drew away sharply from him.

Zampi looked out the window of the bus, and she kicked him to bring back his attention. Obeah was not aphrodisiacs and charms for sour old men. This much he knew.

She looked away, sullenly, then turned to him again.

'But why you so? Since when you get you don't want to do nothing to please people? What it go take out of you if you do a small something for this old man?'

Zampi looked at her first as if he would simply ignore the question and just smile. There were times when he did just that to some of the things she said or did.

But now his mind was clear. He would not simply smile and let it go at that.

'It have some things that you could do and some things that you can't do. Trouble with you is that you ent have no sense—is just the way you is.'

She became more angry at him now. All the more since she had given herself to him, she felt a kind of personal betrayal in Zampi's refusal to grant the driver's wish.

'Is since when you come to know so much 'bout everything? Since when you know what good for people and what ain't good for them? You playin' you is God?'

'It have some things that good for people and some things that ent good for them. Like the way you does dance up with that poor little cripple makin' he heart swell up with joy in front of all them people. You think you makin' him happy? You think he enjoying he-self? I ain't God but I know nuff to tell you that it wrong!'

'Ask him,' she shouted at Zampi. 'Go ahead and ask him who is he friend and who is not he friend.'

'Yes,' said Zampi, 'you is he friend—and Massahood is he friend—but not me.'

'And who friend you is these days?' she asked Zampi. 'I don't think I know anybody who like you any more.'

'Look, I don't want to argue with you in front of the driver. The bus almost reach Marine Square and you should be glad I come to town with you—that is all.'

'But you won't work a obeah for—' She pointed to the driver, who had his ears cocked and waiting for the reply.

'No,' he said finally. 'Is a wrong thing to do. That is not what a obeah man have to do.'

The bus pulled into Marine Square and he stalked out alone. He saw her smiling at the driver, the palms of her hands upturned in a gesture of apology to him.

11

THERE is no street, no stone . . . no place where night meets day . . . where people come as if to watch the walls alone. There is no place that does not have a reason for its being. The Scorpion Tail Club is on one of those small dark streets that run for one block off the Eastern Market. It is a strange street, one of extreme moods and lights. During the day, when the Eastern Market is open, the street is like a busy beehive with vendors scurrying to the small dingy restaurants to get a six-cent lunch or to the Prince of Wales Bar at the corner, or simply on the move because that vast noise of chickens squawking, vendors arguing, whores soliciting, beggars and porters pleading and whining . . . all this has drowned out the thin small sound of life in their own breast, and so they move with the tide, not questioning its flow.

At three o'clock the market rings its great brass bell and by a quarter past three the whole area empties out and at once a strange and haunting silence falls across the place, broken only by the loud slush and hiss of powerful hoses pushing away the debris of broken vegetables, rotten fruit and wilted provisions along the road in a flood of water, and when the noises cease the hum of flies signals their return for their evening feeding before they settle down for the night.

Evening had almost come and the streets about the market were lonely; only one of the sad red-eyed mongrels of the market place stood in the middle of the road licking its body. It stopped as if from habit, looked about in wonder . . . in expectation of the kick it would get from someone ordinarily, and, sensing the strange quiet of the streets, started jogging away with a diagonal trot as though its licking tongue had lost its savour.

By the first darkness a single donkey cart arrives. The animal is unhitched, sugarcane tops are placed under its head, it neighs out loud, twisting its profane lips, baring its brown teeth in its pale pink cotton mouth, then settles down to munch for the night. And then, as if out of nowhere, the streets are lined with donkey carts all piled high with produce from the deep and hidden jungle corners of the island. Darkness begins to fall and they light their hurricane lanterns, and still more carts keep coming. As the evening wears on, buyers come to haggle and barter with the farmers, and the air is filled with a different kind of noise, and when the bartering and buying are done they repair to one of the many little clubs like the Scorpion Tail, one flight of stairs above the streets, to drink there and wait for the dawn.

The vendors wait for the dawn at the Scorpion Tail, but there are others also, who know that people will be waiting there, and since no one likes to wait alone, they have come to join hands till the dawn. They are people of the night for whom the world is a different place.

And Zolda was one of them, for she too was a child of the night, of shadows and half-dark images with their brush-lines smoothed and worn down like seashells. Her body, her life's breath, seemed thin in daylight. Her feelings were deep and ran like flood waters through her tight veins when darkness fell. Her body came to life and fell into rhythm as easily as water flowing. She had only to hear two beats of a rhythm and instantly her arms, her legs, her hips, her feet, all were tuned to it, her face shone with excitement and laughter; her bright teeth flashing, her head thrown back.

Zampi followed her up the narrow flight of steps that led to the Scorpion Tail. He watched how her body moved, how her waist tilted like balances as she mounted each step, the tight string of vine about her waist holding her body in the centre as though top and bottom halves were separate, yet worked together with a smooth rhythm. She paused at the head of the stairs, looking down at him with the same sullen look she had had on the bus.

'It must have something left in the world that could make you get up and run.'

He lowered his eyes and shook his head slowly from left to right. 'When you find it tell me 'bout it . . . maybe I go start running then.' This he said more to himself than to her.

'Why you always mumblin' mumblin' so? I can't even understand what you sayin' no more.'

He stood in front of her, looking her up and down. She was still peeved about his refusal to the bus driver. To her it seemed simple, it was just a refusal to a harmless little old man. What had she always been saying? 'Life have enough hard times and when you could make yourself happy you is a damn' fool to miss the chance.' Could he ever tell her, would she ever begin to understand, why he had to refuse the driver his wish so that he could entice the Diego Martin girls into his bus?

'I say you playing wrong and strong. As soon as you reach the Scorpion Tail you ready to 'buse. Soon as you smell rum and hear calypso you begin to feel like if you own the world and you ain't care what happen tomorrow. I say I want to see you dance till your two foot drop off and I want to hear you sing till your throat get hoarse. Come on now.' He took her by the arm and drew her inside roughly. It irked him more that she should enjoy being treated roughly, it was clear from her eyes.

The place was much larger than it seemed from outside. It was a large hall with a small bar at one end and great wide glass windows clear across the front which rotated on centre pins. The market streets were below. There was painted crudely on the wall an ugly scorpion, its tail curled back upon itself as the legend told . . . when a scorpion became over-angered it arched its tail back and injected its venom into its own back, then died. The scorpion tail motif hung over the bar where a thin man with deep-set eyes stood. His head was something of a triangle; a tiny little pouty mouth, wide-set eyes, and a thin point of a chin. He had that pale nocturnal sadness of men whose flesh has hungered for sunlight.

Across the floor of the hall were small tables with deep chairs made of old puncheons and cut-away casks with arm rests and seats. They were all painted different colours, green, red, orange, white, yet they still had that mellow aroma of rum, and where the metal hoops were rusted or missing there was painted on a ring of colour to simulate the hoop. At the side of the bar were many steel drums decorated and marked off in garish colours, a bass, and other musical instruments. At the other side of the bar was a small dressing room where Zolda went to change into a costume for her dance later on. As she left she said to Zampi again, 'I can't understand why you act so selfish to that poor old bus driver.'

Zampi started to explain. 'Ah . . .' But she had already turned her back before he could say another word.

As he looked about him, the place seemed lighter than when they came in at first. Now he could see people sitting at the nearby tables or moving about in the darkness. The more respectable people of the island clung to the edges of the walls as if to protect themselves from something savage in the room, whereas in the centre of the great hall was a less well-dressed set of people, some of them in carnival costumes which bore marks of the day's toll, creased, sagging, with dark patches of sweat in the armpits, the crotch, around the waist, faded in the ugly way that cheap bright satin colours do in a day of abuse. The large glass windows were open wide, yet there was a cloud of smoke about two feet deep smoothly thinned out below the dark ceiling, and the room smelt faintly of rum, cigarettes, and that odour that hung about gymnasiums.

The place was beginning to liven up, the midnight hour had just passed and people were coming in off the streets. There was a bat man half asleep at one table, his large bat-faced mask facing him, his long dark brown silk wings standing in a corner. There were sailors everywhere, clean and white and starched to coal-black filthy ones. Two highway robbers were arguing at the bar and at one of the tables nearest to the door were huddled together three red dragons with little bright butterfly wings on their backs, arguing animatedly with their hands. Each time the door opened the red dragons looked up as though they were waiting for someone.

'Is the beast,' one of them shouted as Zampi came in with Zolda. And then, seeing that it wasn't, they turned back to their drinks. 'But how the hell we lose the beast man?' they questioned one another as they searched the faces for their beast, a great scaly monster with a gigantic mask. Each frail skin-fitted red dragon had a long rope attached to rings in the beast's heels, his arms and through his nose. They were supposed to keep him in rein as he lumbered along contorting his grotesque face, clawing at his scales with long fingernails, lurching at pretty girls on the streets. The little dragons had lost him . . . They seemed forlorn and lost without their monster . . . all the devilry had gone out of them.

All the tables were taken, and since the dragons had caught the obeah man's eye, he drifted over to their table. There was a loud burst of applause from one of the far tables, followed by a raspy laughter which made Zampi look around. He was sure he had heard that laughter somewhere before.

'You ain't pass a red dragon monster when you was comin' up here?' one of the dragons asked Zampi dolefully.

'What happen, you can't make bacchanal 'less you have your beast with you?' the obeah man teased.

'Man, we just went in the rumshop to chop a liquor and the beast bust 'way quiet quiet quiet without nobody seein' him.'

'Well,' another dragon added, 'the poor bitch must be lonely no ass without we. A beast ain't no good by he-self, he need he assistants.'

87

'I hope we find him before morning break, man!' the other dragon said. 'I hope we find 'em.'

Zampi was smiling to himself. 'Even the devil can't be happy by he-self . . . he have to have people round him,' he thought.

'Everybody need somebody, eh? Even you fellars with all your masquerade can't make bacchanal.'

As he spoke these words, the obeah man felt someone touch his shoulder: he looked round. 'Everybody but me . . .' It was Massahood, the stick man, beaming at him with his full face as though he was very happy to see the obeah man, as though he felt in some way that his boyhood friend was here to join with him in all the bacchanal that they had shared together so long ago.

'Is goin' to be real bacchanal tonight, boy . . . It look as if it take a stronger obeah than yours to bring you out the bush,' the stick man said, laughing.

It was hard for Zampi to tell if he was drunk. Massahood was never what he could call drunk at any time. Zampi was smiling as they walked over to his table. 'You ever get drunk in your whole life, boy?'

Massahood laughed with that deep gurgle that seemed to come from way down in his barrel chest.

'When you see I get drunk, is the rum fault, not mine,' he boasted, drawing the obeah man to his table. Zampi could see the faces now. A few regulars of the Britannia. With surprise he saw the bus driver. Zolda must have mentioned the Scorpion Tail, and here he was. And now the obeah man remembered where he had heard that raspy laughter, for there in the midst of the tight little knot about the table was the cripple.

'Look who comin' to fete with we tonight . . . is Zampi,' one of the men shouted with excitement.

The obeah man nodded, smiling with approval.

'You don't think that is time he come out from the bush?' Massahood asked the company around the table. 'When a man stop in the bush too long and he ain't use certain things they does get cold after a while.' There was a wild uproar of laughter at this. Zampi could not fail to laugh with the others as well.

'Way Zolda? Way Zolda, man? You bring she wid you or you hiding she in the bush?' the cripple asked, his voice filled with excitement.

Zampi jerked his head in the direction of the dressing-room. 'She gone to get dress up for she dance.'

The cripple took a deep puff on his cigar. It was a whole cigar—ordinarily he smoked butts—and the long brown taper seemed incongruous between his fingers, for he smoked by pinching its edges between thumb and index finger just as though it were a butt.

'Is now the fete go really begin, boys. That is what we need to liven up the old Scorpion Tail.' The cripple rubbed his hands together as though he were soaping them up.

Zampi could see some people across the way at a table close to the wall talking and pointing at him. One of them was a very tall blond man who was dressed formally—perhaps he was a tourist. The man with him was as black as coals and spoke English with that pompousness that made the words from his mouth like stones. Zampi turned his attention to the drink which Massahood was offering him. 'It look as if I go have to go a long, long way befo' I catch up with you.'

'Now you beginning to sound like the old Zampi that we uses to know.'

The obeah man tossed the drink down his throat and there was a short round of applause from the little knot of men. It was carnival, and they were drinking all day. Their greatest pleasure was to have everyone about them feeling the same sense of unreality, of swimming, of the possibility of all things.

Zampi was beginning to feel that warm glow of comradeship that he once knew, yet he still felt alone, and afraid that his feet might slip into the quick and easy rhythm of the life about him. Then he would be back on the La Basse with only a bottle of rum from time to time in between. 'Let me stand my hand and buy a bottle,' he offered as he swallowed the second shot that Massahood poured him. The rum hit something in the back of his jaws and snapped at his throat like the crack of a whip.

'Aie,' he gasped as he looked at the bottom of the empty glass.

'*You* can't buy we a drink,' the cripple answered, foraging in his pockets. He always rummaged through several pockets before finding whatever he wanted. He had to slap himself all over, then go through three or four pockets before he could find a match. 'You is a *big* obeah man now,' he said, his eyes lowered to his hands. 'You must only eat, drink, and be merry . . . let other people put they hand in they pocket.'

The cripple found his little purse and removed a few silver shillings from it. Zampi at the same time reached into his pocket, but Massahood held his hand there and nodded his head 'no'. The obeah man did not like the tone of the cripple's voice, yet he smiled. 'Next time, then?' he asked. But the cripple ignored him by turning his eyes to the corner of the bar where Zolda had gone.

And now the bus driver was whispering in the cripple's ear. The cripple's face turned expressionless at first, then serious. 'Why you don't ask him . . . He is the big obeah man . . . not me.'

The bus driver looked sheepish as the cripple spoke harshly at him. 'I mean is not such a big thing that I did ask him for, man,' the driver said more to console himself.

'Well, ask him, man . . . ask him . . . he sittin' right there in front of you.'

'I done gone and ask him already, man . . . A obeah man not suppose to be hoggish . . . he can't handle all them woman in Diego Martin . . . I only want *one* . . . *one* li'l thing to keep company with me when—'

The cripple lost his patience now. 'Listen, man, why you ent keep your tail quiet?' he said, silencing the driver.

Meanwhile Zampi and Massahood bantered back and forth amid the many voices and conversations that filled the room of the Scorpion Tail.

'I bet since you gone and turn obeah man you can't hold your liquor like you uses to,' Massahood dared Zampi.

'I think I could drink with you bottle for bottle and still find my way up to Blue Basin, 'specially as how you see how *you* must be start drinking since morning break.'

'Oh God,' Massahood laughed out loud. 'Boy, what you talkin' 'bout? . . . I just beginning to feel good. You could push a pin in me and I wouldn't feel it. You can't call that drunk.'

One of the men in the little knot who followed the conversation spoke up instantly. 'It have a bottle of Black Cat that say you can't do it,' he challenged Massahood.

The stick man jerked round and almost impulsively accepted the challenge. 'But wait,' he said, and then, 'A bottle of Brown Skin Gal, since you want to lose your money here tonight.'

The man was as surprised as Massahood was at the quick turn of events. He was ready to withdraw the offer. 'No, man, that cost too much . . . but I is a man of my word, you know. I say a bottle of Black Cat and that is all.' He said this with some hope that the stick man would still back down, but Massahood's excitement could not be put out. These were the moments when life flashed through him like a bolt of electricity.

'All right! . . . I go show you . . . for a bottle of Black Cat. Is a bottle of Black Cat you did say?' The man agreed half-heartedly, his jaw hung loose as he nodded. 'Well, a bottle of Black Cat it is.'

The cripple followed the dares and bet with hungry eyes and ears. He volunteered a pin which he had buried with hundreds of other odds and ends he carried about on his person. He rummaged about feverishly and after a few moments of excited shuffling shouted out with glee as though he had found some hidden treasure. 'Look, a pin . . . Look, a pin! . . . I have a pin right here!'

He wedged through the tight knot of men close to Massahood, and the man who placed the bet tried to draw back now from the centre of all this bustle. But the cripple caught him by his sleeve. 'Here,' he said to the man as he backed away nodding his head, trying to recede into the background. The cripple grasped his hand with a kind of anger, of disappointment. 'Take the pin, man . . . here, take it!' he badgered. 'Your blood turn to water or what?' He held the man's thumb and index finger and forcefully made them hold the pin.

Meantime the stick man held out his arm, tensing its muscles, rolling his wrist around and around with a wide smile cast across his face, his eyes glued to a spot on his arm midway between wrist and elbow. He pressed his thumb hard into the spot, then watched the blood race back into it, and then he smiled that inner smile of the pleasure that he derived from feeling all of life buried deep in his body. Any moment now he would feel it touched by the point of a pin and it amused him.

The man was completely cowed now. He turned pale and finally worked up enough courage to back down. 'No,' he said. 'No, man, I can't do it . . . I beginning to feel sick in my stomach . . . must be all the rum I drink.'

'Gimme back my blasted pin!' the cripple cried, feeling its inch length as he rolled it between his fingers. 'You want me to do it for you? . . . eh? You want me to show you how?'

The bottle of Black Cat lay on the table already uncorked, surrounded by small glasses and a pitcher of ice water.

'No,' the man said, 'I don't even want to see it.' He stepped out of the crowd which had thickened up now that some action was focused at the table.

Zampi felt that things about him were going past too quickly. All of this had started very innocently and before he could digest the initial spark from which a situation arose, hundreds of other little sparks had flown out of nowhere and blazed up like a frightening fire out of control. He reached for the silver box he had tied to his arm and, holding it tightly, he concentrated hard on it, bringing all his attention and energies to focus on it. He looked up at Massahood to see if the stick man had noticed this lapse of attention, but Massahood was glancing at the bottle sitting in the midst of the cooled glasses and the white enamel pitcher of ice water. He took the pin from the cripple and looked at its point carefully. The men who were at the table surrounded him and over their shoulders were many other people straining and stretching to catch a glimpse of the stick man and what he was about to do. They left a wide space all around him as though they were all afraid of what he would do, as if they too felt that savage scent in the air, were enticed and repelled by it at the same time.

The stick man now laid the pin flat on his arm. There was a dead silence in the Scorpion Tail and all attention was hard on him, all eyes glued to the spot he had marked for the puncturing of his flesh. The silence was one that everyone joined in creating, a kind of spell which they all knew instinctively should not be broken.

Massahood stood the pin straight in the air, its point pressing delicately on his skin, and then slowly, with that same inner smile he wore at times, he pressed the pin halfway down into his flesh. With his wrist upturned, his fist rolled into a great tight ball, the pin sticking out halfway, he turned completely about so that all could see; and when he had turned through a complete circle, the crowd still as silent as before, he placed his fingers on the underside of his arm, his thumb gently resting on the head of the pin, and with a great howl, 'Hoye-oye-yoye!' he jabbed the pin's whole length into his flesh. Only its tiny metal head shone like a little jewel embedded in a small indentation of his arm.

The spell was broken now, there were gasps and sighs. The bus driver, who was a stranger to this group of men, looked on with the quiet amazement of those who do not belong to such a tight-knit crew and know that he should see, hear, and feel all emotion, but not express a single sign of being present. That low murmur of the Scorpion Tail returned and the stick man caught the head of the pin between his fingernails and pulled it out, staring at the dark red blood on it, then he threw it into the spittoon at the side of the table.

Someone shouted: 'Oh God, man . . . Oh God!'

As he threw the pin into the spittoon, the stick man looked up to the crowd; his face, his eyes, filled with laughter. He snatched the bottle of Black Cat by the neck with a sweep of his hand and . . .

'Fire one on the *Hood*, everybody . . . Ah say to fire one on the *Iron-man!*'

92

12

A LOUD and agonizing scream raced across the hall, and there, standing at the door of the Scorpion Tail, was the beast, the red dragons' monster. He tottered about a few steps, flung his head forward, then rolled it loosely about, screaming like some prehistoric beast in great pain.

Everyone at the Scorpion Tail looked to the door, some left their tables to investigate. The cripple pushed himself up on the arms of the puncheon seat into which he was wedged low down. Zampi turned around, for his back was to the door. Massahood instinctively reached for his stick which lay under the table.

'Ahh . . .' The monster groaned again, and now the little red dragons rushed over to buckle and bind him, to snap their ropes into the heels and nose of the beast. But the beast was wild with agony, drunkenly he lashed out with his long tin claws at the dragons as he saw their ropes. The little red devils pranced about mocking, teasing, keeping at a safe distance. More people had moved to the door, save the respectable folk, who ran to the far end of the hall and lined up against the windows. They were curious, but afraid of that savage thing which hungered in the very walls of the Scorpion Tail. They saw its teeth now and they tried to laugh nervously.

Zolda heard the wild roar and came running out of her dressing-room. She pushed her way to the very edge of the crowd which formed a wide circle about the beast. Zampi, Massahood, the cripple, and the bus driver were all lined up watching the monster. In spite of all his wanderings, he still had his large silver javelin with sharp spikes, and a hatchet, hung from either side of his hips. He used them alternately, swinging wide each time the dragons came close with their hooks. His voice sounded in pain as it muffled through the two-foot mask he wore, and each time he lashed through the air with his javelin the tin scales covering his body made a rustling metallic sound as though his entrails were filled with small metal jingles.

'You stupid beast, you ugly just like you stupid,' said Zolda. 'Why you didn't go and make bacchanal by yourself? You didn't have no dragon to tie you down, no rope to bind you, nobody to pull and tug you this way and that by your nose, kick you in your chest . . . you was free! Why you ain't go your way?'

The monster was leaning up against the wall taking deep loud breaths, his chest heaved up and down and the scales on his body, laid out like a tiled roof, rose up and down along his chest. He bellowed out angrily at Zolda. 'Ahhhhh . . . !'

Then he held his head low, shaking it from left to right, uttering a low moan as though Zolda had wounded him. For he thought of how he had roamed the streets all afternoon and evening alone. Small children pelted him with mango pits and dirty fruit, shouting, 'What kind of beast you is? . . . you ain't have no red dragon.' And other children screamed, 'Where your ropes?' And the beast could only lumber and totter about, working his hands and fingers with their long claws in the air, moaning, groaning as they pelted him with cabbage heads and shrivelled potatoes. The band of dragons would have protected him and he hated them for leaving him alone.

'You playin' mass or you playin' ass?' the cripple asked. 'You have one or two rums in your head and you really think you is a big big devil . . . you walk 'bout whole day playin' devil and now you *believe* you is a devil . . . behave yourself. . . you ugly bitch.'

The beast tossed his head high, looking at the little cripple who was dressed in his costume of the day before: his suit turned back to front, the little stool strapped to his shorter leg and a mask of the most beautiful, the most delicate lines of lips and eyes on the back of his head. And the growl the monster uttered was one of hate as he brandished his javelin. Meanwhile the red dragons darted back and forth waiting their chance to snap their hooks into his heels.

'Look at them! Look at the li'l buggers, eh!' Massahood said, laughing, thumping his stick on the floor, rocking back and forth on his stick. 'They did look so half dead and helpless like if they couldn't walk another step. But watch them now. Watch how they have to catch the beast. They have to chain 'em and hang on to 'em. Worthless scamps. . . they ain't nuttin' without him! . . . Here,' Massahood offered his stick, 'give them a good lick in they ass, boy. You could bust open they head one by one with it . . . it have a master obeah on it.'

The beast dropped his javelin and half reached for the stick.

Zampi rushed the stick man and slapped his wrist before the beast could touch the stick. 'Don't do that,' he said to Massahood. 'What the hell you think you doing at all? Best hads put 'way that stick before something bad happen here tonight.'

Massahood stopped gesturing at the beast with the stick. He looked at Zampi first with surprise, then defiance; now he turned to the beast again. 'Is *my* stick, boy. Here, take it!' he urged the beast, whose hand trembled to take hold of it, for it was longer than either his javelin or his hatchet. But as the beast's eyes caught Zampi's he coiled away, shaking his head with a kind of tiredness that came from being torn and pulled in different directions.

'Why you come here to make trouble?' Zampi asked. 'You come with your own two foot. You *want* them to catch you. Now they catch you, you want to make all kind of noise and fight.'

By now everyone who gathered about had taken sides. No one knew the dragons or the beast personally, but something in the situation struck at some hidden thought in each of them, and Zolda flew at the obeah man. 'Now what you tryin' to say at all? You want to see everybody tie down like you? You think everybody want to be like you? Nobody ain't want to get tie down, is only a fool like me that would wait for you to come out from the bush . . . ha boy! But no more . . . no more of that for me.' And turning to the beast with disgust: 'You is a fool. You had your chance and you didn't take it. Now look at you, you can't make a *note* by yourself.'

Zampi understood what she meant. There were times when he was certain that she was no saint in the past four years. Some women could because of their poor looks, and their dull fires. For that kind of woman temptation was not frequent, but this was Zolda, and the obeah man found himself wishing that he could believe she had waited for him, that she had gone out of the way to remain chaste, that she did not have a lover after him. He was placating in his tone of voice now.

'You can't see that he need them just so much as they need he . . . that without one another neither of them worth a damn?'

The monster was tiring from the flailing of his arms, for the tiny dragons were lithe and quick, and, as though they planned it deliberately, they were wearing him out by coming close enough within his reach, then darting away lightning fast. Massahood laughed at the incident like no one else. He pounded on the floor with his stick, rocking with laughter. His head was thrown back far so that you could see the roof of his

95

mouth and one wide gap in the back of his jaw where a great molar was missing. He drew a flat bottle from his pocket and tilted it to his head, still laughing wildly, and as he took the bottle away he sputtered and then his face became stern and his eyebrows furrowed deep.

'Tell me why that beast need them dragons, *Mister* Obeah Man.' He addressed Zampi with all the irony he could put into his voice.

'Yes, tell we . . . tell we anything. You is a big obeah man, you know everything,' the cripple's voice chimed in from the depths of the crowd.

'Everybody need people, it ain't have nobody who don't need somebody. Not even you,' Zampi told Massahood. The stick man seemed surprised by this remark. He looked at Zampi with an expression of strangeness, as though he were one whose face and voice and character he was meeting for the first time.

'Who need people?' he asked again. 'Boy, why you does talk this kind of funny funny talk? You forget how we grow up side by side . . . Lately you beginnin' to sound like if you is somebody else.'

Zampi knew that he must sound like someone else. He knew two worlds now. The world of obeah, of waking in the morning with happiness as he went about his lonely tasks in the bush, of pleasure when someone made the long journey to come all the way up the waterfall to get some little advice, some little charm because they had heard from someone else what wonders he could work. He also knew the world in which Massahood lived. He remembered the mornings filled with fear. Fear of the running down of time, fear of death, fear of the chill in his heart when nothing seemed bright with colour and all that was left was the Britannia Bar . . . another day like many, many others before.

'A man does change from day to day. That is the way life is,' said Zampi simply, more to himself than in reply to Massahood, who ran his tongue along the edges of his front teeth in introspection, in deep slow thoughts as he scoured Zampi's face, his size, his shoulders, comparing the similarities of their bodies, puzzling over the differences that had come between them.

'Well, I never change! I is the same *Hood*. Ask anybody, I never let nobody down. All my friends could still talk to me and understand me. You? You make yourself a stranger to everybody . . . even to yourself. Is you who need *people*, boy, all I need is this,' pointing to the stick, 'and this,' grasping a handful of his genitals.

'And that is all you need? You never hear 'bout happiness that come from doing something for somebody else?'

'Oh Gawd . . . I want to dead!' Massahood laughed, jeering, sardonic. 'Oh Gawd, but look at how I want to dead with laugh too bad today, man!' And then his face turned serious, as only Massahood's could, in an instant. 'Boy, I give more people happiness than you could ever dream about . . . with these same two things . . . Wait, wait . . .' He swung round unsteadily, facing the bar where several people were standing. 'Aye, Teena!' he called to one of the women at the bar. *'Teenah! Teenah!. . .* come and tell this *big* obeah man who does make you happy in the nighttime, chile.' A small woman with dried-up breasts that she had somehow arranged like pointed icecream cones started towards them in a drunken gait.

'I don't want to hear no slackness,' Zampi said to her. She stood still with her drink in her hand, then went back to the bar when the obeah man turned to Massahood. 'You know damn' well what I mean but you only want to play the fool with all your big talk. You ain't different from anybody else.'

'I *different!'* Massahood insisted. 'I *different different different!'* he shouted. The movement of his head shook his body in sharp jerks as he pronounced these words. 'It ain't have nobody like me. Nobody else in the whole whole world like me. I tell you today, and I tell you tomorrow, I is me!' He rapped his breast with his fist, clenched hard so that it made loud thumps. 'I is *me! . . . me me me me me!* And I don't need nobody. Nooooobody. The whole world could haul they ass! What I have I damn' well have and everybody have to come to me for it. Man-woman-and-chile. I ain't have nuttin' to get from nobody! Fire a rum and stop talkin' like a blasted priest. You have a li'l bit of powers, you gone and turn obeah man. You only want people to respect you and 'fraid you. That is the only reason you turn obeah man. You ain't doin' a damn blasted thing for the island. Who the hell you think you foolin' sittin' up top the waterfall? You squeeze a shillin' here . . . a shillin' there out of poor people and you give them some rubbish to eat and drink and you say you cure them, you make them strong. That is a good life. A man like you should be happy. But don't run-come-sayin' 'bout "Oh, I helpin' people." You helpin' yourself!'

And while Massahood was speaking, Zolda seemed to be listening with her eyes, her mouth, her nostrils. Her sympathies were similar to the stick man's. There was a sudden moment of recognition in her face. Recognition of something that has been so for ages, of having gone past it each day without noticing it. And then one day, when it has been cleared from the landscape, its absence makes it visible. Her face changed as suddenly as a face bolts from one moment to the next with a sharp slap. Her emotions shuttled back and forth, not with indecision, but with a stronger and stronger conviction for each thought, each emotion. Massahood rolled his shoulders, the stick man's great round of muscle worked like balls at the side of his chest. His face was a wide smile of wickedness. Under his lips his teeth shone wet and glistening, a small piece of one front tooth broken away leaving it slightly shorter than the other.

The steel drums and the other musicians had started playing, only slowly now as though each player was seeking out the core of the music, looking for the essence of its meaning before they would burst forth in unison with the calypso of this carnival, and the melody, the rhythm, the emotion of flesh meeting flesh was being probed by the music like hungry fingers in search of the right key to open the door to explosion.

Iron something bend up my something,
Oh . . . Man-Man-Ti-Re!
Iron something bust up my nothing
Oh . . . Man-Man-Ti-Re!

'Fire one!' the stick man announced again to Zampi, who stared now at him, now at Zolda, in that manner of quiet perception as he followed the thoughts of these two people with a deadly accuracy.

Zolda looked him straight in the face. 'You *dead!*' she said to him. You aint *no* good for me, you is a *dead* man!'

The cripple, whose voice and comments rang out from the background, shouted: 'Hear! Hear! Hear!' as he rapped on the floor with the small stool strapped to his foot.

And the stick man smiled at Zolda. 'That is the way I like to hear you talk, girl . . . Now you beginnin' to talk!' and he jutted his bottle in the air.

'Ah say to fire one on the Iron-man!' Zolda reached up and snatched the bottle from his hand before he could bring his arm down. She put it to her lips, her head leaned far back, her waist arched, and small bubbles ran through the dark brown rum to the bottom of the bottle. As she drank, her eyes turned up in their sockets a pale bluish white, the bone in her throat moved up and down, and when she took the bottle away her lips shone wet and sensuous. She ran the tip of her tongue along her lips much as Massahood did, and there was a wicked glint in her eyes as she looked up into Massahood's.

A feeling of conquest raced through the stick man's breast. He turned again to the beast, imploring him to take the stick, to lay low the three dragons with it. The beast reached out his hand to take the stick, but Zampi snatched the end in his hand as Massahood waved it in offering.

'I done tell you not to use this stick to play the fool with,' Zampi warned. He could feel Massahood's determined grip on it. Through the length of the stick travelled the tense pitch of emotion and temper of the two men.

'You think that is your . . . *obeah* what make this stick great? Dat what you sayin'?'

Zampi knew now what it meant to be an obeah man. He should never have placed a hex on Massahood's stick. He did not believe in it, he would not respect any of the taboos, or the responsibilities which went with the power Zampi placed in his hands. Zampi knew too that the stick man did not believe in him. That was his fault because in the beginning he did not know the responsibility of his calling. He knew now that he was responsible, that he would have to answer for Massahood's actions. His attention strayed for a moment as he reflected on this and Massahood tugged hard on the stick, pulling Zampi towards him with a sudden jerk. Zampi's grip on the stick was firm. It pulled him along with it. They stood face to face now.

'You playin' bad-john! Take care I bust a lash in your ass and make you coil up like a old snake here tonight,' Massahood warned.

Zampi slapped both his hands on the stick. 'You want to lash? Well, lash! Go ahead and lash!'

Massahood, feeling himself at a disadvantage holding on to one end of the stick only, slapped his other hand on now as they faced each other. The stick man smiled sardonically, a little more confident than before. He rocked the stick to and fro as he looked deep into Zampi's eyes, testing him, testing the tenseness of the obeah man's grip on the stick, wondering how far he was willing to go. 'You lookin' for trouble, boy . . . bad bad trouble. Why you didn't stop in the bush? You have to come all the way down to Port of Spain to look for trouble.'

As he rocked back and forth holding on to the stick, Massahood felt the power, the determination with which Zampi held the stick, his two fists twined around its midsection.

'I ent lookin' for trouble, but I warnin' you. Don't play the ass with this stick otherwise a bad thing go happen to you. I don't know what you think, I don't know what you want to think. You could believe all what you want to believe . . . that you is the best stick man in the island. You could laugh all you want to laugh, but take care, take care!' Zampi warned over and over again.

Massahood sucked his teeth in disgust. 'I ain't 'fraid no obeah man like you. I ain't 'fraid *ten* obeah men like you. I bust open two fellars' head today. I ain't 'fraid to bust open your head, you know.'

Zampi knew that he had that power now. He could feel it in his thighs. His loins felt taut, his abdomen like rock. He had heard of men who had a sledgehammer hit them in their abdomen, he knew that such a blow could not touch him now. 'You want the stick?' he asked, still holding tight to it.

Massahood nodded.

'You want it? Well, take it!'

They had worked the stick above the level of their heads now. Massahood clenched his teeth and pulled down hard with all his strength. And Zampi, waiting, timing his action to a split second, relaxed his arms only. The stick came down fast, and when it reached breast-level Zampi pushed hard with his legs, running the stick man backward several steps until Massahood fell and the obeah man came down with his knee on Massahood's chest, his eyes cutting deep into Massahood's. 'I *warnin'* you, boy . . . I *warnin'* you *today today!* If you want to live to see another carnival just remember what kind of obeah you playin' with.'

The obeah man pressed hard against Massahood's throat with the stick, then he got up and left the stick man lying on the floor. He could feel Massahood's eyes cutting into his back as he walked away.

'Kill the bitch, Hood. Bust open he head. He beggin' for it for a long, long time. Let we see what he obeah go do for he now.' The cripple's voice cried out above the din.

Massahood stood up sullen and angry. He seemed taller, broader, and more robust. The men about him from the Britannia wore that look of timidity, and fear; fear of what revenge the stick man would take as he stood alone with his thoughts, planning his actions with the acrid chemistry that rushed into his blood. One of the men began dusting off his clothes with a sheepish air. He seemed to be saying, 'Look here, man, Hood . . . we see . . . but we ain't see.' Then he spoke aloud, still as timidly as before. 'Listen, man,' he said, 'you remember how he did freeze your hand at the Britannia yesterday? Don't cross him again. It look as if he really is a *bad* obeah man.'

His eyes still following Zampi, Massahood shrugged his shoulders with indifference. His body stood still, but his mind raced on. What did they say? If you had an obeah man's woman he couldn't have any powers over you? 'But I ain't 'fraid he . . . he or he obeah,' Massahood repeated over and over to himself. Yet the stick man was humiliated. He had never seen a man's face looking *down* at him. He had never known the sensation of his back lying flat on the floor. He could still feel the way the bones in his shoulder blades and the long column of his back-bone felt as they pressed into his skin against the floor. It carried him back ages, it recalled from the deep well of memory how he had once seen the world a long long time ago with Santo Pi's ugly eyes looking down at him, into him, and there was a fear like that, and a hate as well, a flood of many emotions vague and intangible, unhinged to any distinct picture he could recall, only a feeling of black rage that he could not place.

Zampi went over to the beast, who was swinging feebly at the drag-ons. The obeah man stared hard, trying to catch the eyes of the man, which were about the level of the neck in the great mask he wore, but moments passed and their eyes did not meet.

'Aye,' Zampi called. 'Aye, man!' The beast heard him finally and looked about. Their eyes met now. 'The poor man come to think that he is really a devil,' Zampi said to himself. He motioned the dragons to stop prancing about and now he moved in closer. The man in the costume growled and shook as Zampi approached. He held his javelin high over his head, threatening Zampi with it. Zampi placed his fingers on his arm where he had the charm tied. He moved in another step closer.

'Put that down!' Zampi ordered. And as if his words struck the beast's arm, it shook as though it were touched by some hidden hand. 'I say to put that thing down.'

There was something incongruous in the communication between the two, for the monster's eyes in the mask were focused towards the ceiling and yet its movements were directed from eyes low down in its neck. And now the arm was lowering slowly, with the same incongruity, for the beast's mask was ugly, grinning, and vicious, yet inside that front was an exhausted man. His arm descended slowly and Zampi stood in front of him now. His eyes looking hard into the man's eyes. He placed both hands firmly on the mask and lifted it off gently. And there under the grotesque mask was the man's face, covered with sweat; tears were rolling down the folds of his cheeks, then he started sobbing like a child.

Zampi placed both thumbs against the man's temples and pressed them hard for a few seconds as he spoke some words that were barely audible. Then he said to the dragons, 'Carry him outside where he could catch the breeze and come back to he right senses.'

13

THE Scorpion Tail is real to those who inhabit the night. Like a potion which slowly envelops the senses, the Scorpion Tail steals silently under the skins of men until they are one with its easy laughter, its gaiety and abandon, its ability to infect all those who enter with its mood. Men do not ask about the Scorpion Tail, they know by instinct that it will take them like a mother into its arms. They go seeking, they have only a vague restlessness in their blood but they know that here, if anywhere, it will be quieted and that their hearts will rise high. And as the evening wears on they move with its momentum. So closely have they clasped it to their hearts, so closely it has taken them to its bosom. This union grows with time. The pitch of laughter rises, and men feel themselves for all of the things they are. All their stifled emotions, the faces they wear for the street, all melt away, and they feel every inch of power their beings contain and they take pleasure and delight in the sense of their own blood, as they shuttle back and forth with their masks in place.

'I bound to have a woman . . .tonight tonight . . .wait an' see, boy . . . wait an' see!' And indeed there in the corner next to the bar was the bus driver, his hand against the wall, leaning over a saucy girl, her eyes looking up into his.

The musicians, the dancers, even the bar attender whose face seemed unable to smile, all had moved with the evening, creating that particular sound that masses of people can when all is going well. A passerby in the market streets below on his way home from some other fete would hear this sound, this singular sound, and immediately know that the Scorpion Tail was alive, and that he too could, by walking up one short flight of stairs, become infected with its gaiety. Such was the way the evening progressed, such were the ways in which the hall became more and more crowded with people, with new faces, each adding to the joy and momentum that rose steadily in the walls, the floorboards, and in the hungry hearts of men.

'But look how t'ings does happen nuh! I was on my way home down by the Dry River . . . I say carnival over . . . and look at me now!' a voice would exclaim. And then another voice caught up in the swell of the steel band music, smoothed down to velvet by nips of Vat 19: 'Dat is the only kind of fete it have in this world, man . . . the kind that crawl up under your skin sudden sudden sudden . . . fire one before you analyse too much . . . monkey smoke your pipe, then! Ah say to fire one, man . . . fire one!'

And this expression, too, 'Fire one', had an infectious quality about it. Someone would shout, 'Fire one,' and it travelled through the hall like an echo bouncing back and forth until it reached Massahood's ear and he too exclaimed 'Fire one' to Zolda who stood next to him, both of them moving their feet, their bodies, not really dancing, but keeping the rhythm of the steel drums in rein deep down in their bodies. The obeah man glanced at them from the table to which Massahood had brought him earlier on; now they were joined by the two people whom Zampi had noticed across the hall before. The tall blond man, it turned out, was a visitor to the island. He was a painter from England here to do an important mural to adorn the new building which would house the new Government of an independent Trinidad.

The painter was saying how pleased he was at being in the Scorpion Tail, and as his artistic mind went to work, he visualized the two striking figures of Massahood and Zolda as Man and Woman of the Caribbean. He was animated, and he spoke excitedly about his project as though he saw in his mind's eye the vast mural with little side echoes of Caribbean history: sugarcane plantations, green and swaying in the sun, slavery, emancipation, races all colours of the rainbow who came to plant the sugarcane, the music and rhythm of a savage miscegenation forged in tropic sun . . .

'The Spirit of Independence . . . that's what I'll call it,' he said, still drawn by the faces of Massahood and Zolda. He would paint them as they looked now, he thought. Massahood, his feet bare, the lighter brown colour of the sole of his left foot. His trousers registering each muscle of his calves, his legs, his buttocks. Bare from the waist up, his thick neck, the skin of his face honed down smooth and beardless, brown as well-aged rum. The stick man's eyes closed, his lids pressed tightly together, one arm flung out in the air with his stick held high about Zolda, her long braid of hair down the front of her breast, her head thrown back, her breasts firm and high, held in cups of gold satin, her body bent back and forth at each joint . . . head thrown back, chest forward, hips back, knees forward, half standing, half stooping on the balls of her feet, her loins clad in the same satin of gold with black lines of velvet tracing the clefts of her loins and meeting at the crotch.

The obeah man's eyes were on Zolda and he could see all the poses she would assume on such a mural. He remembered how life followed a monotonous pattern from which he could not escape. And then, that day when Jimpy cornered him and drew him into the world of obeah, the narrow track he had shuttled back and forth along was broken. 'She have to see it one day . . . She bound to see it and get away from all this fete fete fete day in day out . . . just because she can't find something to do with she-self.' Zampi was a little disappointed that the painter had found his subject matter here, in the Scorpion Tail.

'So that is what you will show people in your painting? That this is what-all you see here in Trinidad? And this is all what you see in all these islands? You think that you will do we a justice in saying that this is the true "Spirit of Independence"?'

The painter meanwhile thought that he could not have found more perfect subjects. He had travelled throughout the Caribbean islands and in most of them he found a thin kind of calypso borrowed from Trinidad and smoothed down in tone and music, its lyrics deliberately intended for the tourist dollar. The sugar was long dead, the cocoa was stricken with blight, and only because Trinidad was farthest from the tourist route some of its originality still remained in the hearts of men.

The painter looked at Zampi quizzically. He never thought that anyone would question his vision and what he saw and felt. He thought of his work standing strong where thousands of people would come and feel this 'spirit.' As he drank more and more Vat 19 his face reddened, the blue veins in his temples rose high, and his eyes seemed more blue as his bright red blood raced through his face. He felt like anyone at the Scorpion Tail. He knew Massahood, he knew Zolda, knew the islands, he knew its sun and rainy season, he had captured its essence this very evening in this place and he wanted to drown himself in all its ways, then project this glorious world of the islands which had seized his senses on to his mural.

The tourist officer, a huge square Negro with a mouth full of bright yellow gold teeth, was himself so immersed in the din of the Scorpion Tail that he did not notice an immediate kinship between Zampi and his guest. Turning to Zampi, he said in his rocklike British voice: 'And here you see what we call an obeah man. A voodoo practitioner . . . a witchdoctor, if you prefer.'

He leaned and whispered into Zampi's ear, giving him a cutting glance.

'Stand up when you get introduced to white people, boy . . . you forget your manners or what?'

The painter flinched at this remark, although he did not understand the tension between the two men. 'No . . . really, please don't,' he said to Zampi in a voice so pleasant that the obeah man felt a kind of bond with this man in these few words. His mind was set on remaining seated from the time they joined the table, yet now he felt that he would not have minded, that he would have been proud and glad for his sake and for this man's sake.

The tourist officer went on, a little more stern of voice, a little more authoritative than before. 'You see before you the vestiges of the dead past . . . the darkness and the fumblings of prehistoric man to find himself. Culture and breeding take time, my friend . . . time. But it shan't be long now before we rid ourselves of all this nonsense and make ourselves a credit to the Empire.'

'Hear, hear, hear!' the cripple shouted, raising his glass to the tourist officer, then to the painter, who in turn raised his glass to Zampi, and the obeah man raised his glass too, but only to the painter's silent smile.

'Tell me,' the artist inquired, 'what would you say obeah is . . . can you truly work miracles?'

The cripple listened with an air of wisdom and secret knowledge, crouched back in his chair, puffing out thin long streams of smoke between his lips with a kind of philosophical calm, taking in and casting out issues that were too little for him to toy with.

The obeah man glanced across the table, puzzled by his unusual calm, wondering if he might not see in the artist all that was British and become sullen or insulting. But the cripple only smiled on with a kind of smug and pleased air. Zampi wished now that the tourist officer would take his guest away before anything unpleasant happened, for in his own way he wished to impress upon the mind of the outsider, the visitor, the tourist, that the Caribbean was not only the abode of 'Calypso Joe' but that here too men were concerned with questions of destiny, existence, where they were headed and why, even if they did all of these things in their own slow and stumbling ways.

The artist's presence delighted the cripple, for he saw in him a kind of ally. What educated Englishman from across the seas would believe in obeah? He had good reason to be pleased with the company. It meant that ho would not have to argue with Zampi himself. He could sit back nicely wedged in his puncheon chair and laugh at the obeah man's embarrassment and ridicule if he should be foolish enough to try to explain his hocus-pocus. But the cripple had an odd ambivalence towards the painter. The man's colour, his speech, his British air ... all of these things the cripple would detest ordinarily, yet he fell into a kind of servile respectfulness. He felt honoured to be in such company. His fellows of the Britannia would have more respect for him.

Zampi heard the Englishman's question ring in his ear again, and seeing the questioning look in his eyes, realized that he had not answered. 'Well, I don't know if you would call it miracles,' Zampi said. 'And I don't know if you would say that is I who work the miracle. But it have people who believe that, and is mostly *them* who work it. I think that what is the most important thing is that I could make man think that he could do this and that, that I could make him think that he could make himself well if he sick, and he come to me for a obeah.'

Zampi had his head turned in the direction of Massahood and Zolda, yet his eyes had lost their focus on them as he thought hard of what he was saying. He looked at the artist now, who was smiling in a way that pleased him, for although he had not put into exact words all that he wished, he none the less felt that he had made himself understood.

'Well, would you say that you are a kind of ... er ... sounding board, a catalyst?'

Zampi nodded that he did not understand the meaning of the word.

'Well, then, let's put it this way. Do you think that a man could do the things he does without your help? I mean, would you say that you have some special power or talent which other men do not?'

Zampi had his index finger hung from his lower teeth like a hook as he listened and thought carefully of what was being asked him. He found that he did not have ready answers for these questions. They required thought, then associations, then words and sentences which would not only communicate what he meant to the others but which would also contain the essence of what he felt. The obeah man found this difficult, for he never had to explain his thoughts nor how they worked. A man knows a great many things which settle in the recesses of his mind. Through a long period of time he builds a complex latticework of ideas, beliefs, and values which settle into a coherent pattern, enriching his mind, making it ready to accept or reject other thoughts as they come his way—this was the kind of knowledge he had, an amorphous thing that he felt in his bones. But to hit upon a singular thread of this fabric and to ask 'What is it?' is to ask what is life. The obeah man stumbled along, if not for the others' sake, for the sake of the painter, whose interest was genuine where the tourist officer's was offensive.

After this long silence he finally said, 'Well, yes . . . you could say that . . . but is all of that and more.' His reply was more to stimulate conversation than spell out in one sentence what obeah was. It was the first time that the question was put to him, and it was the first time it occurred to him that to try to put into words just what he did was near impossible. But the painter smiled at Zampi as if to say that he could understand what he had told him, and that he could appreciate the position in which he was placed. But not so with the tourist officer, who became more sullen and angry with Zampi.

'This man come from far far up in England to do a big job here and right away you want to tell him what to draw and what not to draw . . . Who the hell you think you is at all . . . a pissin' tail rum-sucker who turn obeah man and giving the island a bad name with all your nonsense.' The officer had two types of speech. He could be more British than British, but when he became excited he spoke in pidgin.

The painter tried to intervene in Zampi's defence by asking the officer to let the obeah man speak up and say what he had to say. But the officer would not let him go on. Instead he said to Zampi: 'Tell the man what and what you does do when people come to you, man! Tell 'em 'bout all the secret powers you have and how you get them . . . all the old chicken bones you does have rattling around in a shoebox!'

Zampi could no longer hold his temper. 'It look as if you know more 'bout obeah than me. If you know so much why you bother to bring the man over here to talk with me? You must be think that I is a animal in a cage that you could bring all kind of tourists to look at and charge them a shilling for a look-see!'

'My boy, you are a young man, and you are still in the bush where your ancestors left you. It will take years before you come out of that wilderness and begin to understand what forwardlooking people have in mind for this island.'

When the obeah man lost his temper he took hold of the little silver box strung to his arm, for he knew that to lose his temper was to lose all. Now he spoke calmly and coldly to the officer so that the painter could hear each well-formed word. '*Sah*,' he said, 'you is the *True Spirit* of *Independence*. This man here should paint a picture of you with you gold teeth and bow tie choking you so you could only talk the Englishman language with a thick black tongue no matter how hard you try.'

The cripple, who had been quiet so far, resented Zampi's cutting remark. Who was he to speak this way to a man of the officer's stature? He did not know his place. Who was he to humiliate a local man in the presence of an Englishman? He threw his rum into his throat as though it were a funnel, then swallowed hard and in his slow, grating, raspy voice he said to Zampi: 'Why the ass you don't hear what the man say? Tell we what is obeah man, tell we . . . tell we! You always sounding like if you know everything . . . Tell we . . . tell we!'

The cripple's voice was thick and drunken. The look in his eyes was not, as Zampi had thought, one of quiet, complacent listening, but that kind of cunning that comes with drunkenness. A dull kind of half listening and waiting for the right remark to lash out.

'I will tell you one thing,' Zampi said. 'Obeah is not what you think it is.' He had taken his stand firmly now. Previously he had thought that the cripple deserved special treatment and gentle handling because of his twisted body. Now he realized that treatment of this kind was not helpful and if it did anything at all it served only as a longer leash which allowed his warped views to go unchallenged. 'If you really want to know something,' he added, 'I don't think it have anything like obeah for a man like you in this whole world because you ain't believe in nuttin' but yourself.'

The cripple's eyes stared at Zampi wide open, waiting for him to finish his last word, and when he was done the little man allowed a small pause as if to ask if he was finished. 'Obeah is *not* this, obeah is *not* that. That is all you know how to talk 'bout, what *not* good and what *not* right to do. *This* ain't true, *that* ain't true. Man, that is all you could say. Tell we what *true* . . . tell we what *right* to do. If you is such a big obeah man who think 'bout so much things the least you could tell we is what *right* . . . tell we what *right*.'

Again Zampi reflected how clever the cripple was. It had not occurred to him before that this was all he had said, what was not, instead of pointing like a determined leader and saying to one and all, 'This is right, this is the way,' yet he felt certain that there was merit in what he thought; he had seen it work miracles, if that was what they were.

'Is enough to know that a thing wrong when you hear it . . . that is plenty! I know that is wrong to have a mind so bitter like gall. I know that only bad bad things could come from your mind.'

The small knot of people around the table had grown as the argument started. Men were standing about behind their women, mincing about to the steel-band music much like Massahood and Zolda with the rhythm in their bowels only as their bodies grazed each other. There was an occasional shrill cackle from a woman's voice shouting 'Stop dat!' or a high-pitched giggle from the back somewhere. Massahood and Zolda had a circle of dancers about them. The stick man had drawn out his handkerchief and used it as a fan which he waved behind Zolda as he followed her footsteps close behind without touching her body, and the cripple, looking in their direction, grinned at Zampi, for he too knew that once a man could have an obeah man's woman he was finished. That much belief he had, or that much fear he still had for Zampi, and then again perhaps it was only hate that he had for the obeah man. With the leering grin on his face he said to Zampi: 'And only good could come from your mind. You sit on your ass, work a little obeah here, work a little there, you think that you is God because you have a few pissin' tail people who come out from the bush and make you feel great. This man doin' something for the island . . .' the cripple pointed to the tourist officer. 'And this man here who come from far away to do a big big honour for we . . . he doin' something for the island . . . you know how much book 'pon book I read . . . just to find out what is what so that I could do something for the people on the La Basse?'

The painter and the tourist officer had taken a back seat in this conversation. The tourist officer was more smug than before now that the cripple took over his defence. The Englishman meanwhile became more sober of his Vat 19, the earlier wild excursions of his mind seemed to fall flat like most sudden inspirations do when the cold light of morning falls on them. He sat intensely concerned with what was going on at the table, and he felt a little bit foolish for the wild imaginations his mind had set loose earlier on. He saw the meaning of the trite phrase 'Melting-pot'; he saw, or rather he felt, a curious bond with Zampi and he asked himself over and over, 'Where's the Spirit of Independence . . . where?' His thought was interrupted by the slow speech of the obeah man, who was saying, as if to himself alone, with his eyes on the glass of rum he was drinking:

'A man have to find the road that cut out for he . . . first thing . . . plenty people ain't know what to do with they-self. First thing come round and they snatch at it. Next thing you know they make other people life miserable.'

The hall of the Scorpion Tail was not a complete chaos of milling people and total strangers as it had been earlier on. As the evening progressed, groups of people formed everywhere, each little group starting mysteriously, growing around some nucleus which gave it a particular quality to which others came, sniffed the air, and if it was the group for them they stayed, if not they wandered off to test the air of some other knot of people. There was no way of making bacchanal by yourself. Every man still carried his loneliness with him, except one or two souls who had had too much to drink and danced about in a self-embrace, or took out their handkerchiefs and waved them back and forth at an imaginary female whom they sang to and followed about the floor in a drunken stupor.

The far side of the hall was still held by the respectable folk in street clothes, ties, white shirts. Around the bar were those who recounted to one another their escapades of the day, what prizes their band had won, how they had been cheated out of first prize over a little thing like having to hold up the king of their pageant when they entered the competition grounds because he had had too much to drink, 'but next year, please God, it will be masquerade for so!' And around the musicians had gathered another kind of crowd. They kept plying the steel-drum players with rum, going into their gyrations in front of the musicians as though their dancing partner was the sound of the music itself. Massahood and Zolda had a group of people about them clapping their hands as they watched Zolda and the stick man dance. At one side near to the wall were Zampi and a group of still different people, those who liked to argue or to be near to an argument, no matter what it was about, and if the cripple were present it was certain to be lively. Zampi was looking at Zolda and the stick man again; his eyes seemed to return automatically to their group each time he completed a thought. Each time he found his eyes in that direction he was a little surprised, for it seemed unusual that his stare did not rest elsewhere when there was a lull in the discussion.

As the crowd clapped hands to the music, Massahood and Zolda became more and more fancy in their steps. The crowd asked for more and more and they both increased the momentum of their steps, improvising more and more new ways and movements suggestive of man and woman copulating. Zolda was in front of the stick man now and he placed his hands around her waist, his thumbs pressed deep under her rib-cage as though he wanted to make them meet. She glanced at Zampi as if to say: 'Look, you fool . . . look. You think you is my master, my owner? Look how free my two foot could move, look how loose my body could swing.' And now she turned around to face Massahood. She placed her hands on his waist and rolled her pelvis in sensuous circles. Each time closer, closer, closer, until her clothes touched the bulge in Massahood's pants. The stick man let out a cry, 'Oyoe oye oyoye!' He slapped his hands behind his neck, he doubled over his tongue and bit hard on it with his head thrown back, and when Zolda turned round, her back facing him now, Massahood stood still, his arms outstretched and the muscles in his breast quivering like blades of coconut palm in the breeze.

Each time Zolda's eyes caught Zampi's the obeah man tried to show no emotion. 'Dance your dance, sing your song . . . when all over and done we go see what you really want.' And she hated him for this. She hated him for the look he threw at her and Massahood, bunching them together as true flesh of the Scorpion Tail. But all of these were merely excuses for the one, the *real*, reason why she hated him. And that was because the obeah man had made a woman of her. No man she ever knew could inspire the desire, the lust and love that sent her nerves cascading in a torrent of screams and passionate oblivion to all the world. With her eyes and her body she was telling him now that Massahood could, that she knew it in her body as only a woman does when she has met a man who could make her do anything.

The obeah man turned his eyes to the motif on the wall and motioned to it with his thumb, and Zolda understood his meaning not because of the motif but because in her own way she knew the picture he had formulated her with. It was not a true picture. It was part what she was, part what he wished her to be, and part mystery. How could she hope to change all of these facets? Yet as she danced she knew that she was dancing for Zampi, for if he had got up and left the Scorpion Tail at that moment all of her actions would have been pointless. She moved about Massahood, her eyes wide with the look of curiosity of a child who has made a sudden discovery of its body and all it can do. Massahood had his handkerchief drawn tight between his hands, he jumped back and forth through the loop, then he shot out its end at Zolda. It struck her on her hips and her body moved with a delightful little motion. He moved closer to her, and his smile, his laughter, his joy, came from deep down inside of him. He smiled outwardly to her. Inwardly he smiled to himself, 'I did always know that you would come beggin' one day . . .'

The painter was looking hard at Zampi. His eyes penetrated deep into the obeah man, searching, questioning. And although it was he who searched the obeah man's countenance, he had a peculiar sensation of being watched from everywhere until he felt caught by his own stare as if it were the obeah man who looked deep into him.

'Tell me,' Zampi said. 'It look as if something botherin' you.'

The Englishman rubbed his hand across his face as if he were tired and sleepy and wanted to rub the sand grains from his eyes. 'It's nothing, really. I just felt as though a cold breath of air passed over my grave . . . Gave me a chill, that's all.' But he had in fact slipped into a strange kind of mood. He had attended the Shango dances and seen people suddenly seized by something unseen, their bodies writhing, their voices different, as if they had gone off into a kind of trance, even speaking a tongue that no one could understand. All of that was in the heart of the jungle and in the dark of night. He did not understand it, but he reasoned that there must be some explanation which he did not have. He looked about at the faces around him questioningly. If there was anything to obeah he would not expect it to come to life here. In the darkness of the bush, late at night, what with all the superstition about, perhaps one's imagination could stretch and wander . . . not here in the Scorpion Tail. He looked up at Zampi questioningly.

The obeah man was smiling a knowing smile at him, as if he had not only read his thoughts but the struggle of ambivalence, of his questioning, doubting mind. 'You think that I could work obeah but you find it hard to admit it to yourself . . . not so?' The painter's mind returned from its momentary lapse. He still felt awkward, a little bit uncomfortable, as he smiled at Zampi's question. 'You remember what I say? That it have obeah for some people but not for other people?'

The Englishman still regarded him with a questioning look in his eyes. The tourist officer and the cripple were also silent. They sat back with a quiet feeling of expectation. The obeah man had backed himself nicely into a corner. He would make a fool of himself any minute now. The hangers-on from the Britannia who stood about the table were on edge. There were among them extremes of opinion. Men drank together, cursed together, whored a little together . . . anyone seeing this clique at the Britannia would lump them together and expect the opinion of one to be the opinion of all. Not so. While some waited in confidence that Zampi would make a fool of himself, there were others who were afraid that he might do something startling, perhaps terrible.

And one man who was nervous and tense felt that he had to say something to contain himself. 'Don't force the man to work obeah here! Suppose he do something bad to one of we, then who to blame?'

Zampi threw him a glance of reprimand, as if to say, 'You don't think that I will really do something to hurt anybody . . . what you think obeah is at all?'

But time was passing, and once people have their hearts set on something they feel that any side talk is hedging and changing the subject at hand. The tourist officer could stand it no longer. He had been insulted and degraded in the presence of his guest—worse, in the eyes of the men about the table—and he was insistent now. 'Tell we what obeah is, man. Show we! Show we something, anything . . . if you know how to do anything.'

Zampi was looking deep into the Englishman's eyes. He saw there a calm and peaceful picture, one that asked in earnest to let him know too, that he was with an open mind and would take anything as proof.

'I will show you if it have or it ain't have something like obeah,' Zampi said to the Englishman. There was a moment of silence and two or three of the men about the table stood back making room for Zampi to pass or to stand back, but instead he remained seated. He took the Englishman's arm, jerked up his sleeve, and pointing to the top side of his arm said, 'Look!'

In the middle of the man's arm between his wrist and elbow was a tiny pin hole exactly like the one Massahood had pierced in his arm earlier on. The cripple and the tourist officer both jumped when they saw the tiny red blood spot against the blue-white skin of the Englishman, who became very pale, his eyes large and sunken deep in their sockets.

'You feel it?' Zampi asked. 'You feel anything hurting you?'

The painter nodded. 'Yes. I believe I do feel . . .'

'All right . . . now watch,' Zampi said. He pressed his thumb on the spot, muttering a few inaudible words, then he moved the man's arm slowly under his eyes as if returning it to him. 'Look now and tell me if you see anything . . . tell me if you feel anything.'

The Englishman first pinched the flesh on his arm to see if he could squeeze blood from the pinprick, and when nothing came he spread the skin this way and that, searching for the small puncture which had been there. The cripple and the tourist officer searched excitedly, then angrily. The murmuring in the little knot of men around grew louder. Some

114

wanted to look at the man's arm, others leaned back as if to say: 'I could of tell them so. They never hear 'bout Zampi or what? The man could do anything.'

Zampi looked up at Massahood and Zolda, who stood among the crowd following each detail, Massahood with his mouth half open in surprise. The obeah man now looked straight at Zolda and the eyes around the table followed the obeah man's eyes as they now cut into her. She felt uneasy and tense with all those eyes upon her. She slipped her arm into Massahood's.

'Come on and let we go from here before this man make bad trouble here tonight.'

The stick man seemed reluctant to go for a moment, but when he saw Zampi's face the look of surprise turned into one of defiance and hate instantly.

'Carry me home,' Zolda pleaded to Massahood, whose mind seemed confused with thoughts that he could not sort out as they shot back and forth in his head. 'I want you to carry me home . . . I tired of everything,' Zolda said again, and they both left, dressed just as they were.

'Aye, Hood . . . Hood . . . Miss Z!' the cripple called drunkenly after them, 'where you goin' . . . wait for me, man, wait for me nuh!'

As he tried to rise out of the puncheon chair he fell back into his seat, his head swung loose and his eyes clamped shut. He uttered an ugly obscenity at the two as they left without him.

14

WHEN the Scorpion Tail begins to lose its darkness it loses its savour and becomes a place of fear and foreboding, for at evening it builds up a savage energy, stores it in its walls, and then, like its bar shelves crowded with bottles, its wooden tubs piled high with cracked ice, its tables and chairs rich with mellow colours . . . all fades and becomes depleted as if used up by the hungry mouths of loneliness that have fed upon its magic, leaving behind only a cold corpse, a rattling skeleton searching for new life. And the same loneliness welling up in the bosom of those who come to wait out the night begins to wake up again, and chase them out into the streets. The creases in the floorboards are wide and worn by early light, the tubs have few bottles, their necks leaning flat on the surface of water left from the melted ice. Water has seeped through the slats of the tubs on to the floor and the thin long streaks are dry from the tub on, wet the other half. The colours are garish and loud and the motif on the wall seems foolish. It is not a scorpion at all, resembling more a half-dead lobster drawn by a child.

Men steal away quietly when daylight falls in the Scorpion Tail, as quietly as if they had made a rendezvous with some woman who has gone on a moment or two before and is waiting for them outside in the early morning shadows. 'We go pick up,' they say to their companions. And that is all. They say this as though they have suddenly discovered a secret which they do not want to share, and slowly, in this secretive, sly, and surreptitious way, the Scorpion Tail empties out after all its life has been sucked dry.

The great wild hall of frenzy and sweat which provoked and compelled violent emotion now became a place of peculiar solitude, a place of recounting with disbelief all that a man had done before. Not only with this evening, which was only one small fibre of his fabric, but with all the evenings of his life. Time stood still and motionless along the long wet and dry streaks of water from the tubs under the bar, as if standing in

wait so that one could recount his past, ask himself if what he remembered doing, saying . . . the very way a man writhed and twisted his body
with all the secret lewdness pent up in his loins . . . came back vividly
with a kind of cringing distaste. As the frightening light of morning came
walking through the streets of Port of Spain, few men remained at the
Scorpion Tail to face themselves. There were no more than a dozen
people about, including the obeah man and the cripple. The obeah man
was familiar with many mornings like this before, but this was the first
time since he had gone into the hills that he would see the break of day
come pointing its cold, long fingers of light. He stayed on as if to dare
the cold light of day to awaken him from the glow of satisfaction he felt
within himself. His nights of fetes and debauchery and Zolda had ended
always with a feeling of loss, of loneliness, and purposelessness. Now he
knew that this day could not rob him of that deep-down joy that fluttered
in his stomach like hibiscus petals.

The bar attender stood at his counter with a dazed look, mechanically
wiping the counter with slow circular movements. His head seemed
shrunken and small. The folds of skin in his face deeper, their crevices
packed with grey. At one of the tables sat two couples. They spoke only
occasionally as they sipped their drinks. They were not cursing one
another, but each remark in their conversation was filled with a kind of
venomous anger and hate. They spoke like people who had done all
varieties of debauchery and lusting with their bodies and their emotions
until their loins and their livers had run dry and tasteless, and now all
they had left was one another's company and a few nips of Black Cat
rum to soothe the ache of dry sand scratching away at their frayed nerve
ends, the sharp teeth of their senses filed down to dull stumps of numb-
ness that made the morning light sour in their mouths.

Zampi was drinking the rum left in his bottle as he surveyed the
Scorpion Tail. There were two men at his table, and the cripple who
dozed with his head down half-drunkenly. From time to time he jumped
in his sleep, uttered an obscene word or two, then dropped off again.
Once Zampi thought he heard him cry out, 'Hood . . . you f***er,' then
later on: 'Miss Z . . . you like it big . . . you don't like me, that Hood go
do for you . . . Them two bitch and them they gone an' leff me all by
myself.'

The men at the table looked at him and laughed, then turned in on their
own thoughts again. They had no need of one another, yet they found a
kind of solace and ease in staying together, and as Massahood would take

pleasure in the shape of a muscle in his arm or thigh, so the obeah man took pleasure in this light of the coming day. He knew that the pangs of guilt and shame some of these people about him were feeling would not be able to touch him. He felt as light as air, and a joy of simply being what he was, an obeah man, warmed him with thoughts of what he had done to become this skilled, with thoughts of what he would do in the days to come. He was aware again and again of the contrast of life in the Scorpion Tail now that morning was breaking. He saw Massahood's face again and he saw that ugly look of humiliation the stick man wore with his back pinned to the floor. He felt that from the beginning as they grew up together there had been a secret that lay buried in his mind, which he hid from himself. The secret was that he and Massahood were very different kinds of men. Tonight that secret had come rushing out of both of them and he felt that sweet pleasure and relief that comes with setting down a heavy burden. He thought of how heavy many men must feel if they have not been able to prise loose all these loads that wear them down.

And as he searched his mind, asking himself one thing after another, he saw how little men understood one another, and at the same time how perfectly well they could understand in a wordless, speechless way as he had felt this evening with the painter. He had tried with all the words he knew to say what he was, what it meant to be an obeah man, and he had not been understood by anyone besides the painter, a man from such a distant and different world. He marvelled at the way they had understood each other with a minimum of words.

This was what Jimpy must have known when he chose him to become an obeah man. It was felt and you could not communicate it to anyone. You could only nod if you happened to see it in someone's eyes, for it was a kind of vision which held all things together and brought them into a crystal focus that should never be explained or explored, but one should only follow its direction, feel the strength of its conviction, allow it to envelop the senses and point the way. All of these things Jimpy, his mentor, had meant, but did not, perhaps because he could not, put into words. For how could he tell Zampi that an obeah man had to divorce himself from the ills of other men's souls, otherwise he would be swallowed up by them and unable to help them? An obeah man had to practise at distancing himself from all things. He had to know joy and pleasure as he knew sorrow and pain, but he must also know how to withdraw himself from its torrent, he must be in total possession of

118

himself, and at the height of infinite joy he must know with all of his senses all that lives and breathes about him. He must never sleep the sleep of other men, he must have a clockwork in his head. He must at a moment's notice be able to shake the rhythm from his ear, to hold his feet from tapping. He must know the pleasure in his groin and he must know how to prevent it from swallowing him up.

And Zampi knew these things, he had his life in rein. He knew now that he would not be plagued with indecision, with the ebbing out of time. He had been accused of everything. By Zolda, because she said he had no sensitivity, no understanding of people and their motives. And yet, if you saw this place in all its lights, as Zampi did, you knew the world. If you felt alien in it at times, at times alone, perhaps outside of it, if you could become infected with the mood and temper of the Scorpion Tail you would know that it is only a matchbox of the world, that you had within you some small grain that could divine the hearts of men. You would know why Jimpy chose Zampi as his follower. The old man had seen Zampi's character change. He had watched him through long hours at the Britannia, at the Scorpion Tail, wrestling with that unseen hand that plucked out melodies from his breast, plunging him deep into the hearts of other men, until he was one with them, feeling all their joy, their exhilaration, and then at times all their lonely melancholy and misery. It took all this to be an obeah man and then it took more, for it meant time and practice and resignation and sacrifice and thoughts as confusing as nightmares and more, and it meant discovery of oneself and being and not being at the same time. Being all the things that another man was, absorbing it, healing it, then purging yourself of it.

How wrong Zolda was. He did understand people. How wrong Massahood was. He had not lost touch with his friends. Changed, perhaps he had, but lost touch and understanding? No.

Time passed this way with the four of them lost in their own thoughts.

'What about a drink, man . . . All yuh boys keepin' so quiet,' Zampi said to his companions at the table.

'Um? . . . Um-hm . . . Um-hm . . . yes, is a good idea,' one of the men said, stirring in his seat. The other man woke up from his reverie too. He stretched both his arms languidly up in the air, arching his body like a snake as he stretched and yawned. The tiredness in his body after carnival was beginning to claw at him.

'Oh Lawd Gawd, have mercy on this po' body of mine,' he groaned as a wide grin of physical delight spread across his face after he had stretched and yawned, then he slapped on the table. 'You say the right thing! That is just what we need, man . . . a rum.'

Zampi poured from his bottle into the men's glasses, then into his. He tilted his head to look into the sleeping cripple's face, then nodded as he was about to pour into his glass.

'Chief,' the man who was stretching said to Zampi, 'it look like as if you frighten them people here tonight.'

Zampi laughed. He was pleased that he had not done anything wild and spectacular. He looked at the faces of the two men, with whom he had drunk before at the Britannia. He thought how strange it was to suddenly discover among his old acquaintances of the Britannia that there were some who knew, like these two men, that he could work obeah. He owed a kind of responsibility to them for this faith and belief. He would have to remain in their eyes all of the things they expected of him.

The cripple, who was dozing meantime, heard the clinking of glasses and the few sentences of conversation. He jumped with a sudden start in his sleep as he had earlier on, and now he began to wake up. He shook his head, and his loose cheeks and lips flapped about while his red eyes stood still in his head, then he began rubbing and slapping his shorter foot to which the stool was strapped.

'Oh God, man, my foot gone to sleep . . . It feel like if it have a million needles sticking it all about.' His voice was still angry, his tongue thick, and like the fox that can be so angered at its own paw caught in a trap, he pounded on his foot as if it were the cause of his pain.

'Wake up, you bitch. You gone to sleep. Wake up! Wake up!' Each of the last words was accompanied by a violent slap of his stretched palm, and then as he thought of Massahood and Zolda again, of how they had gone off and left him, he muttered under his breath: 'Them mother-ass an' them gone an' leff me . . . Wake up!' Slap. 'Wake up!' Slap. 'Wake up!' Slap, slap, slap.

The men at the table smiled at the initial blows the cripple showered on his foot. Now he was no longer the centre of attraction and they resumed their conversation with Zampi. 'Chief, is not you who is the obeah man what give the Hood that stick with a *master* obeah on it?' one of them asked.

Zampi thought that as he bore some responsibility to these men who believed in him, and his obeah, so he bore a responsibility for the gift, the power he gave to others. No matter what had happened between him and

Massahood, he was responsible for any misuse of the stick.

'Yes,' Zampi answered thoughtfully. 'Was me all right . . . Was a long time gone now since I put a obeah on he stick.' He would have liked to add that if he knew the meaning of obeah then as he knew it now he might not put such a power in the hands of someone like Massahood. The cripple stopped slapping his foot abruptly. He threw a cutting glance at Zampi, then sucked his teeth and began patting his foot again. The obeah man reflected again that to Zolda too he owed something. Simply because she did not understand why he would not work obeah left and right was no reason to let her go the way she had walked out with Massahood in a moment of anger. No matter what she did, she was doing it to get back at him for leaving her all alone after he had awakened desire in her, which her body had never known before. He knew that she would be unhappy by the time this night was over. It was he who had conquered and cornered pride, he who should go in search of her. It was too much to expect her to come to him. Some people found it difficult to say that they were sorry, to admit that they had made fools of themselves. For Zolda it would be impossible.

'Chief, you think that a obeah could turn back on a man? I hear that if a obeah man make a mistake and he slip . . . he slide. And then monkey smoke he pipe.'

Zampi was looking outside through the large glass windows. The trees in the market yard across the way were beginning to lose that mass of darkness they were earlier on. They were slowly becoming a pale pink latticework as the sunlight burst out of the sea beyond like a distant explosion whose pale light lit up the morning skies.

'How you mean that?' Zampi asked.

The man was thrown into a dilemma now. He searched for a way to put his question more clearly. He scratched the back of his head, tilting his old felt hat forward over his eyes.

'Well, supposin' . . . and is only suppose I supposin'. Suppose like the Hood try to bust open your head with that same stick that you put your own own obeah on?'

The cripple was wide awake and alert now. The way he looked at Zampi made the obeah man feel that he must still have some small ray of belief in him.

'That can't happen in donkey years,' Zampi answered confidently. And turning to the cripple, 'Why you don't let me do something to that foot of yours before you break it up with blows?'

Mention of the cripple's foot threw him into a vicious rage. His eyes blinked quickly, his little pointed tongue shot out like a snake as he wet his dry lips with quick licks left and right. 'You think that just because you have two good foot-and-hand you know everything? Boy, I read 'nuff big big books to know that this obeah of yours is a lot of nonsense. And you know who write them books? Scientific people all about the place . . . big big men up in England and America. They know you, boy. They know all your tricks. Them fellers up dey know all 'bout you and your worthless obeah. They say that you can't cure a dog, far less people. I have my head on, you know . . . I ain't like some of these foolish people who have they head screw on backwards.'

The obeah man could not help but notice the cripple's choice of dress for carnival, for it was just the reverse of his expressed opinions. His suit was on backwards, the coat buttoned down his back. His trousers were reversed, his fly buttoned down his seat, and his mask placed at the back of his head gave the impression of someone going backwards when the cripple walked. He wondered how the cripple who had come pleading to him to straighten his deformities could reverse so completely. Was it because he had faith in him then? Zampi saw again that a man's life was not pointed, directed, then shot out into the world. He could follow many paths. He knew now that if he could not have helped his body he could have helped his mind, and in not doing this he had destroyed what faith the cripple had in him. A man whose presence could inspire faith in others had a responsibility, and Zampi was such a man, an obeah man. If only he had known then what he knew now he would not have lost that faith, that trust which the cripple had in him. It was he, Zampi, who had driven him to Massahood, for faith lost gropes blindly in the dark, lashing itself to the nearest mooring like a kind of hunger, a special kind of lust that pains at feeding time, not questioning the nature of the food, crying out only to be fed. The obeah man could only listen to the weird tangents along which bitterness had driven the cripple's thoughts as he went on.

'Oh, no, boy, God ain't make me like you. You know why? He make me like He-self. I look more like God than you. You think God have two good set of foot-and-hand? *Eh?* Answer me that. You think God have straight straight foot-and-hand like yours?'

'I don't know God that good,' said Zampi, his eyelids hung low over his eyes as he looked at the cripple's gnarled hands, their small marble bones strung like small black berries on a vine, the skin of his palms dry and leathery with deep crevices that had remained that way since birth for want of opening and closing like ordinary hands. Then the obeah man's eyes travelled to the cripple's feet dangling from the puncheon seat which was too high for him so that his feet could not reach the floor. The cripple saw him looking at his legs, and his anger increased.

'You bitch . . . you lookin' at my twis' foot, well look at it good! You don't know God, eh? Well, *I* know God! *I* know how He does feel inside He belly. *You* can't know that. You can't *begin* to know that. And you know why? Because you could jump into bed with a woman whensoever you please. You could walk 'bout the street whatever hour you want. Nobody notice you. You could have all what you crave and still you can't be like me, you can't begin to feel like me. You invisible! That's why. You is a invisible man and it does haunt you. That's why you gone and turn obeah man. I have more feelin's in this little toe than you have in your whole body. I feel for a woman more than you. I feel for a liquor stronger than you. I feel my own two foot-and-hand every time I walk down the road, and when you see it quiet quiet quiet in the mornin' and I walkin' home I could hear my own footsteps. You hear what they call me? Hop-and-Drop? Well, it like a music in my brain that always with me and I know that I is *me*, day and night! What the ass you know? God make cat, and he make dog and all kind of jackass like you first. And when He see He mistake, then He make *me*. With *all* He feelin's lock up inside of me. I is the last last last . . . the last thing that God make, boy.'

He started scraping his long tongue against his front teeth as though he tasted something vile and bitter, then through the wide gap between his stumps of teeth he sent a thin long stream shooting out into the spittoon, and as it landed there he looked about with a kind of satisfaction, as if that final action proved beyond a doubt that his statements were so.

The two men at the table, the obeah man, all three men remained silent when the cripple blew up. Although his remarks were aimed at Zampi, the other men felt as if the cripple was angry at them simply for being alive. They watched him try to get out of his seat, then fall back into it cursing, then rise up again and limp away in the direction of the lavatory, leaving at the table his little stool which he had unstrapped as he pounded on his foot. Three or four people looked round in the direction of their table as the drunken voice of the cripple rose higher and louder, but their interest seemed only to fix in their minds the place and the face from which the voice came, then they fell back to their sullen silence again.

'Chief . . . it look as if that man hate you for *so*,' one of the men said to Zampi after the brooding silence returned to the Scorpion Tail.

'Is not he fault,' Zampi answered, thinking how a great many things could happen at times when a man was not ready or capable of handling them. Although all was done and past, it still remained for him to right the consequences, for it was not the act alone which made guilt, but all its results in subtle and unseen corners of the mind waiting only to seize the landscape again like some malignant weed or parasite. He would have to stand close to all those lives which touched his in the smallest way, that too was obeah, and as he thought this he knew that he would have to go to Zolda. He would try to tell her all these things. Perhaps she would understand that all of these things had come late, and he hoped that it was not too late even now. He looked in the direction where the cripple went, still hoping to say something, anything, to him that might make his hate a little less venomous, not only towards him, but to all the world.

'It look as if Hop fall in,' one of the men said to Zampi, laughing, as the obeah man looked at the stool which he expected the little man to return for.

'You think he gone and drop asleep inside there? . . . He did look as if he could go to sleep on a tramcar line when he get up from here,' the other man suggested when the cripple did not return.

Zampi got up and walked across the hall. He rapped on the door.

'You in there?' There was no reply. He rapped again. Still no answer. He began to think that what was said at the table might have more truth than jest. Had the little man really dropped asleep in there? He pushed open the door gently. The small room was empty.

The men at the table were looking in his direction for an answer to their curiosity. Zampi spread his hands in the air, indicating that the cripple had disappeared, then he waved out to the two men as he set out for the La Basse to look for Zolda. 'We go pick up,' the men called out in unison, then looked at each other with surprise for having chosen the same phrase, speaking it with the same tone of voice. '*We* go pick up. . . *We* go pick up . . . We go pick up . . . We go pick up, man!'

15

WHEN they turned off the Eastern Main Road they left the last street lamp behind throwing its yellow cone of light which stood in the early-morning darkness like a pyramid of pale yellow stone. Morning had not come yet, small insects of the night were still screeching in the ditches and trees, they called from under the great green leaves covered with crystal balls of dew.

Desire welled up in them, slow and deliberate desire, the kind that could be put away to sleep because of the tiredness in their bones, the screaming of their flesh for sleep, for rest. They looked at each other's face in the light of the stars which peppered the heavens. Massahood's body shone like pale grey silk in the starlight. Zolda walked arm in arm with him and he could feel the movement of her body against his. He had his arm about her waist, his fingers reached as far forward as her navel. He kept drawing her closer in, his fingers intent upon reaching the centre of her waist. He had never felt the movements of a woman's body this way before; each step of hers moved her hips. Now they were close and caressing, now they shifted. His hand grasped her flesh just above the waist, and she looked up at him pleadingly, asking him with her eyes to wait, and then they walked on. There was no one on the La Basse at this hour, they heard only thin leaves of water splashing irregularly against the land beyond, the scuttling of crabs as they dodged their mates in a curious foreplay, making a noise with their claws against the earth which was different from hurry or escape. The air smelled of the sea, for it was still night. The breeze fanned small fires that burned eternally on the La Basse, wafting their peculiar odours of sea and garbage burning. They walked slowly on, savouring, anticipating each other's lust, and all the pleasures they would yield up to each other, yet they did so secretly, each one possessed with the same thoughts, the same desires and images of the same secret, the secret of love. Massahood's hand left her waist and grasped her breast so tightly that she felt a twinge of pain. She placed her hand on his and pressed it close to her bosom. He stood in front of her now, his thumbs in her armpits, his fingers arched like crab's claws into her shoulder blades. She felt that in his insistence he might lift her off her feet this way. She moved her bosom from left to right and was disappointed that it did not yield as much pleasure as the lower part of her chest did where their naked skins touched. And in an effort to find that pleasure she moved her hips, pressing hard against him until she could feel his desire mounting and throbbing like a heartbeat against the walls of her loins. The light was on her full face now as she looked up to him. All the races that had lingered lost in these islands blossomed in her face making her feel that she was woman, a small part of all the women of the world. She clasped her hand flat against the back of his neck, drew him closer, and kissed him.

'Come,' she said, 'come on before somebody see we.'

'It ain't have nobody here to see we this hour,' he replied, loosening his grip on her. He stooped down to pick up his stick which he had dropped to the ground, then they walked on as before, moving through the pale silver light like one body with one movement. With each step they took the stick man felt closer to the answer of a question that recurred in his mind with the persistence of wayside weeds that rushed from the earth as fast as they were cut down, trampled upon, or burnt out by fires. The question was Zampi and the stick. But Massahood's questions did not seek answers for answers' sake, they sought only to put an end to themselves. If it was indeed Zampi's hex on his stick which gave it such power, if Zampi was an obeah man of the first order, if Zolda was really in love with the obeah man, if she was doing all this to spite the obeah man . . . Massahood was of one mind. If he could once have her Zampi's obeah would no longer be a question in his mind. The desire he felt for her was not singular, it had in it a complexity of motives. And then which man could turn away from this creature whose every movement was calculated to house and harness all the desire a man could possess? There had always been a strange kind of antagonism, of friction, between himself and Zolda, yet together they elicited a kind of response from onlookers as they danced, or fought, or cursed each other. The stick man had known love. His experience was collected like a cream skimmed off the surface of a rich broth. His women were women of the streets, each one of whom loved and desired like none other, and he, Massahood, was the repository of this vast and varied storehouse of knowledge. It was clear to him from the very beginning that Zolda would come begging one day . . . and this was the day.

She was silent now as they walked along. Her head hung down, looking at her feet and Massahood's. It raced across her mind that she would never be the same to Zampi after tonight. That much she knew about him, but he had neglected her, laughed at her, all but told her to go away. She thought: 'Damn him . . . Damn him in hell anyway. He want too much from people, he want them to be a saint.'

She saw Massahood lift his stick quickly. 'You see something move past down there?' He was pointing with his stick at one of the small fires in the distance. She looked up. 'I could swear I see somebody run 'cross down there.'

'How you could see anything? . . . It still so dark.'

They looked at each other again, and now that they were close to Zolda's hut, and the long night of waiting was so close to its climax, they both shut out their previous thoughts. 'It must be one of them blasted dogs that does hang around here at all hours of the day or night,' Massahood said, drawing her closer to his side.

Zolda was untying a string that ran through the latch in the door. 'If anybody want anything in here I don't want them to break down the door to take it,' she had always said to the cripple, who made sure that all his belongings were bolted and barred.

The task of keeping watch over Zolda's place was a kind of special privilege which the cripple had somehow come to assume. No one remembered how or when, but these things were so, like the way Zolda always favoured him with a dance at the Britannia. Everyone accepted it, for it seemed that it had always been so.

As she lifted her arms to reach the latch, Massahood put his hands on her breasts, pressing his body hard against hers. Her mind went racing, tumbling, and she leaned into him, turning her head towards him, offering her lips, but the stick man already had his lips on her shoulder just below her neck, and she felt his teeth on her flesh, she felt its pleasure, its pain sink slowly throughout her body as it unfolded like a ripple flowing through her bosom, her waist, her thighs, and thinning out as it came to settle down her calves and feet. 'Oh God,' she uttered, almost in pain. Massahood drew the hanging string from the latch with one sharp tug and Zolda, who had in mind to first light the candle or the kerosene lamp, felt herself being lifted, moved. Massahood held her by the small of her waist and she felt powerless, for her feet were off the ground. She could only shout, 'Wait . . . wait!' Then she was pushing him away.

The stick man was laughing that deep-down laughter that came from his chest sounding like laughter that was housed in a barrel, having the same kind of thickness and echo as it rumbled out of him. Was there ever a woman who wanted to be loved by coaxing and cajoling? Her resistance to his love-making only doubled his appetite like a delicious aphrodisiac. 'Yes,' he shouted, 'yes! Tonight-tonight! You goin' to give it to me.' He had her on her bed now, her legs hanging down the side, and she felt the thick strong fingers foraging at her loins. It would be simple to undress her. He had only to get his fingers slipped through her costume which was no more than two or three inches wide at its narrowest between her legs. He had watched her dance, he had watched her body move, he had rehearsed over and over in his mind just how easily the object of his desire would be laid bare. His hot and hungry hands were moving with instinct now, following a pattern, his body had already slipped into its instinctive lurches and withdrawals. He heard her voice coming to him as if from the distance. She must have cried out several times before he finally heard what she was saying. As she struggled with him on the bed, his singular thought was that she would fight with him to the bitter end. He enjoyed the way she tried to repulse him. By pushing his face away, their bodies pressed together. He had always known that she was not the kind of woman to give herself easily and he would have been disappointed if she had given herself to him that way. He wrestled with her until he had both her arms pinned to the bed, the full weight of his body upon her, and only then did he hear her say, 'Let me . . .'

He stopped his wild pursuit for a moment to ask her, 'Let you what?'

'Let me light the lamp. I don't like to . . . I 'fraid the dark.'

He wanted to say no, to press his advantage. He felt that his chance might be lost for ever, yet from the way she fought with him he knew that she was powerful enough to push him away or at least to deny him his pleasure. He rolled over on the bed and let her get up. He could see her vaguely in the shadows. She moved like a nude figure in the dark, her clothing scant and close-fitting, outlining her body with even deeper indentations and more voluptuous lines as she moved about searching for matches in the dark. He heard her shake the matchbox from habit to check if it was empty. Each little sound like the matchbox brought him closer to the moment he had long awaited. He lay on the bed devouring the silhouette of her body in the shadows. His body answered with reactions to hers as though she were indeed in the nude and now he had forgotten that she was dressed, so that when the thin tongue of flame caught in the kerosene lamp, throwing a feeble light in the hut, he was surprised to see her figure emerge clad as she was in the dance costume. She stood looking at the flame with a faraway expression on her face which Massahood did not like.

He rushed at her and before she could turn around he had felled her to the floor, going down on top of her. Now he tried to turn her body over. She reached to cover up her breasts in protection and he slipped his hands around the small of her waist swiftly, then rolled her over, and now her hands and arms were confused in their attempts to cover or shield herself, as though they did not know where the stick man's lust would thrust next.

'No!' she shouted. 'No!'

There was a noise outside. It sounded like a prank of one of the La Basse children who would bang on a door, then go racing away to hide when someone came to investigate; but the door flung open, and Zolda, writhing on the floor, her shoulders pinned by Massahood, her long legs flying through the air, saw only the wedge of pale orange light coming through the doorway. She tried to lift her head and shoulders, but Massahood, his left hand still foraging at her loins, floored her by pulling hard on her hair until her head was on the ground again. Then she heard two noises. One like a grunt, the other a low muffled moan.

The former came from the cripple as he plunged his knife blindly into Massahood, missing his chest by inches but leaving a deep white hole in his shoulder. The groan and the escape of air making a sound of relief came from Massahood as the knife cut into him. She felt the weight of Massahood's body thrust against her as the cripple plunged his knife, throwing the whole weight of his body with it. He tumbled over the pair and landed in a corner of the hut where Zolda kept her pots and dishes and charcoal brazier. The stick man, still lying on Zolda, supporting himself on one elbow, looked at the cripple.

'So is you . . . you worthless little bitch. After all I done gone and do for you,' he shouted at the little man who was sprawled out in the corner. He pressed his right hand on the cut to keep his blood from seeping out. His face had no expression of pain, but one of disgust, disgust with the wound that would take time to heal.

'She didn't want you!' the cripple cried out. 'She don't want you . . . who tell you to force she? She belong to me . . . to me . . . *me!*' The little man jabbed at his chest with the knife which he still held, as he insisted, 'Me me me!'

With all the strength in her waist Zolda gave a sudden lurch upward to lift up and throw the stick man off, but he pushed her down again by squatting hard on her stomach. He looked hatefully at her now as if she had been responsible for the cripple's actions and, as he floored her, the cripple began twirling about in the cocoon of his clothes, collecting his limbs like a puppet whose strings were drawn slowly. As he came to his feet, he held his knife at the level of his abdomen, preparing to rush Massahood again. The level at which he held the knife and the level at which his eyes were focused suggested to Massahood that the cripple's aim was at his genitals or his bowels.

In an instant the stick man had his stick. He shot up like a man who has stayed below water to test how long he could go without air, and he hit the cripple across the small hump of his back. 'Take that, you bitch . . . is woman you want, and you can't even do a thing for them!' The blow made a dull sound as if it landed on a sack of clothes, and fine motes of dust shot out of the little man's cocoon into the shaft of morning light coming through the doorway. The dishes, pots, and pans rattled and scattered as the cripple fell into them.

'Oh God, Hood . . . is you, is you! I did always know that I have to give my life to you,' he groaned.

Zolda grabbed at Massahood's ankle with an iron grip. The stick man turned, lifted up his other foot and came down hard on her neck with his heel. 'That is what goin' on all the time? You want that twis'-foot break-back bitch? You don't want me. I should'er know it all the time.'

She released his ankle as the sharp pain from the blow on her neck raced throughout her body, crippling her hands. 'Oh God, no . . . no . . . no, no . . .' she cried as she rolled on the floor, massaging the painful soreness in her neck while the cripple rattled about in agony among the scattered tin-can pots and pans.

Massahood stood over him and his mind reeled insanely. It was he, Massahood, on the floor, as a child; it was Santo Pi standing above him with his walking stick. The noise of the cripple falling among the pots and pans blurred everything. It carried him back to the time he fell among the red lanterns in Santo Pi's cabin and an old buried vision shot out of the hidden shadows of his brain, one of hate and resolution. He swung his stick through the air and it made a low hiss before it landed on the cripple's head with a crack that sounded like the explosion of a dried-out calabash in the hot night as it pitches out its hundreds of seeds.

'Oh, God . . . you kill him . . . you kill him!' Zolda screamed.

Massahood turned to her. His face was grotesque. She thought that murder was written on it and that anyone looking into his face from now on would plainly see it.

'You want him?' Massahood asked, pointing to the dying cripple with his stick. 'Go on, go ahead, take him since you love him so much.' He stood over the cripple in case he should try to get up again, but there were only quick sharp tremors from the fingers of the little man's right hand, and then in a moment only his little finger twitched in irregular spasmodic jerks, and then he was still.

Zolda rushed past Massahood and began shouting: 'Murder Murder! Murder!' The first light of morning was breaking as she raced hysterically between the small shacks, and although there was enough light outside as she ran screaming, rapping on a door here, pounding on another, small lights went on in the houses and people began moving out of them clad in their scant sleeping clothes, some of them half naked.

At first only men were coming out of the houses, then as word went back and forth that Massahood had killed the cripple more and more people were awakened, women wondering where their men had gone, children who had been left alone, all moved towards Zolda's hut where she lay on her bed crying hysterically. Everyone wanted to see the cripple's face and they had to walk around his body which still lay on the floor, twist their heads at an awkward angle to see his face which had drawn into his clothing like a turtle draws its head into its shell.

Massahood was applying saliva to the cut in his shoulder, and as each application dried he rubbed on some more. The gash was deep red now and the bleeding had stopped. It looked like a neat incision in his flesh, placed there with the skill of a surgeon. He looked at the crowd with disgust on his face. 'Why the ass all you people ent go home . . . you ent have nothing better to do? The man dead! Dead! That is what you come to see? You never see a dead man face befo'?'

The crowd began to get surly now. Who was he to deny them their curiosity? They all knew the cripple. He was like a brother to this one, a father to that, a grandfather to some of the children. He was their political spokesman. He had had his photograph in the *Trinidad Guardian* as the unofficial Mayor of the La Basse when the City Council wanted to clear the place of squatters. The cripple had embarrassed the city fathers by asking pointblank where they would house the La Basse dwellers, and they had no answer so they forgot the clean-up programme quietly while the cripple grew in the esteem of his fellow residents. He was a man of legend. People knew, remembered, and heard of innumerable acts of this kind that the cripple had done, and they knew only one thing about Massahood—that he had killed the little man with his stick.

'Who the hell you think that you is at all . . . Governor? You best hads look out when the police come.'

Massahood looked up at the man who spoke to him. 'I markin' your face . . . don't let me catch you by yourself, otherwise is bust-head for you today-today, boy.' Mention of the police did not disturb him. He stood firm and strong on his ground. His encounters with the police before were always simple. Someone had challenged him to a stick fight and he had wounded them. Each man was equally armed in a kind of contest. He did not feel any different about the cripple's death.

Ugly Wednesday, Ash Wednesday. You've stretched all the thin frail fibres out to fractured frayed-out fuzz. You've drained the small sugar sacks of your syrups and sweetened sauces. The pale limp flesh surrounds your bones, as dry and tasteless as excelsior, you can hear it rustling dry and stark as you move through the morning light. Sleep has been hiding in the hill where the cool valleys of St Ann's and St Clair bury themselves. Sleep and rest has been for full firm bodies, accustomed to food and feeding of the flesh. You have only your thin juices to feed upon in the La Basse. The thin pale juices that keep you going when the pot runs dry. You have only the high-standing blue-black veins on your well-worked hands to tell you that there's a lonely foolish heart as small as a pound of raw beef in the Eastern Market that some trick of existence has kept pumping along this far. And then you have carnival, bacchanal. Once a year fete like fire and you could haul ass with all your talk 'bout tomorrow. And if you see that you can't make the grade this 'bout . . . well, next year, please God . . . Next year, please God! But I have like a something inside my belly that make it want to boil over like rice water that cook too long and it have to have a little something before the boiler explo'. . . So you mustn't tell me that my body can't take the strain because that is all I make from for two days . . . my body and all the sweet sweet things that it crave. So hear my singing . . . 'Iron something bend up my something, Oh Man-Man-Ti-Re . . . Iron something burst up my nothing . . . Oh Man-Man-Ti-Re'. Two days for me, boys . . . two whole days! I save up for the whole year to play red dragon . . . I save up six months' pay . . . I want to be the best mask in Port of Spain, these two days belong to me . . . and I is King. I is anything that I want to be . . .That is what carnival mean . . .Tell me I dead when I dead . . .don't talk ass now. Tell me tomorrow when Ash Wednesday come. . . don't talk ass now . . . Tell me when I wake up from my long, long sleep that the world make this way and that, but don't talk ass now. Let me sleep, man, sleep; let me sleep now sleep till the morning come . . .

The morning came too soon to their senses and they hated its rude light, these men who had closed their eyes only moments ago. They were sullen and angry at the stick man, they were angry at anything that could come with its wicked hands and drag them from the dark night of sleep. They would curse in the streets tomorrow, they would hack their spit in round green balls at their bosses tomorrow, they would drown rum with rum, they would race back to a moment of the day before when the sunlight caught their bats' wings, red dragons' tails, *Bad Behavior* suits, they would hear a single bar of the great steel band, they would see a pair of eyes that they caught in their moment of glory as their band crossed Frederick Street and Marine Square, and they would curse the evanescence of faces that they knew they could have held in a moment and told them all, told them all the hidden lust in their loins; and they would have said yes come with me . . . I know a place . . . what make me lose that face? I will never see she again . . . never . . . and now they turned with all the feeling of loss, with all the feeling of anguish that they could not put in its proper place. They were all one now, all together against this devil thing that had robbed them of the joy of sleep and dark night and void, and they saw the stick man for all of the things they had always thought about him.

'The big bitch like to play Bad John! He is best stick man. Hai aye aye, boy! This time he gone and put he foot in he own mouth. No more carnival for you, boy. You gone and kill a helpless cripple . . . you ain't have no shame? What that po' cripple gone and do to you? You uses to be he best friend . . . always buyin' he a liquor . . . this is the way you have to show your colours? This is the kind of friendship you did have for him? Police should put you in jail and throw 'way the key in the sea.'

Massahood was wild with rage. He felt powerless against the crowd. Could he tell them that the cripple was jealous, that he wanted Zolda for himself, that he was tortured by the sight and the thought of the pair as he discovered them rolling about the floor? The crowd would only laugh at him and his ridiculous ideas. He wasn't sorry for what had happened. He thought back to several incidents where the cripple was more than possessive about Zolda and it was clear to him that the little man loved her, desired her in his silent, sheepish, thieving glances and gestures. In a moment it all came clearly to Massahood. 'The little humpback bitch . . . he got what he had comin' to him for a long, long time!' he said to himself.

Meantime the crowd grew and grew. People from neighbouring districts, the worst rogues of John-John . . . Laventille and Rose Hill were filtering in to the La Basse as the tale of what had happened and how it had happened spread through the crowd. Some of the stick men whom Massahood had whipped threw looks and remarks of scorn at him. Insults came from the crowd of faces faster than he could mark the faces from which they came.

'All you nasty bitches . . . come on one by one . . . see if I ain't cut up your ass for you in little pieces.' He rapped on the ground in front of him with the stick, striking the earth with venom and anger. But the angry crowd which had admired, bragged, claimed Massahood as *their* stick man, would not calm down, nor would they go out singly to curse him. They discovered suddenly that none of them liked him, that it was well enough to have him in their midst at the Britannia, or in some remote section of the city where they were strangers but that was all!

'Go on, Hood, bawl . . . Let we hear your voice. Let we hear how you go bawl like some old cattle when the gallows pop your neck,' a voice jeered at him.

Massahood's eyes jerked up in search of the voice. His eyes were red, swollen out of their sockets as they moved across the faces that stood about, finding no one face from which the remark came.

'You think that I is a *coward*?' he screamed with all the force in his lungs. There was light tittering in the background somewhere. '*Coward! Coward! Coward!* . . . All you 'fraid to dead, but I ain't 'fraid.'

There was more giggling in the rear of the crowd. They sensed that they had this huge monster of a man in a situation which none of them would ever be able to handle by himself. They could anger and twist him this way and that, like you could most men. They had never thought that Massahood had any place in his life where ordinary men like themselves could insert the knife and twist with glee. And this new little sharp-toothed instrument was played like a subtle flute. They angered, teased, insulted just so far, then they let up; then they started again from a different corner of the crowd each time.

'All you 'fraid to dead, but I ain't 'fraid . . . not me. It ain't have nuttin' that could make me 'fraid. Nuttin'! Why you ain't come out here?

. . . Come out and show your face one by one or two by two.'

Again there was soft giggling and hushed cackles in the crowd from those who enjoyed the teasing. There were men whose anger rose high and did not care to tease but who wanted to see Massahood punished, and indeed if any one of them could singly take the law into his own hands he would have rushed the stick man and dragged him by his feet to police headquarters. But as the crowd continued to anger him, as he insisted on daring them to come out in the open, his great bulk heaved with his heavy breath, his powerful body seemed to have lost that inner framework that made it hold its shape. He was a loose hulk, blinded by his emotions, unable to find the voices in the dark that hurled pointed darts at him. Another wave of laughter and jeering quieted down again and still another voice from still another corner shouted out, 'Everybody 'fraid to dead, boy . . . even you!'

Massahood ran his hand over his hair, then his face, kneading and wringing his features. 'Who say that? Who? If you name *man* come out here today-today and face me like a man.' The veins on his great neck stood out like green knotted vines that fell from the trees in the bush. There was a smoothness of his chest and arms which had raised veins too but not with the prominence of his neck and forehead.

'Is the gallows they goin' to bust in he tail . . . Oh God, man!'

They baited him on with calculation. The hecklers might have run if the stick man rushed blindly into the crowd and started raining blows with his stick, but in the amorphous mass of the mob there was a feeling of safety, a feeling that if he did rush in to attack the angry men, the really angry ones who remembered the cripple for all the times he had been helpful to them would all jump together at the chance to pummel the stick man. The crowd knew its makeup, it knew its temper. Each man by himself knew his own courage, his own fears, and his own strength, yet he knew too that there was a certain strength in their numbers and they played it on and on.

'I ain't 'fraid!' Massahood shouted like a madman. He struck the ground as hard as he could with his stick, tossing up small bits of earth with each blow. 'I ain't *'fraid 'fraid 'fraid*,' he repeated and the blows travelled up his stick, hurting his shoulder where the cripple had stabbed him.

'Somebody should bust the bitch mouth open like he do to so much people . . . then see how he go like it,' someone jeered.

And then: 'He like woman, always playin' like if all the woman in the

135

world belong to him, but all of that go come to a end now . . . this time monkey smoke he pipe for good, the worthless bitch.'

With this last comment from the crowd, its temper changed, slowly, but perceptibly. Each man there could feel the change in the mob. They were no longer content to jeer, curse, and joke from a distance, and as if the few women in the mob sensed this changed attitude they began filtering back and away, still looking over their shoulders to make sure that they might not miss any of the violence which their whole being anticipated, not knowing what form it might take, but knowing with their intuition that something swift, violent, and frightening was about to take place any moment now . . . and from the edges of the crowd, the swimming, moving, throbbing crowd, as the women moved away you could hear their voices calling their children to safety. 'Tommy Tommy Tommy . . . Boysie . . . Boysie . . . where that boy gone to at all?. . . Boysie, you can't hear me callin' you? . . .'

And then someone threw a small pebble. It shied past Massahood's foot. It was just another way of teasing him, not really intended to strike him, its aim was bad and deliberately so. But its effect was strange on Massahood. Whether it was the stone or the shift in the mood of the mob that gave him a puzzled look was hard to say, but the stick man was struck dumb, he was bewildered. He gripped his stick fiercely, clutching it in front of his chest as if it were the only friend he had here as he surveyed the hateful eyes watching him with a bitterness he never suspected anyone could have for him.

And then another stone. This time it hit him on the shoulder and bounced off his body as though it were made of rubber. He turned to look at the stone where it had fallen, then another stone hit him before he could turn around, and when he did turn round he held his stick like a bat and swung at the next stone, but they were coming faster now until there was a shower of stones falling on him like a sheet of rain. He lifted one arm to protect his face from the stones as he backed away slowly until his back came up against Zolda's hut while the noise in the crowd grew and grew as they pelted stone after stone at the stick man, cursing out with each stone they hurled at him. 'Take that, you bitch . . . that is for Hop-and-Drop . . . this is for Mabel.'

There was no sound, no word from Massahood, he had backed up against the hut and each stone seemed to pin him to the wall until, finally, he slid down to the ground. His body shook with each new blow and he was bleeding in many places. As he fell to the ground, his eyes closed, and hidden by his arm, he made one final lurch to get to his feet and he swung blindly with his stick which flew out of his hand. Then he fell back to the ground again, and now the angry savage mob moved closer in for the first time, and each man emptied his hands of the stones he had picked up from the ground upon the stick man, who must have been quite dead already.

16

THE railroad station starts opposite the Britannia Bar at the foot of Frederick Street; and since all of life roots along the route of the railroad tracks, the main roads and arteries laid out by the founding engineers of the island follow parallel to the train lines. Such a road is the Eastern Main Road. If you miss the 'Midday Special' to the depths of the bush, you could hail a cruising taxi and race it to Barrataria. If you miss it there you are sure to catch it at San Juan four miles up the line. So close are the towns along the Eastern Main Road . . . so hungry are the quiet people who inhabit the bush to seek that confusing, bewildering thing called the city, Port of Spain, that they have fled the bush even though leaving it meant life on the La Basse, the lowlands, the dumping grounds of the city. And then again perhaps it was the 'Yankee dollar' which left men shiftless when the war was over, forgetting their rural skills and preferring the shanty town and the garbage dump to their small plot of soil in the country where they farmed. The city had called them from the hills, and now the city was finished with them . . . but they weren't finished with the city, they waited on its edges for its dregs. Whether it was the call of civilization to the inhabitants of the La Basse, the vague dream of fame and fortune; whether it was purely the war, as people said; whether it was the fault of the city fathers for not housing them after their quick moment of usefulness was spent . . . no one knew. They were part of the city of Port of Spain. A sick and sore spot on the city which visitors were led away from. Yet the La Basse was there and, wish as they would that all was well in Port of Spain, they had only to look with their own eyes and see that the La Basse was real, that men lived out their lives there, that in short it was a world peopled with human beings who had not profited from the war, but who none the less led their lives with the same kind of hopes and aspirations as those who entertained the Premier up in St Ann's, St Clair, and in the great mansions around the Queen's Park Savannah . . . so resistant is this blight called hope once its licelike feet have pierced the surface skin.

At first the train, or the Eastern Main Road, goes through the dark and ugly switch yards of the TGR . . . the Trinidad Government Railroads. Beyond are small craft bobbing up and down at anchor, mostly fishermen's boats waiting for the tide with that smell of tar that they dip their nets in. There is also the smell of charcoal and axle grease mixed with hot steam, a smell that never quite leaves the pitted walls of the station corridors and walls. Farther up the line the train goes past rows of abattoirs and factories, tanneries, all lying between the railroad tracks and the stagnant sea beyond with its putrid odours and lime-green scum idling on its surface, the swimming pool of children who grow up on the La Basse. And as the train goes past, their happy faces ring out some greeting to the passengers in the train which meets with disgust and a quiet turning of the face, and now the train is going past the La Basse, dotted with shacks all the way down to the sea.

You must cross the railroad tracks to get to the La Basse and it is at this point the road bed ends, broken up by the constant grinding of steel wheels on the mule carts and other dumping vehicles that must pass here. No automobile nor taxi would venture farther.

'You want me to bust up the tyre on my motorcar or what? I can't go down 'cross the tracks at this hour. I can't even see one hole in the road from the next,' the taxi driver said to Zampi as he let him off at the crossing.

The obeah man stood looking at the two large white gates swung across the road. They were closed now, their red kerosene lanterns hung in warning of danger. Off to the side of the gates was the watchman's shack which was occupied by Santo Pi, Massahood's grandfather, who had left the TEB and gone over to the TGR. On Armistice Day he got dressed up in a tattered soldier's uniform and went majestically to the parades with several smooth old worn-down medals pinned across his breast. Some said that he had actually been to the Great War, crossed the seas, and fought on foreign soils. Others said that he was just plain crazy. He would close the gates at his own discretion, and sometimes after a good fifteen minutes had elapsed and no train had gone past he would open them up, cursing and swearing at the mule cart drivers, pushing open the gates as though they understood his curses.

Zampi rapped on the door of the shack, but there was no answer. He then made his way between two great hinges on which the gates swung where there was enough room for a person to squeeze past. He had to lift

139

off a piece of chicken-coop wire with which the old man had sealed up the passage to prevent people from crossing the tracks; and later on when they took to cutting out a path up along the tracks where they crossed over he retaliated by pelting them with small stones that formed the road bed. 'Why the ass you can't wait till the white people train pass . . . *eh?*' And he would pelt a stone with such might that the strength of the pelt usually threw him off balance, resulting in a very bad aim, and the stone went shooting off in the wildest tangents away from the villain who crossed the tracks. He boasted to everyone about his grandson Massahood. 'Is me who teach him to be a stick man, you know . . .' And wagging his finger, 'He ain't too big for me to give 'em a good cut ass, you know . . . he still 'fraid me like a cat!' But everyone knew that the old rascal was afraid of Massahood's shadow, for if the stick man happened to be coming out of the La Basse past the watchman's hut Santo Pi would run into the hut and hide until the stick man was well past. Sometimes children from the La Basse would shout, 'Aye . . . Santo Pi . . . look, Massahood comin' up the road.' And when the watchman ran to hide in his shack they would laugh out loud at him. The old man would then emerge from his hiding and begin stoning and cursing them angrily.

Zampi called out, 'Santo Pi . . . Santo Pi,' but there was still no reply. Sometimes the old man went about in the early morning to check the crab traps which he had set out, and it was not unusual for him to lock the gates whenever he went to do his little errands. Perhaps he had gone to Charlie Chan's rumshop to get a nip. The Chinaman was always ready to accommodate customers after hours for a few cents more.

As Zampi walked on deeper on to the La Basse he could see clumps of darkness in the distance. The sun had not climbed out of the sea yet, there was only a burst of light where it would emerge from its night-long sleep. And then as he got closer he could hear voices rising from the dark blotches about Zolda's hut.

'Something happen . . . something bad happen,' he said to himself as he doubled his pace into a trot. He had had a feeling of danger, of impending disaster, all evening long. The past two days of carnival and all that happened about him shaped themselves into a complete picture, and each time his mind was about to grasp it and focus it the images dissolved into one another. He could see them only as single incidents, yet he felt his mind stretching, groping, reaching out to find a key, a pattern to all that had happened in the past two days. He was moving faster and faster; he ran until he came to the crowd in front of Zolda's hut. He squeezed past between them and there in front of the shack he saw Massahood lying on the ground, dead.

At first he wondered if Zolda had killed the stick man. He saw the cut on his shoulder, then decided that it could not have caused the stick man's death.

Now he looked Massahood over carefully. He was stretched out flat on the ground, his legs wide apart, his arms flung out. Zampi looked questioningly at the faces about in the crowd.

'He dead,' a man said. 'They stone 'im till he dead.'

The stick man had dark bruises on his bare chest, his head was swollen in small bumps in one or two places. His skin was covered with dust as though someone had emptied out a bag of sand or dirt on him, and the dry dust of the stones helped to cover the welts and bruises, although there were small patches where he had bled. The stick man's face was turned away as if he was looking below Zolda's shack, which stood on short stumps about a foot from the ground.

The obeah man heard soft sobbing coming from inside the hut. He turned and stepped up into the doorway. Against the far wall lay the cripple. Zampi thought that the sobs were coming from him, then he turned in the direction of the sound, where Zolda lay curled up on her bed, her arms wrapped around her head covering her eyes and her ears. Her body jerked with short quick spasms as she sobbed quietly.

The hut was the same. The bed they had dragged off the La Basse, a black iron bedstead with curls and swirls of wrought iron. The room was lit up in a pale pink light that bathed the odds and ends of wood, already seasoned with a silken hue by the wash of the sea, in a warm glow. They had found an old broken kerosene lamp such as watchmen sit about when there is an open ditch in the street; together they had filled its red glass chimney with melted-down ends of candles and paraffin. She was so happy with it that she had said to Zampi long ago, 'I will only light it when you come to see me.' He felt strange in this room which he had come into and gone out of as his own. He had thought that all of this was he at one time, or rather he and Zolda, for they had put the place together with whatever little pieces of cast-offs they could make into roofing or decor. A piece of fisherman's net, a large purple and blue conch-shell, the skeleton of a white-boned fish sanded down to a marble polish. And even the odour of the hut reminded him of himself. He had come to associate the odour of his body with this place. He smelt like that, or it smelt like him. He felt a wonderful feeling of exhilaration come over him at the thought that nothing was changed, that Zolda had not thrown out any of the things that they had made together with so much pleasure and joy. It was a sweet feeling to be surrounded by things, even the faintest of odours, that could draw you back in time and almost make you relive a moment of the past when you were really happy.

Zampi sat on the bed next to her and took her head in his arms. She sobbed aloud as he held her, his lips moving across her face, caressing her cheeks, her hair. He wanted to ask her what had happened, but she began to tell him herself how she had come away angry at him and then before she could sort out her emotions all of this had happened.

'And how he get here?' Zampi asked, pointing to the cripple who lay in the corner of the hut.

She told him how Massahood fought with her and how the cripple broke in and what the little man had said, that she was his. 'I never realize he feel that way 'bout me.'

The obeah man shook his head with remorse. 'Is not your fault,' he said. 'You couldn't know.'

'But it is my fault,' she insisted. 'You tell me long time gone that I encourage him, and that I encourage Massahood too, and you was right. Look what happen here today. I used to think that nobody like him because he small and twist' up and that I was he friend and I used to dance with him, but I didn't mean anything by that, Zampi, I didn't . . .'

She started sobbing again and the obeah man held her close to his bosom, whispering in her ear, 'Shh . . . shhh.' And as he looked at the cripple's dead body in the corner he felt a strange compassion for him, for the quick and sudden way in which his life was snuffed out. He had spent an eternity in pursuit of something that he only vaguely understood. He had collected hundreds of books, thousands of newspapers and magazines, he had nourished himself on vast quantities of knowledge. He hungered for learning, for enlightenment, he treasured his findings above all things. How he worked, wearing his frail body down to the bone, always trying to possess that something that would hold all of the loose ends of information he had gleaned together. Now suddenly that taut-wound spring of his life which sought the universal glue which would hold his world together had snapped, pitching out the intricate cog wheels that went rolling away in their different directions. He had held arguments that sounded coherent and whole. But only a few pieces of his fantastic jigsaw puzzle formed some semblance of a picture, and when you thought about other fragments of information each picture cancelled out the previous one. He had not found that adhesive, that single thread on which he could string the billion-beaded boxfuls of information he possessed.

And Zampi now saw that what the little man had he had come by at a tremendous cost. He saw how hard men worked and drove themselves, making only small segments of their lives bear truth, and how they hid away the next peg of information, the next fact that might disrupt the small pattern. They collected, sorted, arranged, and pressed together an infinite jumble of jetsam, forcing their twisted order upon them, while other men had, at the time of their birth, a string like their umbilical cord on which they strung simply, their beads taking to the string with ease, enlarging their tapestry until its patterns blazed with beauty in wholeness and perfection.

The cripple lay on the floor with his arms and legs drawn up tightly like an overturned bug that could not right itself. His figure was a strange sight. It looked like a puppet with its head twisted back to front, its arms and legs wrenched out of kilter in the back-to-front carnival costume.

Meantime, Zolda was looking at Zampi's face. She felt that she could read all the thoughts that sped through his mind. And deep within her she felt a guilt, a feeling of shame, a feeling that insisted in the back of her mind that she was in some way responsible for what had happened, and she was not satisfied to simply say as she had said before that she was this way, or that, that people should learn to take her for what she was; and yet she knew that Zampi was right when he said that it was not her fault. She loved him for that, for the feeling he gave her of not being alone, not being directly at fault. Most men who tried to get close to her were afraid of her. Even now she could hear the whisperings of some in the crowd outside blaming her. Her kind of woman was always to blame, always at fault, and doubly so with the men she did not allow to have their way with her. All the moments of pleasure she knew, all the reck-lessness that drove her, left her now, and she felt as though she were in an empty house where all manner of debauchery had been acted out, leaving behind only the dirty confetti, the flat limp streamers that she, Zolda, was now left to tidy up, to be haunted by the emptiness, the hollowness, the sight of the two dead men. In her own way she saw now what Zampi must have felt, she could understand why he had taken himself away from the Britannia, and the Scorpion Tail, and the La Basse. There was only one reason why Zampi came to the city, and Zolda knew it. The reason was love, and that was all there was, after all. There was nothing else left in the world. In his presence now she felt that he had communion, power over the earth, and she felt pleasure in her bosom, in her thighs, in the nipples of her breasts, she felt a strange pleasure in the thought that this man was hers, had always wanted her, had come out of the bush hungry with desire to claim her, and that in all he had done and seen, in all of the days that must have been filled with a million thoughts, all had led to her. In this moment of emotions dumped like distant stars upon one another . . . when she wept and cried she wished to throw herself in his arms, to have him possess her with thrusts like lightning bolts that would scorch her loins.

'Carry me far away from here,' she pleaded. 'I want to see all of the things you do, hear all of the things that you hear in the bush. I want to see what the nighttime like when it get dark and quiet up in Blue Basin. I want to see if I can't find you again and know you like I used to know you.'

Zampi looked at her face with an expression of satisfaction. How many times he had wondered if she, Zolda, would ever leave the city, would ever want to come away with him. There were moments when he was sure that he could persuade her, when he saw her just like this, wanting to go away with him. It did not seem strange in his imagination then, and now here it was and he felt surprised to hear her ask to go with him.

He looked at her as if to allow her time to think of what she was saying, of what she was asking, but she went on and on. 'You will show me all them things that you did have to do before you turn obeah man?' she asked. 'Tell me 'bout all the things that cross your mind while you was away? I feel as if I would give anything in the whole world to walk in the same road that you walk, live in the same house that you live in during those days . . . I feel as if I miss a big fete for all of the times you must be sit down by yourself up there and cook and eat and sleep and I wasn't with you.'

Outside the hut there was a new outburst, a different kind of energy in the crowd. Nothing as loud and riotous as before, but a low mumbling and chattering of voices growing and spreading. Now and then a single voice stood out while the others fell silent as if listening, then the grumbling started up again. The obeah man left Zolda's side and went to the door. There were two Negro constables in black uniforms, and an inspector, an Englishman, in khaki uniform swinging his short swagger-stick. One of the constables was questioning people in the crowd who still stood about, although most of the men who stoned the stick man had gone away. The inspector was rubbing a red insect bite on his arm with the tip of his stick. A little boil on his skin stood around a grain of gold-red hair on his arm, and as he rubbed it with the stick the skin broke. He seemed annoyed that the insect should have chosen that particular spot as he examined the small sore, first with a look of disgust, then questioning . . . would the hair drop off? He only half heard the questions the constables were asking the men.

'So you mean to say that all of you people livin' here and all of you was sleepin' and nobody ain't see how this thing happen?' one of the constables asked. The other constable had gone into the hut to talk to Zampi and Zolda. Instead of answering the questions put to them, people turned to one another asking, talking, mumbling. One man turned to another, the second to a third. Policemen and the law were always dropping down on the La Basse to make trouble. People shunned them, their black uniforms and heavy steps meant only one thing—trouble. The law did not mean protection to these people, it meant punishment. In their own way they took pleasure in looking on at the helplessness of the police, the way their questions went unanswered, tossed about the crowd like footballs until their bounce fizzled out.

'It must be some of them bad bad bad stick men up in John-John,' someone in the crowd offered, impersonally, as a suggestion only. There was implicit in the tone of the voice that it was not a statement for the record, merely a thought. And then the crowd broke into cackling fits of laughter again. Which policeman dared go up to those districts? They could come down here on the La Basse and drive up with their jeeps and flash their brass buttons and molest the La Basse people, but they would be run out of John-John and Laventille with their coat tails flying. Women, men, even children, took the sight of a black uniform with laughter, then a quick search for anything that could be hurled at them, garbage pails, rotten vegetables, occasionally a chamberpot was emptied from a window.

The constable who went into Zolda's hut came out and whispered to the other who was asking questions in the crowd. Both turned up their palms, then one of them stepped up to the inspector. 'Nobody seems to know how it happened, sir.'

The inspector kept his eyes fastened to the little sore on his arm, playing with the grain of hair. 'I'm not surprised . . . always the same story,' he said without looking up. Seconds passed, then he looked across at the dead body of Massahood and clenched his teeth hard with a grimace. 'Well, turn in your reports when you get back to headquarters, you chaps . . . Come on, let's go.' As they walked back to their squad car, the inspector walking ahead of the constables was shaking his head in puzzlement. 'I don't understand it,' he muttered to himself. 'God knows we've put the King's English in their mouths.' Then he climbed into the back of the car, the two constables in front, and they drove away.

Even a mob will loosen up, move back, and open up a space, provided some reward is given them, some tears from an eyelid, some blood from a vein, some human cry of pain or anguish. The hardest of hearts will soften and swallow his push, and the harsh voice of bully and bravado will begin to whisper, as it happened when Santo Pi, the stick man's grandfather, came slowly through the crowd. He did not have to squeeze or wedge his way through, the crowd made an opening for him. Those who knew that the old man was Massahood's grandfather nudged others who stood tightly in the crowd. No one had to tell them who he was; there was an instant understanding in the mob that they should step back and let the old man through. And Santo Pi, dressed in an old blue-black conductor's uniform of the TGR, moved with a tired trudge up to the dead body of his grandson. He stooped down on to his knees, took off his conductor's cap, and laid it on the ground, then his eyes travelled up the stick man's body, pawed at his face, then moved down to his feet. In a broken voice he said, 'Oh God, my grandchild dead.'

The crowd looked on in silence, even the children were whispering to their parents. There was an intense feeling of sympathy in the crowd, but their sympathy was for the old man, who wailed on and on. 'He d-a-i-d . . . Dis po' boy daid an' gone from the worl'.' The old man's saddened face never left Massahood's body. He never lifted up his eyes to direct his sorrow or his tears to anyone. He wept alone, and for himself; even his sobs were so soft he seemed to keep them just low enough for his own ears. 'I ain't have nooooobody . . . nooooobody,' he said over and over, rubbing his small wrinkled hand on Massahood's shoulder with a feeling of tenderness. And then bewilderment and confusion spread over his face as if he could not understand how this body, this lifeless mass of muscle and bone, could really ever die, lie still like this never to move again. 'You is the onliest flesh-an'-blood that I did have leave in the world, boy . . . an' now you gone . . . you gone and leave your Gramps all by he-self . . . all by he-self!'

In the faces of the onlookers there was no pity, no sympathy nor love for the stick man. They had taken pride in having him in their midst, many of them had stood him drinks at the Britannia, or they had threatened other men by mentioning his name. 'Don't play the ass with me, you know . . . I come from the La Basse and if you talk too hard I make Massahood bust up your ass for you.' But now no one was moved with any sorrow for him, and the words, the very formulated phrase, they let fall was: 'The bitch dead . . . dat good!' or 'He should'er dead long time gone!' and 'Is so they does always go. Well, he play the ass long enough.'

Those who felt any guilt at all knew in their hearts that it was not because of Massahood's death but because of the old man, and his tears, which came running out of his body, lashing them with surprise that in his small, dry, wizened bundle of bones there could be any juice or moisture of pity or love. And as he cried the old man did not question how or why Massahood had died. He accepted it as something he always knew would happen one day. His hands, which were too large and incongruous with their small wrists, touched the cuts on the stick man's face, trying to close the flesh where it lay open.

And then the old man's expression changed suddenly. His face became filled with scorn, his eyes drew together, and his wet nose flared and stiffened. His tears still ran down into the folds of his cheeks, but his body tensed from its limp pose. He flung Massahood's body away from him and slapped his face with a black rage. 'Why you gone an' dead?' he questioned the dead man. 'Why you gone and dead befo' me? I is a old man! Why you didn't wait a li'l longer . . . you damn' blasted fool!' And here he slapped the dead man again. 'You worthless good-for-nuttin' scamp . . .' Slap! 'You can't even answer me now. I did want you to cry for *me*! For *me!*' He slapped Massahood's face, and with each slap the dead man's head swung from one side to the other as Santo Pi struck now with the palm, now with the back of his hand. 'Cry . . . Cry. . . . Why you don't cry?' he screamed as he slapped the dead man's face. 'You can't even cry for me no mo'.'

The La Basse dwellers, some of them standing about half naked as they had slept, began mumbling among themselves. There were still among them some whose stones had killed the stick man, but each one individually disclaimed the crime. Since no one stone had killed the stick man, conscience was divided.

'Aye, man,' someone shouted from the crowd. 'It ain't good to hit the dead . . . is a bad bad thing that you doin'.'

'But how you ain't have no feelin's for the dead . . . and your own gran'chile too-besides.'

'You gone crazy or what?' they asked from the depths of the crowd.

And now Santo Pi began crying again, his body jerking with short, quick, spasmodic sobs. 'Oh God, Hood . . . you gone . . . you gone, boy. You gone and leave me all alone in the world . . . Why you gone an' do it to me, boy? . . . Why?' Santo Pi cried out again. He put his arms around the dead man, pressed his face into the hollow of Massahood's neck and shoulder, and began rocking him back and forth like a baby as he wept softly now, speaking words in the dead man's ear that were soft and sweet and whispered so low that no one could hear. Not even the crabs that had done with their mating and their scraping claws and gone into their damp dark holes to sleep through the day.

Let a firefly glow in the evening . . . let a bullfrog call.
Let the crickets scratch their thighs to screeching.

Let love live like a lonely lost thing locked up in the heart. It will surface, shine, and see itself again as Zolda saw it now. She would walk along the paths that led up to the waterfall at Blue Basin, she would see all of those things that Zampi had seen without her. She felt that there was a gap between them that she wanted to fill in, and she waited to go with him right away with all of her senses open so that she would not miss the smallest sound that the winds make when the great sea calls them back from the land.

'It have anything in this house that you really want . . . that you can't do without?' Zampi asked.

She looked from one corner of the room to another, then she looked at Zampi and nodded. 'Come on and let we go, then,' he said as he watched her hesitating, pleading with her eyes. Yes, there was something she wanted to take with her. Zampi nodded to her, then she went and took the red hurricane lantern filled with paraffin. She held it close to her bosom with a childish look of embarrassment.

And as they left the hut the obeah man took the stick which lay at Massahood's side. He swung it over his head until it buzzed as it sliced the air, then he let it fly into one of the smouldering fires on the La Basse. Seconds later there was the sound of a small explosion from the fire that sent the stick shooting into the air, snapping, crackling, blazing . . . then it fell back into the flames, hissing like some rich and volatile substance that would consume itself to the last black ash.